英文
學術論文寫作
WRITING ACADEMIC PAPERS IN ENGLISH

•—•— 講解與作業 —•—•

董崇選——著

作者序

　　在今日，英文已是全球的共同語言。在學術界，英文更是發表論文的最重要語言。在使用中文的華人世界裡，經常有人要用英文來撰寫論文或把中文的論文翻譯成英文。可是，英文的學術論文，依學科的不同，有不同的寫作模式。這點許多人並不瞭解。此外，許多以中文為母語的人，他們的英文往往不夠好，所以他們所撰寫的英文學術論文往往有疏漏或錯誤，有的甚至於造成語意不清或含義扭曲，令人不解或誤解。知道這種困難的人，寫完英文論文之後，常常會找行家幫忙修改潤飾，但真正的「英文行家」並不易找到。懂普通英文的人，可能不懂某科系的英文專門術語；懂某些英文專門術語的人，卻可能缺乏普通英文的寫作能力。

　　目前，在以中文授課的大學裡，很少有為自己單一的科系開設「英文學術論文寫作」這門課的。有些學校是有開設類似「英文科技論文寫作」的課，來供相關的科系共同選修。但實際的狀況是：往往找不到妥適的授課者，也往往找不到妥適的教科書。英文系的老師往往只能教普通英文，因為他們不懂其他科系的術語。自己系內曾經出國留過學，而且在國外教過書、寫過許多英

文學術論文的教授，卻又不會想要開「英文學術論文寫作」這門
課。就算有人想開，也往往因為找不到現成而且合適的教科書而
作罷。

　　理論上，各科系是應該運用本科系的英文術語來為自己編寫
「英文學術論文寫作」的教材。如果這點辦不到，權宜的辦法便
是：用一本泛論「英文學術論文寫作」的教科書來授課。畢竟，
無論何種科系，用英文撰寫論文，都有共通的地方。而英文不好
的華人，也有同樣類型的英文錯誤。本書便是基於這種認識而編
寫的，希望對大家有實際的幫助。

　　本人出身英文系，在大學裡教過「英文學術論文寫作」的
課，深知授課的困難，瞭解學生想要學習的地方，也發覺沒有好
的教科書可用。於是，利用退休後的閒暇，編寫出這本「心得之
作」。全書有十二章，外加三個附錄。每章有講解，有作業，適
合一學期的快速授課，或兩學期的從容授課。本書除了講述論文
寫作的要點之外，也安排提升英文寫作能力的教導。除了可以當
班上的教科書之外，本書也可以當個人參考書用。只是：瞭解論
文寫作要點，一時並不難；提升英文寫作能力，卻是長久的事。
好的英文寫作能力並非一本書所能完全教好的。

　　本書於2013年10月初版時，並沒有序文。今再版之際，除了
修改疏漏與調整版面空間之外，特加上此前言，一方面感謝使用
者的厚愛，同時也告知本書的性質與撰寫本書的背景，希望能增
加本書的效益。

　　　　　　　　　　　　　　　　　　董崇選　謹識

contents 目次

第一章

概説

講解

　　在今日的學術界，無論學者或學生，大家都常常需要寫「學術論文」（academic papers）。學術論文有很多種，有的是大學者發表特殊見解的「冊論」（tract）、「專論」（monograph）、「論說」（treatise, discourse, or essay）、「批判」（critique）、或「評論」（review），有的是學生為取得學位所寫的「博士論文」（dissertation for a doctor's degree）或「碩士論文」（thesis for a master's degree），有的是一般學者與學生所發表的「期刊論文」（journal paper）或「研討會論文」（conference paper），有的則是老師要求學生寫的「學期論文」（term paper）或「研究報告」（study report）。

　　每一種學術論文，不管用中文或英文寫作，通常都有一定的內容、寫法、與長度。學術論文的內容當然受限於學門或學科：物理學的論文只能探討物理的問題，心理學的論文只能探討心理的問題。各種學門或學科在寫作論文時，其書寫格式（writing format）與文章長度（article length），往往都有明言的或共識的規範。大學者出版書籍時，為了樹立其獨特的風格，或許不會全然遵守那些規範。但是，一般的學者與學生，卻都必須遵守那些規範才能使論文被接受、被刊登。每種期刊或研討會，通常都會規定寫作的格式。例如，英文的期刊可能會要求跟隨MLA或

APA或IEEE或其他學術組織所訂的寫作規範[1]。

　　不同的語文有不同的用字（wording）、用詞（phrasing）與不同的句法（syntax）、語法（grammar），也有不同的標點符號系統（system of punctuation marks）。中文與英文是兩個極不相同的語文，其字、詞、語、句乃至標點方式都有極大差異。所以，慣用中文寫作的人，如果沒有同時精通英文寫作，便很容易用詞不對，語法有誤，甚至連標點也弄錯。其實，在使用英文的世界裡，「英式英語」（British English）和「美式英語」（American English）之間，除了發音之外，其拼字（spelling）、用詞、語法、與標點方面，也有不少差異。有些期刊使用英式英語來編輯，有些則使用美式英語。這一點，要向期刊投稿的人，應該也要特別注意[2]。

　　學術論文的長度有的長至幾百頁，有的短至三、五頁。一般的英文期刊論文或期末報告通常是5至30頁之間。但不管長度如何，每篇論文都必須要有「標題」（title）。標題就像招牌，好標題才能清楚標示內容，而引起興趣。有的時候，一個標題裡還會含有「主標題」（main title）和「副標題」（subtitle）。標題的訂定，也是寫作學術論文的一項學問。

---

[1] MLA（Modern Language Association）有 *The MLA Handbook for Writers of Research Papers*，APA（American Psychological Association）有 *Publication Manual of the American Psychological Association*，而IEEE（Institute of Electrical and Electronics Engineers）有線上的 *Editorial Style Manual*，提供寫作規範給相關學門使用。

[2] 有關英式英語和美式英語在拼字、用詞、語法、與標點方面的差異，請參考本書附錄一：書面英式英語與美式英語的對照。

有些論文會被要求要附上「摘要」（Abstract）和「關鍵詞」（Key Words）。通常「摘要」和「關鍵詞」放在「標題」之後，而接著便是「全文的主體」（the main body of the text）或「主文」（the main text）。在主文中如果標有「註記」（notes），那些註記便要以「腳注」（footnotes）或以「尾注」（endnotes）的方式呈現。在「主文」與「注釋」（Notes）之後，通常也要有一項稱為「參考書目」（Bibliography）或「參考資料」（References）或「引用著作」（Works Cited）或「引用文獻」（Literature Cited）的這一部分。最後，全文如果還有「附錄」（Appendix），便也要附上。此外，有些學術論文還會加上「謝詞」（Acknowledgements）或其他聲明。可見，一篇完整的學術論文，會包括許多部分，而每一部分都是寫作時要注意的環節。

　　學術論文的主文本身，也可以再分成幾個部分。它通常有起頭有結尾，起頭是提供研究背景、問題、與目的之「引言」（Introduction），結尾是總結研究發現、心得、與建議之「結論」（Conclusion）。在引言和結論之間，依論文的長度與內容方面的差異，會有不同的安排。在許多自然科學與科技類的期刊論文中，除了「引言」和「結論」之外，便是「材料與方法」（Materials and Methods）、「結果」（Results）、和「討論」（Discussion）的部分。在不使用「材料」而使用「資料」（data）的學門裡，「材料與方法」這一部分當然會變成「資料與方法」（Data and Methods）。在有些人文學科裡，可能既不使用材料也不使用資料，因此論文中要交代的可能只是「研究題材」（study subject），而其研究的方法其實是研究的「途徑」或「手法」（approach）或研究所根據的「理論」（theory）。總之，主文要分成幾個部分，每一部分要標上什麼題目（heading），都由作者自行斟酌，自由決定。要緊的是：一定要說清楚研究的背景、問題、目的、範圍、材料（資料、題材）、方法（途徑）、過程、與結果（發現）等等，也要有妥善的討論和明白的總結。另外，或許還要加上可行的建議。

　　不管是「主文」的什麼部分（是引言或結論，或是材料與方法、結果、討論等），也不管是哪種「副文」（sub-text），是標題、摘要、關鍵詞、注釋等，或是參考資料、附錄、謝詞等，反正「文中都是書寫的語言」。英文的學術論文，到處都是書寫的英語（英式、美式、或其他方式的書寫英語），而書寫的英語和口語的英語是不一樣的。書寫的英語是比較正式（formal）的英語：它不用口語的isn't, it's, can't等，而用書寫的is not, it is, cannot等。它比較會用正式的字眼，如investigate, constitute, decrease等，而比較不去用口說的成語，如look into, make up, go down等。這點，寫英文學術論文的人，都必須要知道。

　　學術論文講究的是精確（accuracy）、清晰（clarity）和簡要（simplicity），它不要文學裡的含糊多義（ambiguity）。寫英文的學術論文，便是要用最精確的英文詞語和語法，以及用最清晰的英文表達方式，把論文的學術內容簡要的寫出來。可是，要如何才能把英文寫得精確、清晰而簡要呢？那當然要英文好才辦得到。一般而言，以英文為母語的人，只要受過良好的教育，要寫好一篇英文學術論文是不會太困難的。而以中文為國語的人，除非他也精通英文，否則要寫好一篇英文學術論文並不容易。

「學術的英文」（academic English）並非「普通的英文」（ordinary English）。「學術的英文」是在「普通的英文」裡，夾雜著「英文學術用語」（English academic terms）的英文。今天，在英語教學界所謂的ESP（English for Specific Purposes），是為各行各業之「特定目的」而傳授的英文，那種英文包括商用英文、新聞英文、觀光英文、科技英文、醫療英文、航空英文、藝術英文等等許多「專業的英文」（professional English）。不管哪一種專業，它的「專門術語」（technical terms），用在學術界時，也就是「學術用語」。而各行各業所講的英語「行話」，或各個學術圈所寫的英文學術論文，都同樣是「普通英文 夾有英文專門術語」的英文。那種英語要行內或圈內的人才容易聽得懂、看得懂。

既然「學術的英文」裡頭有「普通的英文」和「英文學術用語」，寫英文學術論文的人便要同時熟悉「普通的英文」和「英文學術用語」。要熟悉「普通的英文」，就必須長時間在各種場合不斷聽、說、讀、寫普通英文。要熟悉「英文學術用語」，也必須在學術圈裡經常聽、說、讀、寫英文學術用語。任何一種語文，任何一類用語，都必須練習慣了才能夠運用自如。只有多看多寫英文學術論文，才能看懂寫好英文學術論文。

雖然「學術的英文」並非「普通的英文」，但兩種英文都遵守同一套語法。因此，科技英文除了有科技術語之外，並沒有特殊的科技英文語法。普通英文說"Room 10"，科技英文同樣也說"Protein 53"，不會說"53 Protein"。普通英文說"Peter is capable of buying and selling various goods"，科技英文同樣也說"Protein 53 is capable of activating or repressing various genes"，不會說"53 Protein is capable to activate or repress various gene"。所以說，寫英文學術論文時，如果有語法的問題，可以回歸普通英文的語法，可以同樣用一般的語法為準則。

學術論文是發表給學術圈內的人看的。在學術發達的今天，每一個學門學科都是術語充斥。因此，屬於不同學術圈或不同行業的人，很難看懂別人的論文。在大學的科系裡，有許多教授在以英文為官方語言的國家留學過，甚至於任教過，他們既懂普通英文，也懂自己本行的專門英文。另外，他們還看過並寫過不少英文的學術論文。那種教授最適合教自己系內的學生如何寫作英文學術論文。在英文科系任教的老師，則通常只能教普通英文，不宜教其他科系的英文論文寫作，因為他們可能不太懂其他科系的英文術語。

理論上，既然各科系有各科系的術語與寫作規範，各科系便應該編寫自己的「英文論文寫作教材」。不過，不管什麼科系，寫作英文論文還是有許多共通的地方。在那些地方，大家使用的是共同的普通英文。或許，這些地方的普通英文，便是一般英文老師都可教導的範圍，而那也是泛論英文論文寫作的書籍可以發揮的所在。

作業

1. 請找出一種你最常用的英文學術期刊來看，據此回答下列問題：

   a. 該期刊的名稱是什麼？

   b. 該期刊要求寫作格式要跟隨什麼學術組織所訂的規範？

   c. 該期刊是用「英式英語」或「美式英語」來編輯？

   d. 該期刊裡，一篇文章的長度大約幾頁？

2. 請找出一本英文的碩士論文或博士論文來看，據此回答下列問題：

   a. 該論文的英文標題是什麼？

   b. 該論文有Abstract, Key Words, Notes, References, Appendix,和
   Acknowledgements這幾部分嗎？

   c. 該論文的main text裡有Introduction和Conclusion的部分嗎？

   d. 該論文的main text裡還另外分成幾個（章節）部分？有
   Materials and Methods, Results,和Discussion這些部分嗎？

3. 請找出一篇英文的學期論文來看，據此回答下列問題：

　　a. 該論文的英文標題是什麼？

　　b. 該論文裡有can't, couldn't, won't, wouldn't, isn't, aren't, it's, they're等等這種口語英文的縮寫字嗎？

　　c. 該論文裡用了類似look into, make up, go down這種口說成語來代替比較正式的語詞（investigate, constitute, decrease）嗎？到底它用了哪些口語？那些口語代替什麼正式的字？

　　d. 該論文整篇讀起來是不是很像在說話而不像在寫文章？

4. 請拿出一本你們上課用的英文教科書來看其中一頁，據此回答下列問題：

　　a. 該頁的英文有達到accuracy, clarity, simplicity等學術文章的要件嗎？

　　b. 該頁有哪些technical terms使它成為學術的英文而不只是普通英文？

　　c. 該頁的英文應該算科技英文嗎？或是哪一領域或行業的英文？

　　d. 該頁有任何不符合一般英文語法的詞語或句子嗎？

5. 仔細看下列各句英文，確定它是否為「純普通英文」。如果不是，找出它因為有什麼technical terms而成為「學術英文」。

a. For health one should drink pure water, not alcohol.

b. Water is composed of oxygen and hydrogen.

c. The conclusion Einstein arrived at was the equation: $E = MC^2$.

d. The word "morphemes" contains three morphemes: two bound morphemes ("morph-" and "-eme") and one free morpheme ("-s").

e. Marx and Engels formulated the principles of dialectical materialism. They maintained that economic structure is the basis of history, and determines all the social, political, and intellectual aspects of life.

f. We found calcium levels to be decreased by RA and D3 but increased when AG1296, in addition to RA or D3, was given.

g. Quantum phenomena are particularly relevant in systems whose dimensions are close to the atomic scale, such as molecules, atoms, electrons, protons, and other subatomic particles.

h. The aerostructures are for horizontal stabilizers, engine nacelles, fan cowls, etc.

第二章

標題的訂定與寫法

講解

人需要有名字（name）或稱謂（appellation），有些人甚至於有外號（epithet）或頭銜（title）。同樣的，學術論文也需要有名稱或放在論文前頭的名銜。不過，論文的名稱或頭銜，通常是用以「標示題目」（indicate the topic）的「標題」，因此它的名稱或頭銜就是標題。在英文裡，"title"一字就是指名稱、頭銜、或標題，而"heading"一字也是指標題。只是，大家通常用"title"來指稱整篇論文或整本書的標題，而用"heading"來指論文裡各部分（part）、各章（chapter）、各節（section）、或各段落（paragraph）的標題[1]。

在公開發表之前，每篇學術論文都必須訂出標題。通常成書成冊的大論文只需要一個標示大題目（big topic）的「廣大標題」（broad title）就好，而一般的期刊論文或學期報告則必須把大題目約化成探討小題目（small topic）的「狹小標題」（narrow title）。例如，一個歷史學者可能寫出一本很寬廣的書，叫《中國史》（*The History of China*），而他的學生則可能交給他一篇狹小的期末報告，叫〈漢朝百姓對「吉日」的想法〉（"People's Ideas of 'Auspicious Days' in the Han Dynasty"）。廣大的標題通常只標示研究的大範圍，狹小的標題則標示探討某特

---

[1] 其實，"chapter heading"和"chapter title"以及"section heading"和"section title"，在一般英文裡都是同樣常說的詞語。

殊問題的小範圍。

其實，在每一次做學術研究之前，學者或學生都必須先確定「這次要研究什麼」。一開始，研究者可能只想到研究的方向（direction）、範圍（scope）、對象（target）、或題材（subject matter）。例如，一個文學家可能想到要研究莎士比亞的《暴風雨》，而一個生化學家可能想到要研究植物的「葉綠素」。可是，在深入思考那個研究的方向、範圍、對象、或題材之後，針對目前的某特定問題，那研究者就會擬出一個題目（topic）來引導或制約整個研究的活動。例如，那文學家可能擬出「莎劇《暴風雨》裡的後殖民思想」（"Post-colonialism in Shakespeare's *The Tempest*"）這個題目，用以引導自己來專心探討「莎劇《暴風雨》裡有何種後殖民思想」這個問題。同樣的，那生化學家也可能擬出「葉綠素在光合作用中的功能」（"The Function of Chlorophyll in Photosynthesis"）這個題目，用來制約他的研究方向，讓他自己專注在「葉綠素如何促進光合作用」這個問題。像這種「基於問題的題目」（problem-based topic），如果把它放在論文裡面當頭銜，便是論文的「標題」（title）。通常一本大著作會等於幾個小著作的集合，也就是說：在大著作的廣大標題之下會隱含有幾個小著作的狹小標題。

近來有些學者或學生，尤其是生命科學界的研究者，他們所訂的標題往往不僅是「基於問題的題目」而已。他們所訂的標題常常變成「針對問題的解答」（solution to the problem）。他們在研究之前可能已經訂了「假說」（hypothesis），研究之後也可能證實了那假說，而那假說或研究的「結論」（conclusion）便成為他們的標題。例如，一個研究「第一型之人類免疫不全病毒」（type 1 of human immunodeficiency virus）的人，在假定並證實「那病毒的基因體是由gag, pol和env等三種主要的基因所組成」時，他的論文標題可能就不只是「人類免疫不全之第一型病毒基因體的主要成分」（"The Main Components of the HIV-1 Genome"），而可能是類似「人類免疫不全之第一型病毒基因體包含gag, pol和env等三種主要基因」（"The HIV-1 genome consists of three main genes: gag, pol, and env"）這樣的標題。

　　從以上解說我們可以得知：現行的論文標題可以分成兩種，一種是指明「要研究什麼」（what to study）的標題，另一種是告訴「發現了什麼事實」（what fact has been found）的標題。從英語的文法觀點來說，前一種是「片語型的標題」（phrase title），由某名詞為核心加上那名詞的修飾語；後一種是「句子型的標題」（sentence title），裡頭有主詞有動詞，形成完整的一句話。例如，"The Main Components of the HIV-1 Genome"是以"Components"為核心加上其他字為修飾語的「片語型標題」，而"The HIV-1 genome consists of three main genes: gag, pol, and env"則是有主詞（"The HIV-1 genome"）有動詞（"consists"）的「句子型標題」。其實，前一種標題可以說就是標題前面省去了"I/ We want to study"這幾個字，而後一種標題則是省去了"I/ We have found the fact that"：

(I/ We want to study) The Main Components of the HIV-1 Genome.

(I/ We have found the fact that) The HIV-1 genome consists of three main genes: gag, pol, and env.

換句話說，前一種似乎是「研究前而未見成果時」所訂的標題，後一種則好像是「研究後而看到成果時」所訂的標題。

既然句子型的標題是告知研究者得到的（過去與現在皆然的）事實，標題中的動詞，不管主動或被動，當然會用現在式。而那標題有可能是一個「肯定的陳述」（affirmative statement）。例如：“Coffee consumption *is associated with* a lower incidence of fatty liver in middle-aged men”。它也可能是一個「否定的陳述」（negative statement）。例如：“Taking supplemental antioxidants *may not help* prevent SARS”。有時，它還可能是個「問句」（question）。例如，像“What roles *do* reactive oxygen species *play* in ovarian toxicity?”或“*Is* HIV/ AIDS just a young person's disease that needs nursing care?”這種標題。

不管是片語型或句子型的標題，有時一個標題還可以分成兩部分，前一部分是「主標題」（main title），後一部分是「副標題」（subtitle）。通常加上「副標題」是為了進一步告知論文的焦點（focus）。例如，在“The post-release fate of hand-reared orphaned bats: survival and habitat selection”這一個標題裡，主標題告訴我們這篇論文的研究方向：人手養大的蝙蝠孤兒，將其釋放後之命運。副標題則進一步告知論文的焦點在那些蝙蝠的「存活度」（survival）和「棲地的選擇」（habitat selection）這兩方面。

有時候，副標題只是進一步告知論文的屬性（attribute）而已。例如，在"The effects of uncertainty on the roles of controllers and budgets: an exploratory study"這個標題裡，副標題只是進一步告訴我們：那篇論文是「一種探索性的研究」（an exploratory study）。有時候，所告訴的屬性是研究的「手法」（approach）或「方法」（method）。

有時候，主、副標題之間形成一個類似「問與答」的關係。例如："Do Local Governments Save and Spend across Budget Cycles? Evidence from North Carolina"。有時候，主、副標題之間則「有題有問」。例如，"Neuroblastoma therapy: What is in the pipeline?"便是。

主、副標題之間，通常由冒號（：）或破折號（一）隔開。例如，"Conceptual and Functional Diversity of the Ombudsman Institution: A Classification"和"Who Transcends What and How—A Re-reading of Emerson"便是。

英文學術論文的標題，在寫出或印出時，從「字母大寫」（capitalization of letters）的習慣上，可以分成三種。第一種是標題內每一個字的「每一個字母全都大寫」（with all letters capitalized）的模式。例如："LINKING A LAND-USE CELLULAR AUTOMATA WITH A WATER ALLOCATION MODEL TO SIMULATE LAND

DEVELOPMENT CONSTRAINED BY WATER AVAILABILITY IN THE ELBOW RIVER WATERSHED IN SOUTHERN ALBERTA"。這種標題比較不普遍。

有一種比較常見而看來似乎也比較正式的標題是「有大寫各重要字之首字母」（with capitalized initial letters of important words）的標題。這一種模式是：除了標題第一字的首字母要大寫之外，其餘在標題裡的每一個重要字，其首字母也都要大寫，除非它是「似乎不重要的小字」。

在寫作英文標題時，所謂「似乎不重要的小字」，可以分成如下幾類：1.冠詞：a, an, the等三個字。2.連接詞：and, or, but等三個字。3.前置詞（介系詞）：as, at, by, down, for, from, in, into, of, off, on, over, to, under, up, upon, with等等許多字。4.其他像via或versus (vs.)這種原為拉丁字的前置詞。不過**請注意**：像against, among, before, between, beyond, despite, during, except, since, through, toward(s), without等等，這些看起來好像比較有份量的前置詞，很多人有時不會視之為「似乎不重要的小字」，但你視之為「似乎不重要的小字」也未嘗不可。

另外**請注意**：一個英文字不一定只屬於一個詞類，如"but"可當連接詞或前置詞，而"as"可當連接詞、副詞、前置詞、或代名詞。但不管這些「不重要的小字」是當什麼詞，在「通常有大寫」的標題裡，不會大寫其首字母。

在英文的文法裡，冠詞、連接詞、和前置詞，通常都被列為不變換形態的「質詞」（particles），或列為主要在扮演語法功能的「功能字」（function words）。這些字常常被算做似乎不重要的「虛字」，而非很有內容而比較重要的「實字」（content words）。這裡請特別注意：we, you, he, she, it, they; am, are, is, was, were; this, that, these, those; both, all; either, too; if等字，看起來小小的，但在論文的標題裡，它們都不算「似乎不重要的小字」。因此，在「有大寫各重要字之首字母」的標題裡，這些字通常也都要大寫其首字母[2]。

另一種也比較常見的標題是「通常無大寫字母」（usually without capitalized letters）的標題。這種模式是：除了標題第一字的首字母要大寫之外，其餘在標題裡的每一個字，其每一個字**母都不要**大寫，除非它有「原本就必須大寫的字」。所謂「原本就必須大寫的字」是指：在日常的英文裡通常會大寫其首字母的字，或通常會大寫的縮寫字（abbreviations）。例如：Monday, Sunday, Canada, Japan, John, Smith, H(= hydrogen), N(= nitrogen or north), UN(= United Nations), SOS等等。這些字，就算出現在「通常無大寫字母」的標題裡，該大寫的字母也照樣會大寫。附**帶請注意**：在各行各業裡，各種物料或品類的英文名稱都有「字母大寫小寫」方面的成規。例如，在生物學界，動植物及微生物的分類學名，常常是兩個斜體的拉丁字，其第一字的首字母通常會大寫。例如：*Schindra chinensis*是一種schisandra或magnolia vine（五味子）的學名。

---

[2]　不過，有時也有人把it, is,這種小字當成「似乎不重要的小字」而不大寫其首字母。

英文學術論文之主標題，其第一個字之首字母一定要大寫。副標題的第一個字之首字母通常也會大寫，但也可以小寫。在「通常無大寫字母」的標題裡，副標題的第一個字之首字母通常比較會跟著小寫。

　　英文學術論文的標題，不管是哪一種，其第一個字如果是冠詞（The, A,或An），則該冠詞可以省略，也通常會省略。例如："The effects of uncertainty ..."這個標題，會改成"Effects of uncertainty ..."；而"An Investigation into ..."這樣的標題，會改成"Investigation into ..."這個樣子。

　　以上是在寫作標題方面，有關英文學術論文的一般規範與說明。下面就「有大寫各重要字之首字母」與「通常無大寫字母」這兩種標題，再舉一些實際的例子，請參看理解。

　　「有大寫各重要字之首字母」的標題：

a. "Ecophysiological, Genetic, and Molecular Causes of Variation in Grape Berry Weight and Composition"

b. "Whether and How Virtual Try-On Influences Consumer Responses to an Apparel Web Site"

c. "Restrictive Measures Adopted by the European Union from the Standpoint of International and EU Law"

d. "Coffee Consumption Is Associated with a Lower Incidence of Fatty Liver in Middle-aged Men"

「通常無大寫字母」的標題：

a. "Successful changes in plant resistance and tolerance to herbivory"

b. "Effect of different concentrations of *Bacillus subtilis* on growth performance, carcase quality, gut microflora and immune response of broiler chickens"

c. "A closer look at the effect of preliminary goodness-of-fit testing for normality for the one-sample *t*-test"

d. "Soil water potential does not affect leaf morphology or cuticular characters important for palaeo-environmental reconstructions in southern beech, *Nothofagus cunninghamii* (Nothofagaceae)"

　　本章最後要提醒大家：標題既求精確、完整（exactitude and integrity），也要引人、有趣（appealing and interesting）。為此，有兩點要特別注意。第一點：標題的長度要適宜。成書成冊的大著作，既然只需給個標示大範圍的廣大標題，它的名稱自然是短短幾個字就好，不必像十八世紀有些英國的文學作品那樣，把書名拉得很長。相對的，一篇期刊論文則可能需要長一點，因為除了標示研究的方向、範圍、對象、或題材之外，它往往也要進一步告知研究的特定問題或屬性與該論文的焦點。

　　不過，期刊論文的標題也不能太長。例如，有一篇叫"A honey bee odorant receptor for the queen substance 9-oxo-2-decenoic acid"的論文。在那標題裡，已經告知研究的對象是蜜蜂（honey bee），研究的特定問題是有關「氣味接受器」（odorant receptor），

接受的氣味是「女王物質」（queen substance），而那物質就是9-oxo-2癸烯酸（9-oxo-2-decenoic acid）。這樣的標題已經很好了，但如果加上一個副標題來告知那研究是運用「基因體功能學的研究手法」，同時又加上一些字來告知在研究過程中使用了「某特定覺知化學成分的微陣列以及電流生理學」，結果把標題改成"Identifying a honey bee odorant receptor for the queen substance 9-oxo-2-decenoic acid by using a chemosensory-specific microarray and electrophysiology: a functional genomics approach"，這樣便是太長的標題。研究的材料、方法及其他細節，如無必要，通常在文中說明就好，不用在標題中交代。

其實，太長的標題既不容易記得，有時也沒空間可以把它全部印出來。因此，有些場合，長標題必須縮成短標題（short title）。在期刊的編輯上，有所謂「頁眉小標題」（running title or running head），那種標題會限定「全部的字母數」，像APA就把一個標題限定在40個字母以內。

在這裡要請大家注意的第二點是：中文的標題常有「...之研究」這種寫法，英文則通常不需"A study of ..."這種寫法。"The effects of uncertainty on the roles of controllers and budgets"就是"*A study of* the effects of uncertainty on the roles of controllers and budgets"，加上"A study of"只是多餘。不過，如果用類似"A critical study of," "A comparative study of,"這種詞語來告知那是某種特殊類型的研究（批評的或比較的），則可以接受。

本章的結語是：訂定學術論文的標題是一種學問，寫英文學術論文的標題也是一種學問。大家要多看多學、多寫多問，才能訂出並寫出一個很好的英文學術論文標題。

作業

1. 請找出一期屬於你們學門的（紙本的或電子的）英文學術期刊來看，據此回答下列問題：

   a. 該期刊的名稱（title）是什麼？

   b. 該名稱是否就是「只告知大範圍」的廣大標題（broad title）？

   c. 這期期刊裡的各篇論文是否都是「探討小題目」的狹小標題（narrow title）？

   d. 這期期刊裡有幾篇論文有副標題（subtitle）？

   e. 這期期刊裡的標題有哪些是「片語型標題」？哪些是「句子型標題」？

   f. 這期期刊裡的標題是「每一個字母全都大寫」嗎？是「有大寫各重要字之首字母」嗎？或是「通常無大寫字母」？

2. 根據「有大寫各重要字之首字母」的模式，下列標題有哪些「字母大小寫」方面的錯誤？請指出。

a. "Stress And Depression among Latina Women In Rural Southeastern north Carolina"

b. "Lagged Associations between overall TV news Viewing, Local TV news Viewing, and Fatalistic Beliefs About Cancer Prevention"

3. 根據「通常無大寫字母」的模式，下列標題有哪些「字母大小寫」方面的錯誤？請指出。

a. "circulating insulin-like growth factor binding Protein-1 and the risk of Pancreatic Cancer"

b. "Pattern of migration: how paleo-indians crossed beringia and settled in the Americas"

4. 下面的標題是不是都太長？其畫線部分是不是可以刪除？為什麼？請討論。

a. "<u>An</u> Exposure Assessment of Mercury and Its Compounds <u>by Dispersing Modeling</u>: A Case Study <u>in the Sea of Japan Coastal Area</u>"

b. "Hybrid Materials: Monodisperse Hollow Supraparticles via Selective Oxidation <u>Using an in situ Assembly Method</u>"

c. "<u>The</u> liver function in humans <u>with borderline liver dysfunction</u> is improved by a mixture of schisandra fruit extract and sesamin: <u>a randomized, placebo-controlled study</u>"

d. "<u>A Study of</u> a photon-fueled gate-like delivery system using i-motif DNA functionalized mesoporous silica nanoparticles"

5. 你最近想研究或正在研究的題目（topic）是什麼？如果把它的英文標題寫出來，是否為片語型的標題？請用下面兩種模式寫出來。

a.「通常無大寫字母」的模式：

b.「有大寫各重要字之首字母」的模式：

6. 你最近已經研究過什麼題目？得到什麼發現（finding）或結果（result）？如果用那發現或結果寫出一個英文標題，是否即為句子型的標題？請用下面兩種模式寫出來。

a.「通常無大寫字母」的模式：

b.「有大寫各重要字之首字母」的模式：

第三章

引言的內容與寫法

講解

　　在擬定研究的題目之後，研究者當然就要去進行研究。等研究結束時或研究告一段落時，研究者便可進行論文的寫作。通常，論文的最前面是個「引言」（Introduction）。如果那是一篇成書成冊的大論文（專書或學位論文），那引言可能是一個專章。如果那只是一篇普通的小論文（期刊論文或期末報告），那引言可能只是一個或幾個段落（paragraphs）。有時候，為了節省（寫作或編輯的）篇幅，引言也可以縮短成一、兩句話，甚至於完全省略掉。不過，沒有引言的論文，畢竟很少，也容易讓讀者感到「莫明來由」，而產生"Why this?"（幹嘛寫／研究這個？）的疑問。

　　「引言的部分」通常用來簡單地告訴整個研究的「背景」（background），所以在英文的論文裡，「引言的部分」有的標上"Introduction"的標題（heading），有的則標上"Background"的標題。其實，論文的起頭標上"Introduction"或"Background"，或標上其他字，或沒有標上任何字，往往都一樣：都是在「引言」，在說一些有關研究背景的話來把讀者引入研究的題目裡。

　　「引言」或「研究背景」通常就是論文的前端事項，包括「緣起」（cause）、「動機」（motivation）、「目的」（purpose）、「問題」（problem）、和「假說」（hypothesis）等。不過，有些引言也會述及論文的中間事項，像研究的「對象」（target）和「過程」（procedure），研究所採用的「理論」（theory）、「手法」（approach）或「方法」（method），以及研究所用的「材料」（material）或「資料」（data）等。甚至於有些引言也會先簡單的說出屬於論文末端的事項，比方說研究的「結果」（result）或「發現」（finding），研究的「貢獻」（contribution）、「價值」（value）、「含義」（implication）或「應用」（application），以及「建議」（suggestion）等。

其實，通常只有在大論文的「引言專章」（introductory chapter）裡，才會完整地把論文的前端、中間、和末端事項都簡述一番。在大論文的引言專章裡，甚至於還會有論文「結構」（structure）或「組織」（organization）方面的說明。在一般的小論文裡，引言確實只是簡述一些有關研究背景的前端事項而已。中間事項通常放在「材料與方法」（Material and Method）或其他牽涉到「所做工作」（the work done）的部分，而末端事項則放在「結果」（Result）、「討論」（Discussion）、和「結論」（Conclusion）的部分。小論文也通常不必說明論文的結構或組織。

學術研究者不會無緣無故地做研究（do research）。自然科學家可能因為看到某自然現象（natural phenomenon），而想探索（explore）其中的某問題。社會科學家可能因為看到某社會情況（social situation），而想調查（investigate）其背後的因素。人文學者則可能因為看到某文化的特徵（cultural feature），而想考慮（consider）其優缺點。總之，研究都有「緣起」：為了某緣故某起因，研究者才有研究的「動機」，才想去study，去探索、調查、考慮、檢視（examine）、分析（analyze）、評估（assess）、運算（calculate）、評價（evaluate）、說明（explain）、闡釋（elucidate）、細察（scrutinize）、深究（probe into）、或普查／量測（survey）某事物。在寫論文的「引言部分」時，通常就是要先交代這種緣起與動機。

　　研究的「緣起與動機」有百百種。面對問題（problem）、疑問（question）、或議題（issue），碰到需要（necessity）、需求（demand）或要求（requirement/ request），或感到興趣（interest）、困難（difficulty）、或引誘（temptation），統統會引起研究某事物的動機。有一種很常見的「緣起與動機」是：看到別人的研究不對或不夠，因此想加以更正或補充。這種「緣起」不只是因為看到某自然現象、社會情況、或文化特徵而已，另外還因為看到別人發表的某篇論文或因為參考了不少相關的文獻（literature），因此才觸動了靈感，引發了「進一步研究」（further study or research）的動機。

　　在大論文裡，有時會有「文獻回顧」（Literature Review）的專章，用來回顧一大堆跟這次研究主題相關的論文資料。在小論文裡，文獻回顧則通常只是幾段話，用來談幾篇發表過的著作而已。有時，小論文裡也會沒有文獻回顧，或只針對一篇文章的某論點來加以引述或批判而已。總而言之，在評述別人的著作時，往往會連帶揭露自己的研究動機。例如：在稱讚某人在某篇論文裡關於某事"has presented a plausible case"（已提出一個有理可信的案例）之後，接著可能說"However, the paper has no adequate discussion about ... Therefore, the mechanism underlying ... is still unclear"（可是，該論文關於……並沒有足夠的討論。因此，在……底下的機制仍然不清楚）。於是，研究者便說出他要研究什麼，藉以補足前人的缺憾。

在此附帶**請注意**：在引述別人著作時，雖然該著作之出版是在過去，作者也在過去說出他的論點，可是因為他的文章在現在以及到未來都還可以看見，而他的話語也隨時寫在那裡，所以我們會用現在式（而非過去式）來說他在某篇文章裡「說」什麼。例如："In his ..., C. T. Wang *says/ states/ holds/ suggests/ proves/ contends* that A is less important than B."（「在他的……[某文章]裡，C. T. Wang說／講說／堅持說／提示說／證實說／爭論說A比B不重要。」）

另外，某人研究後所說的結論（例如"A is caused by B"）通常用現在式的動詞來表示那是個恆常的事實。因此，就算你用有過去式動詞的話（如"Last year he proved that"）來說那事實，你也一樣要讓那恆常的事實保持用現在式的動詞來陳述。例如："Last year he *proved* that A *is* caused by B."

既然研究的「緣起與動機」有百百種，用英文來寫「緣起與動機」也就有百百種寫法。不過，因為「緣起與動機」往往牽涉到研究者的過去經驗或遭遇，所以講述起來常會有表示「過去某時」或「最近幾時」的「副詞」或「副詞片語」。例如：
"in the past"（在過去）、"on July 4, 2011"（在2011年7月4日）、
"at some time last year"（在去年某時候）、"in 1950's"（在1950
年代）、"recently"（最近）、"over the last 30 years"（在最近30
年間）、"in recent years"（在最近幾年）、"since the 19th century"
（自從19世紀以來）。

跟隨「過去某時」的動詞，通常是「過去簡單式」（past
simple tense）。例如："On July 4, 2011, I *read* a report on parades
in the world"（在2011年7月4日，我讀到一篇有關世界各地閱兵
的報導）。跟隨「最近幾時」的動詞，則通常是「現在完成式」
（present perfect tense）。例如："Over the last 30 years, the cases
of AIDS *have increased* rapidly"（在最近30年間，愛滋病的案例
已經急速增加）。

附帶**請注意**："recently"和"lately"兩字都是「最近」或「近
來」之意，兩字都可接過去簡單式或現在完成式的動詞，但前
者比較常跟過去簡單式，而後者比較常跟現在完成式。例如：
"Recently we *met* a problem."；"The condition *has* not *improved*
lately."

講述「緣起與動機」的人可能是「我」（研究者／論文發
表人單獨一人），也可能是「我們」（一個研究團隊／發表論
文的群體）。因此，英文的句子會有"I read," "We met" "I think,"
"We believe"這種字眼。不過，在許多論文裡，許多話都不喜歡
用「主動的」"I/ we do something"的模式來講述，而喜歡用「被

動的」"Something is done"的模式。原因是：說了"I/ we"，通常就只指涉到研究者／論文發表人，而不能含蓋其他人。例如："I/ we do not understand the problem"是說「我／我們研究者／論文發表人不了解這問題」，而"The problem is not understood"則是說「那問題不為（眾）人所了解」。

其實，說太多"I/ we"也會顯得太自我、太主觀。例如：說"Online porn films are a source of contamination in our society"（「線上色情影片是我們社會的一個污染源」）就好了，前頭不必加"I/ we know"，變成說「我／我們知道 線上色情影片是我們社會的一個污染源」。好像那件事情只有我／我們才會知道呢。

其實，英文"we"也常用來泛指「眾人」。例如："As we know, the earth is round"（如我們[即眾人]所知，地球是圓的）。用了"we"，有時會分辨不清是指研究團隊／發表論文的群體，或指眾人。例如，"But the problems of 'in what way and to what extent online porn films have contaminated our society' *are still unknown*"這句英文是說：「可是，『線上色情影片已經以什麼方式污染我們社會和污染到什麼程度』這兩問題，仍然不為人知。」說這樣的英文也就好了，不要說"But we still do not know the problems of 'in what way and to what extent they have contaminated our society'"（「可是，我們仍然不知道『線上色情影片已經以什麼方式污染我們社會和污染到什麼程度』這兩問題」）。因為，這樣說，讀者會分辨不清"we"是指眾人或是指該研究團隊／發表論文的群體。

不過，只關聯到"I/ we"的事，還是要用"I/ we"來說，不能用泛指眾人的被動語態。例如：前兩段所說的兩句有關線上色情影片的話可能接上"We, therefore, think it worth while to make a sample study of that sort of contamination in our community"（「因此，我們認為值得對那種污染做一個在我們社區的樣品式研究」）。在這句話裡，認為值得做那種研究的是「講述者／整個研究團隊」，不是「所有大眾」。所以不能改成"It is, therefore, thought worth while to make a sample study of that sort of contamination in our community"。

　　從上面講述色情污染的例句，我們還可以知道：講述「緣起與動機」時，通常由「泛論的話」（general statement）轉到「特定的問題」（specific problem）。上面那三句話中，第一句"Online porn films are a source of contamination in our society."是泛說「線上色情影片是我們社會的一個污染源」，第二句則轉到線上色情影片「已經以什麼方式污染我們社會和污染到什麼程度」這兩個特定的問題。於是，接著講出第三句話，也就是研究的動機：為了要回答那兩問題而去" make a sample study of that sort of contamination in our community"。

　　在此，我們比照這個憂慮心靈污染的話，可以給一段話來說出要研究環境污染的緣起與動機："Waste metals are a source of pollution in our environment. But the problems of 'in what way and to what extent waste metals have polluted our environment' are still unknown. We, therefore, think it worth while to make a sample study of that sort of pollution in our living area."這段話講的是:「廢五金是我們環境的一個污染源,但是『廢五金已經以什麼方式污染我們環境和污染到什麼程度』」這兩個問題仍然不為人知。因此,我們認為值得對那種污染做一個在我們生活地區的樣品式研究。」

有研究動機之後,就會去研究。在進行研究時,一定會懷有目的(purpose),有時還訂有目標(aim or goal)。有些論文可能不講緣起與動機,而直接講目的或目標。但**請注意**:所謂「目的」或「目標」,可能指當初做研究的目的或目標,也可能指現在寫這篇論文的目的或目標。前者等於要回答"Why was this study made?"或"Why was this research done?"這問題,所以會有"This study was (made) to ..."或"This research was (done) to ..."(「(做)本研究要……」)這種句子,用來講述研究的目的或目標。後者等於要回答"Why is this paper written?"這問題,所以會有"This paper is(written)to ..."(「(寫)本論文要……」)這種句子,用來講述寫論文的目的或目標。

附帶**請注意**:因為"study"既可指研究的工作,也可指研究的論文,所以英文"this study"或中文「本研究」一詞,既可指「本研究的工作」也可指「本研究的論文」。指前者時,會跟過去式的動詞;指後者時,則跟現在式的動詞。例如:"This study aimed to ..."是說當初「本研究(工作)的目標要……」,而"This study aims to ..."則是說現在「本研究(論文)的目標要……」。

用英文講述寫論文的目的或目標有許多種方法,下面便提供一些常見的模式供參考:

The purpose of this paper/ study is to investigate...

（本論文／研究的目的是要調查……。）

Our aim in this paper/ study is to explore...

（我們在本論文／研究的目標是探索……。）

In this paper/ study, I report on／deal with...

（在本論文／研究中，我 報導／處理……。）

In this paper/ study, we address the problem of...

（在本論文／研究中，我們應對……的問題。）

This paper/ study considers/ describes/ analyzes/ examines/ assesses...

（本論文／研究 考慮／描述／分析／檢視／評估……。）

In this paper/ study, the problem/ issue of ... is probed into.

（在本論文／研究中，……的問題／議題被深入探究。）

做研究或寫論文的目的常常是為了考慮、探索、調查、檢視、分析、評估、運算、評價、說明、闡釋、細察、深究、或普查某「問題」（problem）。而「問題」不外乎何人、何事、何物、何時、何地、何因、如何、與是否的「問題」。用英文說，就是"who, what, when, where, why, how, and whether"的問題。所以，我們會看到類似下面的說話模式：

This paper is to discuss/ explore *(the problem of) who/ what* ...

（本論文要討論／探索誰／什麼……的問題。）

In this paper, we aim to analyze *(the problem of) how/ why* ...

（在本論文中，我們的目標是要分析……如何／為何……的問題。）

In this study, we hope to answer *(the question of) whether or not ...*

（在本研究中，我們希望回答……是否……的問題。）

Herein, we address *the problem of when ...*

（在此，我們應對……在何時……的問題。）

Herein, we are concerned with *the issue of where ...*

（在此，我們關切……在何地……的議題。）

This paper is focused on *(the problem of) how/ what/ whether or not ...*

（本論文的焦點在於……如何……／什麼……／是否……
[的問題]。）

　　當然了，要討論、研究、分析的事物，用英文寫出來不一定是由who, what, when, where, how, why, whether等字所構成的片語（如how to learn English, why to reduce oxidation）或子句（如how we can synthesize A and B, where the geological features are found）。那事物更有可能只是一個（以某名詞為核心的）英文字群所代表的事項。例如：某論文可能要研究"the effect of A on B"（A對B的效用），或運算"the probability of A leading to B"（A導致B的或然率）。另一論文則要了解"the mechanism by which A induces B"（A引起B的機制），或確定"the role A plays in B"（A在B裡頭扮演的角色）。

　　明確說出研究的目的與問題之後，「引言」就差不多夠了。不過，有些引言會進一步說出研究者有什麼假說（hypothesis）。

因此，會有類似"Our hypothesis is: ..."或"It is hypothesized that ..."這種話語。有時候「引言」也會列出一些疑問（questions）來告訴研究者所要回答的重點。因此，文中會有類似"In this paper, we address three questions"或"Two questions are dealt with herein"這樣的話語。然後那兩、三個疑問便被列了出來，例如："First, what ...? Second, how ...? And third, is ...?"或"One question is: where ...? The other question is: why ...?"

　　以上有關英文學術論文之「引言部分」的解說，不算詳盡，但已經談到了不少重點。我們的結論是：引言的長度要看論文的篇幅而定，引言就是背景的陳述，引言以講出研究的問題與目的為重點，其他事項往往比較可有可無。不過，寫英文學術論文最要緊的還是：把英文寫對。只有好的英文才能讓英文的「引言」有正確的引導而真的引人入勝。

作業

1. 請找出一本屬於你們學門的英文學位論文或英文教科書來看，據此回答下列問題：

   a. 該著作的第一章或正文的最前面部分是不是「引言」？

   b. 該「引言」就叫Introduction嗎？或有什麼別的heading？

   c. 該「引言」是不是先有泛論再轉到細節，由通盤轉到特定問題？

   d. 該「引言」有沒有說明整個著作的結構或組織？

   e. 該著作有「文獻回顧」（Literature Review）的專章嗎？

2. 請找出一期屬於你們學門的（紙本的或電子的）英文學術期刊來看其中的一篇論文，據此回答下列問題：

   a. 該篇論文的最前面部分是不是「引言」？

   b. 該「引言」就叫Introduction嗎？或有什麼別的heading？

   c. 該「引言」是不是先有泛論再轉到細節，由通盤轉到特定問題？

d. 該「引言」有沒有說明整篇論文的結構或組織？

e. 該「引言」有講到研究的「緣起」（cause）與「動機」（motivation）嗎？

f. 該「引言」有講到研究的「問題」（problem）與「目的」（purpose）嗎？

g. 該「引言」有提出研究的「假說」（hypothesis）和列出「疑問」（questions）嗎？

h. 該「引言」有講到研究的「對象」（target）、「過程」（procedure）、「理論」（theory）、「手法」（approach）、「方法」（method）、「材料」（material）、或「資料」（data）嗎？

i. 該「引言」有講到研究的「結果」（result）、「發現」（finding）、「貢獻」（contribution）、「價值」（value）、「含義」（implication）、或「應用」（application）嗎？

j. 該「引言」裡有「文獻回顧」（Literature Review）嗎？

3. 請拿出一篇你的或你同學的英文學術論文來看，據此回答下列問題：

a. 該篇論文有Introduction嗎？

b. 該「引言」有Literature Review嗎？

c. 該「引言」有講到cause of the study嗎？如果有，該動機是因為面對問題（problem）、疑問（question）、或議題（issue），碰到需要（necessity）、需求（demand）或要求（requirement），或感到興趣（interest）、困難（difficulty）、或引誘（temptation）才產生的嗎？

d. 該「引言」有講到purpose of the study嗎？講出「目的」的那一句（或幾句）英文是什麼？

e. 在那「引言」裡，有用到表示「過去某時」或「最近幾時」的「副詞」或「副詞片語」嗎？如果有，在句中配合的動詞時態用對了嗎？

f. 在那「引言」裡，講述者是"I"（研究者／論文發表人單獨一人），或是"we"（一個研究團隊／發表論文的群體）？在文中有用太多"I/ we"或不當的"I/ we"嗎？

4. 請閱讀下段英文，再回答文後的問題。

Over the past two decades, the crucial role A plays in B *has become* a topic of practical interest. Available evidence suggests that if A increases in amount, then the welfare of B is increased as well. However, it is noted that the amount of A cannot grow unlimitedly. It may bring danger if it grows to a certain extent. Now, the question is: what is the extent? We have probed into this question, gathered enough data, made a good analysis, and provided an answer, which may be convincing to those interested in this topic.

a. 文中為何用"has become"而不用"became"？

b. 文中為何說"it is noted that ..."而不說"I/ we note that ..."？

c. 文中的前兩句是不是泛論（general statements）？

d. 文中的第3、4、5句（"However"~"extent?"）是否帶出特定問題？

e. 文中最後一句（"We"~"topic."）是否只直接說出「研究目的」而已？

f. 文中最後一句是否簡述了整個研究的作為？

g. 文中最後一句的"We"是指眾人或指整個研究團隊／發表論文的群體？

h. 文中最後一句能不能改成"This question has been probed into, enough data have been gathered, a good analysis has been made, and an answer has been provided, which may be convincing to those interested in this topic." ？

5. 請閱讀下段英文，再回答文後的問題。

A is an infectious viral disease associated with chickens. It is caused by B, a virus belonging to the family of C. In 2010, a spread of the disease *was found* in the area of D. In that same year, some biosecurity measures (生物安全措施) were taken to control the spread. However, the control was not very effective. Some time later, some scientists found that the outbreak of the disease *is* mostly due to certain vaccine-related strains (與疫苗有關的類型) of B. We, therefore, made an attempt to confirm the fact.

a. 文中前兩句是泛泛地在介紹A這種傳染病，第3、4、5句（"In 2010"~"effective"）是具體說出一個想控制那傳染病的案例，第6句（"Some"~"of B"）指出前人有關那傳染病的發現。這些話是不是研究的「背景」？

b. 這段話的最後一句（"We, therefore, made an attempt to confirm the fact."）是不是「動機」與「目的」？要"confirm"的"fact"是什麼事實？研究者是想改正或補充前人的缺憾嗎？

c. 文中的"was found"改成"has been found"可以嗎？會合於文法嗎？

d. 文中的"some biosecurity measures were taken"改成"we took some biosecurity measures"可以嗎？不會改變含義嗎？

e. 在"some scientists found that the outbreak of the disease *is* mostly due to certain vaccine-related strains"這句子中，"is"可以改成"was"嗎？

f. 文中"We, therefore, *made* an attempt to confirm the fact."這句的"made"可以改成"make"嗎？全句可改成"Therefore, an attempt was made to confirm the fact"嗎？

6. 在一篇談論「歐聯限制措施」的文章裡，我們看到四段話組成的"Introduction"：

第一段有兩句話，一句談到：限制措施一直是歐聯的一種最重要的外交政策。另一句講到："限制措施have been imposed on a large number of occasions, including ..."

第二段話講到："採用限制措施has raised several difficult legal questions, including ..."

第三段話講到："本文章discusses ..., including ... , and examines ..."

第四段話講到："本文章is structured as follows. First, ... Finally, the article analyses ..."

請問：

a. 在這四段話裡，哪一段是泛談情勢？哪一段是指出問題？哪一段講到目的或目標？

b. 在這四段話裡，第四段在講文章的結構嗎？那是不是小論文的Introduction常有的內容？

c. 為何第一段裡要說限制措施"have been imposed"而不說"were imposed"，也不說"we have imposed restrictive measures"？

d. 從第四段裡的"analyses"一字（而非analyzes），你可以推論說那期刊是用美式英語或英式英語在編排？

第四章

寫出研究的經過

講解

　　有研究動機與目的之後，研究者便會進行研究工作。在寫論文時，寫完「引言」（Introduction）之後，便要報告研究的經過。可是，論文有大有小，各學門各科系的研究經過又各有相當差異，我們如何概說「研究的經過」（the study work done）呢？一般而言，大論文要把研究的經過說詳細一點，小論文則可以把研究的經過說簡要一點。最大的問題在於學門的差異：有些人的研究工作只是找資料、看資料、和思考，有些人則必須做實驗、做實習、做田野調查、做實地觀測、做挖掘發現、做搜尋捕捉、做參觀面談、做問卷調查、做儀器分析、做樣品收集、或做其他任何不可或缺的工作或活動。只看書和思考的人，可能認為：根本不需要交代研究的經過，只要把看到的與思考到的加以分析整理，然後分章節（在大論文裡）或分段落（在小論文裡）把心得寫出來就好。相對的，有做實驗或做其他用到特殊場地、工具、人員、設備、儀器、材料、或方法的人，便必須把整個研究的經過加以交代，不論所寫的是大論文或小論文。

　　有的研究（research）要先徵求（recruit）人來做「研究的對象」（study subjects）。這種研究，在論文裡，便要先報告有關"the recruited human subjects"（徵求到的做為研究對象的那些人）的人數，以及那些人（跟該研究有關）的各項重要資料，如年齡、性別、習慣、病歷、教育背景等。如果那些人有加以分組，也要說明分組的情形。接著當然就是要說明如何針對那些人來做研究。

有的研究不是針對human subjects，而是針對animal models（動物模式）。這種研究會拿某種動物（rats, mice, rabbits, frogs, zebrafish, etc.）來當「模式」（models），有時還會加以分組（如分成the control group and the experimental group）。寫論文時，所用的動物類別和品名當然要清楚說明，如BALB/ c 就是一種常用的白色小鼠。至於分組研究的經過，當然更要清楚交代。

研究的對象除了人與動物之外，當然還有植物和礦物。其實，研究的對象可以大到宇宙的黑洞、銀河系、或某天體，也可以小到某種細胞、某元素、或某原子裡的質子、中子、或電子。無論如何，研究的對象必有英文名稱。有些東西除了有英文的俗名之外，還有學名。寫論文時，為了精確起見，通常要提俗名又給學名，例如：the southern beech（*Nothofagus cunninghamii*）就是「南方欅」之英文俗名及其（拉丁文的）學名。有時，除了俗名與學名之外，連其化學的分子式也要告知。例如，俗稱明礬的礦物，其英文俗名為alum，其學名為hydrated potassium aluminium sulfate，其分子式為$KAI(SO_4)_2 12H_2O$。

在英文的論文裡，各種動植物及微生物的學名（屬名、種名、或亞種名）通常都用斜體的拉丁字來表示，例如：*Connochaetes gnou*是一種白尾牛羚，*Eichhomia crassipes*是一種布袋蓮，*Anthrodia cinnamomum*是一種樟芝，*Trebouxia*是一種綠藻。另外注意：化合物名稱裡的化學元素代號，通常也用斜體字。例如：*N*-acetylcysteine 就是有氮（nitrogen）的乙醯基半胱氨酸。其實，各科系對各種物品或物質之英文名稱的寫法都有慣例，寫論文時，照例寫出便是。例如：在生物科技的領域裡，基因的名稱用斜體字（如*p53*），但基因表現的蛋白質則用正體字（如p53）。

研究有對象之外，也有針對的問題。例如，以台北地區為研究對象，可以研究其人口老化的問題；以某大樓為研究對象，可以研究其結構安全的問題；以火星為研究的對象，可以研究火星上有無水之存在的問題；以某種癌細胞為研究對象，可以研究控制其增生的問題。在寫論文時，通常在「引言」的部分一定會先提到研究的對象與問題。只是，在報告研究過程時，那對象與那問題往往需要再加以詳說。

詳說研究的對象與問題之後，還要告知使用的「材料」（material）。如果使用的材料有兩種以上，英文"material"一字便可改成"materials"。材料在研究的過程中，通常有特定的使用「方法」（method）。方法也可能有兩種以上，所以"method"也會變成"methods"。在一篇論文裡，可以把「材料」部分和「方法」部分分開報告，也可以合併報告。總之，在英文的論文裡，報告「材料」的部分和報告「方法」的部分，如果合成「材料與方法」，則其英文的heading有可能是"Material and Method"或"Materials and Method"或"Material and Methods"或"Materials and Methods"，視材料與方法的單複數而定。

有關材料與方法的說明，要盡量詳盡。例如，有一篇論文以某種「花瓣兩側對稱的罌粟花」（a zygomorphic-flowered papaveraceae）為研究的對象，而其研究的問題是：在那種花裡，「病毒引起的基因靜默」（virus-induced gene silencing）為何。在那篇論文裡，有一部分叫"Materials and Methods"。在那部分，首先詳說的是：以那種花的種子（seeds）、盤盆（trays and pots）、和自來水與液態肥（tap water and liquid grow）為材料，來栽培那種花的方法（包括種子來自何方、一盤放幾盆、溫度控制、移放花苗的情形、與施肥的細節等）。另外，還詳說一些細節，包括：以立體顯微鏡（stereomicroscope）切割花與花序（inflorescences）放在乙醇（ethanol）中、脫水（dehydration）後用 Balzers 隔膜乾藏、以及「看基因表現」和「分開定序兩種基因」的細節。

如上面的例子所示，在陳述所謂「材料與方法」時，往往會把工具、儀器、設備、空間等都一併說出。如果使用的工具、儀器、設備、或空間是學門之內所熟悉的，就不必另外說明，否則就要另外補充說明。例如：某研究團隊自製一套「免疫測試」（immunoassay）的系統，用以測定人體暴露於殺蟲劑的情形。在論文裡，他們便詳細說明那是如何裝置、有何功能、如何使用。

同樣的，研究的手法（approach）或實驗的技術（technique）如果是平常的，論文中一經提到，行內的人就會知道。如果那是創新的或特殊的手法／技術，就必須詳加介紹，否則同行的人也可能不會瞭解。例如，在分子生物學界，你說Southern blot,

Western blot,或Northern blot，大家就知道那是何種檢測（蛋白質、DNA、或RNA）的技術。如果你用一種新的、鮮為人知的檢測技術來研究，論文中就必須加以介紹。

其實，有很多學門並不太使用所謂的「材料」，而是使用所謂的「資料」（data）。他們的資料來自調查、觀察、普查、搜查、面談（investigation, observation, survey, search, interview）或其他管道。不管如何，在論文中，資料的來源一定要清楚交代。目前，在人文與社會科學界，很流行透過「問卷調查」（questionnaire）來搜集資料。在論文裡，除了交代發問的對象、發出問卷的份數、與回收的份數之外，也要把問卷的內容與目的說清楚。通常，整份問卷會放入主文中或附錄裡。

材料要準備（prepare）；資料要收集（collect）。準備好的材料要用方法或技術加以處理（deal with or treat），收集到的資料則用方法或技術加以分析（analyze）。在論文裡，除了報告材料如何準備或資料如何收集之外，也要說明如何處理材料或分析資料。在很多學門裡，資料會用統計學（statistics）的方法來分析。統計分成「有參數統計」（parametric statistic）與「無參數統計」（nonparametric statistic）兩大類型，而其方法與模式（methods and models）有很多種。在論文中，有必要把使用的統計方法與模式說清楚。另外，統計分析都會有平均質（mean）和標準差（S.D., standard deviation）。報告分析結果時，常要說出平均質與標準差，如A,B,C三種澱粉含水量的平均質與標準差為：$2.15\% \pm 0.08\%$。

資料中常有一大堆數據。在論文中，為了清楚起見，常常會把數據列成「表」（table）或繪成「圖」（graph）。圖的樣式有很多種，包括line graph, pie charts, bar graph, curve graph, scatter plot, histogram等等。這些或畫線條、或畫切餅、或畫欄柱、或畫曲線、或畫落點、或畫連續柱。但無論如何，在英文的論文裡，要把所有的tables（表）和graphs（圖）加以分開編號而依序印出。所以，Table 1（表一）當然出現在Table 2（表二）之前，接著是Table 3（表三）等等。不過，所有的graphs（圖）通常不會稱做Graph 1, Graph 2, Graph 3或Chart 1, Chart 2, Chart 3等等，而稱做Figure 1, Figure 2, Figure 3,等等，有時會把"Figure"縮寫成"Fig."。所以，"Fig. 1," "Fig. 2," "Fig. 3"等等也就是「圖一」、「圖二」、「圖三」等等。

不管是table或是graph，每一個圖表都要在編號後，加上幾個字當heading（標題）。例如：Table 2. Numbers of the Alumni in the Last 10 Years（最近十年的校友數）。Figure 4. Comparison of boys with girls regarding their sleeping habits（男孩與女孩有關睡眠習慣之比較）。從這兩例子可以看出：這種當標題的英文字，通常是一個名詞片語（nominal phrase），用「有大寫各重要字之首字母」的模式或用「通常無大寫字母」的模式都可以。但「表」好像比較常用前一種模式，「圖」則通常用後一種模式。而且**請注意**：表號及其標題通常放在表前，圖號及其標題則通常放在圖後。另外，表或圖都可在後頭附帶告知資料的「來源」（source）及加上必要的「注」（note）。例如：

Table 2.	Numbers of the Alumni in the Last 3 Years		
2009	Total: 761	male: 320	Female: 441
2010	Total: 765	male: 325	Female: 440
2011	Total: 772	male: 348	Female: 424
Source: From ABC University			

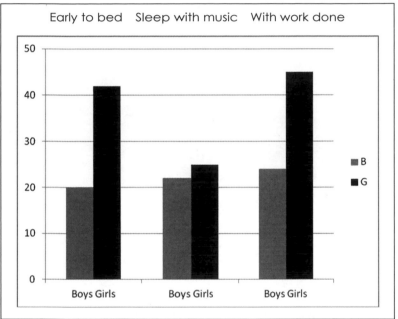

Fig. 4. Comparison of boys with girls regarding their sleeping habits
Note: Fifty boys and fifty girls were chosen at random from ABC University for this comparison.

在論文中，除了列表或繪圖之外，一定要有配合圖表的文字說明。所以，英文的論文裡常常會出現如下的詞語：

As shown in Table 1/ Figure 1, ...

（如表一／圖一所示，……）

As Table 1/ Figure 1 shows, ...

（如表一／圖一所示，……）

... is/ are shown in Table 1/ Figure 1.

（……顯示於表一／圖一）

... is/ are provided/ given in Table 1/ Figure 1.

（……提供／供給於表一／圖一）

... is/ are plotted/ presented in Figure 1.

（……繪製於／呈現於圖一）

Table 1/ Figure 1 shows ...

（表一／圖一顯示……）

Table 1/ Figure 1 provides/ gives/ presents ...

（表一／圖一提供／供給／呈現……）

Shown/ Given in Table 1/ Figure 1 is/ are ...

（顯示／供給於表一／圖一的是……）

事實上，show(n), provide(d), give(n), plot(ted), present(ed)
這些字眼也可能用demonstrate(d), display(ed), illustrate(d),
indicate(d), list(ed), report(ed), reveal(ed), suggest(ed), summarize(d)
等等許多其他字眼來取代。

在說明資料時，常常會做比較。在英文的論文裡，會常看到
如下的「比較用語」：

More/ fewer men did something *than* (did) women.

More/ Less water was found ... *than* (was) oil.

As many/ Not as many / Twice as many men did something *as* (did) women.

As much/ Not as much/ Twice as much water was found ... *as* (was) oil.

Ten percent more/ fewer men did something *than* (did) women.

Ten percent more/ less water was found ... *than* (was) oil.

A larger/ smaller percentage of men *than* women did something.

A larger/ smaller percentage of water *than* oil was found ...

Slightly over twice as many men *as* women did something.

Slightly over twice as much water *as* oil was found ...

Close to three times as many men *as* women did something.

Close to three times as much water *as* oil was found ...

Men *exceeded* women in something *by a ratio of* 1.8 to 1.

Water *exceeded* oil in something *by a ratio of* 2.4 to 1.

Compared with/ to X, Y showed *more/ less* ...

　　在說明資料時，也常常要提到變化。在英文的論文裡，會常看到如下的「說明變化的用語」：

Something *increased/ decreased a lot/ a little* when ...

After an initial increase/ decrease, X then *decreased/ increased gradually.*

After the gradual increase/ decrease, X *reached a maximum/ minimum of* ...

An upward trend/ A downward trend was found when/ after ...

A rise/ fall in something was found when/ after ...

The trend of something *rose/ fell/ remained steady* during ...

The trend of something *reached a high/ low point* during ...

There was a sharp rise/ steep fall when/ after ...

The trend of something *leveled off/ fell off/ declined* ...

It *reached a peak of* ... and then *fell to the bottom of* ...

There was a local maximum/ minimum before *a local dip/ peak.*

We found *a kink*（紐結）during ..., and *a spike*（尖頂）during ...

A sharp decline followed *a slow rise* until ...

　　論文裡，在報告研究過程的部分，除了交代「材料之準備及使用」或「資料之收集及分析」之外，其他跟研究相關的工作或活動（不管做實驗、做實習、做田野調查、做實地觀測、做挖掘發現、做搜尋捕捉、做參觀面談、或做樣品收集等），都要盡量清楚說明。在英文的論文裡，其使用的英文太廣泛太多樣了，在此無法一一詳說，只能說一些通則。

　　論文發表之前，研究工作應該已經結束，所以報告研究過程時，通常都會用過去式的動詞來講述任何事項，不管是主動或被動語態。例如：

We used it/ It was used as our basic material.

We applied the theory of .../ *adopted* the method of ...

This theory/ method *was applied/ adopted* to ...

They *were divided* into two groups by age.

They *were collected* and *classified* according to places of origin.

We *put* them in tubes and *stored* the tubes in a freezer.

We *conducted* the experiment to see the effect of ...

X *was extracted* from/ *replaced* by/ *added* to Y.

These acids *reacted* effectively on the metals.

　　當研究結束時，通常會有「結果」（result）或「發現」（finding），有時得到的「結果」或「發現」不只一項，因此"result"或"finding"會變成"results"或"findings"。在一篇英文的論文裡，有時會有標示為"Result"或"Results"的這一部分，用來報告整個研究中所發現的事實。其實，有些圖表也在顯示那些發現的事實或結果。但不管當時的「結果」或「發現」有幾個，講述那「結果」或「發現」的動詞通常還是過去式。例如："We found that x *had* a great effect on y"或"It was found that x *led* to y"。不過，有些人（有些學門）也會把研究的「結果」或「發現」當成恆常的事實（而非只是當時的事實），因而用現在式來講述。例如："As shown in Table 5, x *has* a great effect on y"或"As Fig. 5 shows, x *comes* from y and *leads* to z"。

　　每一個事項都有人去做，但做的人是誰呢？有時不知道，有時知道了也不方便說。在那種情況之下，英文的句子通常會用被動語態。例如，有一篇研究雞（chickens）的論文就有如下的句子：This study *was carried out* in ... The chickens *were housed* in ... Floor pens *were assigned* to ... The distribution of ... pens *was arranged* to ... ... Each pen *was equipped* with ... to ... New ... shavings *were used* ... The ... temperature *was held* at 31℃ ... 在那些句子裡，既不方便說出進行研究的是哪些人，也很難說出誰把雞放在舍裡、誰來分雞舍、以及誰來設給食器、弄雞窩、調室溫等，所以動詞都用被動形式。

不管是講材料或資料，不管是說儀器或工具，不管提到空間或設備，不管報告結果或發現，在英文的論文裡都會用到各種詞類的英文字，而每一種詞類的每一個字都要遵守語法。在名詞方面最傷腦筋的是：英文字有「可數」（C, countable）與「不可數」（UC, uncountable）之分，可數的名詞又有「單數」（singular）與「複數」（plural）之別。而且，名詞之可數與否、單複之形狀如何，都不是完全有規律、有邏輯。因此，非以英語為母語的人，在寫英文論文時，便要特別留意名詞之可數與否、單複之形狀如何。不清楚時，一定要查字典。像中文「傷害」譯成英文時，有hurt, harm, injury, damage, lesion等字可用，但這些字中，harm和damage通常是UC，lesion是C，hurt和injury則是C & UC。又像information和evidence這兩字通常是UC。而data原是datum的複數，但今天變成C & UC，當C時本身是複數，其複數並非datas。

英文字常有「同義字」（synonym）與「相反詞」（antonym）。要寫好英文，就要挑對用字。如increase, augment, enlarge, enhance

等字都是「增加、加大」，而decrease, reduce, diminish, lessen等字都是「減少、變小」。在寫「結果」或「發現」時，如果要說某地在某段期間「隨人口增加，社會福利反被減少」，其英文便是"As the population increased, the social welfare was reduced/ decreased"比較對，而"As the population was augmented/ enlarged/ enhanced, the social welfare diminished/ lessened"則不太對。

相對的，如果要說某藥物「隨其價格被增加，其效用反而減少」，則其英文便是"As its price was increased/ augmented, its effect decreased/ diminished/ lessened"比較對，而"As its price enlarged/ enhanced, its effect was reduced"則不太對。因此，除了看thesaurus（類詞字典）之外，大家也要養成辨認用字的習慣。各行各業在各種場合都有常用的語詞，跟著用那些語詞就對。

要寫好英文，除了要挑對用字之外，有時也要變化用字。像"X has a great influence on Y"這句話中的"great"可以改為considerable, huge, marked, noteworthy, pronounced, remarkable, significant中之任何一字而含義略同。如果把"a"改成"an"，則enormous, evident, obvious等字也可取代"great"。附帶說：在很多場合，considerably, markedly, remarkably, significantly, evidently, obviously等，也約略等同greatly。如"X is greatly/ evidently/ significantly higher than Y."便是。

本章講「寫出研究的經過」，從研究的對象、問題、材料／資料、方法／手法等講到圖表、結果／發現等研究的環節與論文的部分。我們並沒有把一切細節都說完畢，只是指出一些重點而已。在英文寫作方面，我們也只挑一些跟本章比較有關係的話題來講述而已，其他要點留待本書後面詳談。

作業

1. 請找出一期屬於你們學門的（紙本的或電子的）英文學術期刊來看其中的一篇論文，據此回答下列問題：

   a. 該篇論文有沒有報告研究經過的部分？

   b. 該部分是不是包括「材料與方法」和「結果」？

   c. 「材料與方法」的heading是**Material and Method**嗎？
   如果Material變Materials，或Method變Methods，是為什麼？

   d. 「結果」的heading是**Result**或**Results**？為什麼？

   e. 該論文如果沒有報告「材料與方法」和「結果」的部分，為什麼？

2. 在某篇談論「歐聯限制措施」的英文期刊論文裡，在**Introduction**之後，並沒有**Material and Method**的部分，也沒有**Result**的部分，而是有幾段話標題為Restrictive measures as defined by the European Union，也有幾段話標題為Relationship between international law and European law with regard to restrictive measures imposed by the UN Security Council。

請理解：

a. 該篇論文為什麼沒有說明研究的「材料與方法」？

b. 該篇論文為什麼沒有說明研究的「結果或發現」？

c. 其他類似該篇的法學研究，是不是通常也都沒有報告研究的經過？

d. 該篇論文為什麼要對restrictive measures的definition加以說明？

e. 該篇論文為什麼要說出international law和European law在限制措施方面的關係？

f. 「下定義」和「比較說明」是「研究的經過」嗎？
   如果不是，它們是「研究後的瞭解」嗎？

3. 在某篇談論氧化物與抗氧化物的論文裡，有個含有許多化學分子式的graph。在那graph下方，假定你看到的是如下的英文：

   FIG. 1. Generation and detoxification of ROS

   ROS are formed by ... forming ...

請瞭解：

a. FIG.是否等於Fig.或Figure？

b. 把FIG.寫成Graph，會合乎慣例嗎？

c. FIG. 1.後的那一行英文字（Generation ... ROS）是否為該 graph的heading？

d. 那heading下方的英文，是否為note？

e. 不寫"Note"這個字，而直接注釋，可以嗎？

f. 從"FIG.1."可知這個graph就是論文中的「圖一」，不是嗎？

4. 在某篇論文的Materials and methods部分，在講到*Plant material* 時，有下面幾句話："At each site, a single branch ... *was collected* from ... Thus, material *was collected* from ... All branches *were collected* ... Numerous cuttings *were made* from ... by ..."
請研究：這些句子中的動詞為何都是was/ were + p.p.（過去式與被動語態）？因為是過去的行為而且行為者不明，不是嗎？

5. 在同一篇論文的Results部分，其第一句話的語式為："x was highly dependent upon y (P <0.0001), but it was also strongly dependent upon z (P <0.0001; Table 1)."
請瞭解：

a. 在這句話中，動詞為何用was而不用is？是指過去發現的情況吧？

b. 說x was *highly* or *strongly* dependent upon y不就好了，為何還要加上（*P* <0.0001）這個括弧與數據？是為了給具體（科學化）的證據嗎？

c. 在句尾的括弧中，除了有*P* <0.0001這個數據以外，還有"Table 1"這兩字，那表示什麼？是「表1」或「圖1」？

6. 有一篇論文以「肉雞」（broiler chickens）為研究對象，而研究的問題是「餵枯草桿菌（*Bacillus subtilis*）給那種雞所產生的效用」。假定論文的RESLUTS部分有如下的兩句子：

The boilers fed with *B. subtilis* supplementary diets gained much more body weights than the control group (Table 3). ... No significant difference in body weight was found, however, among those groups which received different *B. subtilis* diets, when they were compared with the control group.

（註：這些英文經過虛擬、改寫，並非直接取自原文）

請瞭解：

a. *B. subtilis*即*Bacillus subtilis*嗎？為何要斜體？

b. *Bacillus subtilis*（枯草桿菌）是研究的material嗎？

c. 該研究有沒有divide the boiler chickens into groups？

d. 句中the control group是指受控制而沒吃枯草桿菌的肉雞嗎？

e. 該研究中的experimental group只有一組嗎？

f. 句中""those groups which received different *B. subtilis* diets"是否就是指實驗組，而且表示不只是一組？

g. 第一句中"much"可否用"significantly"取代？而第二句中"significant"可否用"great"取代？

h. 句中為何用"gained"和"was found"而不用"gain"和"is found"？

i. 第一句後面為何印上"(Table 3)"？

j. 出現"than ..."和"compared with ..."時，都跟著有比較級的字眼嗎？

7. 假定有篇論文以cell-phone worm（手機蠕蟲）為研究對象。研究的問題是：那種蠕蟲在cellular networks（手機網路）中如何透過opportunistic communications（隨機通訊）來擴展蔓延。假定在報告研究過程時，並無標示所謂Materials and Methods

的部分，但卻提到利用Markov model來設立自己的theoretical models，然後進行simulation（模擬）的測試。

又假定，該論文的某一部分以SIMULATION AND NUMERICAL RESULTS為大標題。該大標題之下又分成*Simulation Result*與*Performance Analysis with Numerical Results*兩個小標題。在前一小標題裡講兩句話。一句說：「我們run several simulations時，用的是the Opportunistic Network Environment (ONE) simulator」。另一句說：「我們的模擬is based on the Random Waypoint (RWP) mobility model」。而在後一小標題裡講到類似這樣的話："As Figure 5 shows, if the worms kill nodes ..., they may bring ... Furthermore, if the anti-virus software becomes ..., the worms will bring ..." 根據以上的假定，請瞭解：

a. 利用Markov model來設立自己的theoretical models，是不是就像利用某theory/ approach來開發自己的theory/ approach？在論文中報告研究過程時，應該包含像這樣的細節嗎？

b. 被使用的the Opportunistic Network Environment (ONE) simulator，是不是就像別的學門所使用的科學儀器或設備？在論文中報告研究過程時，也應該包含像這樣的細節嗎？

c. 模擬所根據的the Random Waypoint (RWP) mobility model，是不是就像別的學門所使用的assay（測試法）？在論文中報告研究過程時，也應該包含像這樣的細節嗎？

d. 在論文中，把某一部分再細分成若干部分，並分別給標題，可以嗎？給heading的字體（大、小寫，或粗、細體，與正、斜體之分），有硬性規定嗎？像這裡的SIMULATION AND NUMERICAL RESULTS分成*Simulation Result*與*Performance Analysis with Numerical Results*，可以接受嗎？

e. 這裡全用現在式的動詞（run, is, shows, kill, becomes等）來講述研究的過程與結果，這是電子學門的普遍作法嗎？你們的學門也都這樣嗎？

f. 既然有Figure 5，該論文應至少有五個graphs，不是嗎？

g. Figure 5的heading如果寫成Simulation result with RWP mobility model可以嗎？要把這heading放在圖前（上方）或圖後（下方）？

h. Figure 5是不是應該顯示"if the worms kill nodes ..., they may bring ... Furthermore, if the anti-virus software becomes ..., the worms will bring ..."這兩個事實？

第五章

討論與結論

講解

　　研究者在進行研究時，就可能會有一些「心得」（understanding）；在研究結束後，研究者通常會得到某種「結果」（result）或甚至於有所謂的「發現」（finding）。在寫論文時，研究者通常會根據研究的心得、結果、或發現，來進行「討論」（discussion）。在討論完之後，通常也會下個結論（conclusion）。

　　有許多學門的論文，在論文中會有標示為「討論」（Discussion）的部分，那部分有時候會有好幾段話，有時候也可能只有一大段話而已。不過，也有不少學門的論文（通常是人文社會科學的論文），在論文中並無標示「討論」（Discussion）的部分，而是在「引言」（Introduction）之後，便分章（chapters）或分節（sections）在討論各項問題了。那種論文似乎以「討論」為重心，雖然沒有標示「討論」（Discussion）的部分。

　　不管有沒有標示「討論」，討論都要針對研究的問題，把研究的心得、結果、或發現拿來跟「相關的事情」（relevant matters）說一說。在說一說的過程中，可以客觀引述各種事證與各種說法，也可以解釋自己的結果與堅持自己的看法，而讓討論（discussing）變成爭論（arguing）。但是，千萬不要扯得太遠，不能讓討論變成離題（digressing），變成離開了研究的問題。

　　討論是為了結論（Discussion is for conclusion）。在許多「相關的事情」（relevant matters）中，有助於達到（可能的）

結論的事項，就要說一說；無助於達到（可能的）結論的事項，就要放棄掉。討論是為了讓人能接受結論。所以說，討論是結論的準備工作（Discussion is preparation for conclusion）。

每篇論文都有它特殊的內容，「討論」的部分跟著不同的內容就可能有不同的寫法。一般來說，討論要先提一提當初研究的目標或問題，接著要說出這次研究的結果或發現，然後要講這個結果或發現是否合乎研究前的期望或假定、是否合乎一般的理論或想法、是否應驗了某種機制（mechanism）、是否跟前人的研究結果一致、是否受到了某種（材料、方法、或其他的）限制（limitation）、是否有特色或缺點、是否有應用的價值、是否有特殊的意義、是否有進一步研究的必要等等。在講是或講否時，同時要檢討為何是或為何否。在檢討時，常常會引別人的話或提別人的成果，也常常要拿別人的東西來比較。最後，在檢討、比較、論說之後，就要下結論。

下結論時，可以說幾段相關的話之後才下，因此論文中會有標示「結論」（Conclusion）的部分。其實，結論應該是可以用一句話來講完的事實。如果真的用一、兩句話便要講完，這時的「結論」便可以和「討論」結合在一起，成為「討論與結論」（Discussion and Conclusion）的部分。但是，在大論文中，有的「結論」很長，它是一個專章。在那個專章裡，前面各章討論的重點會被總結地再說一遍，然後才講出真正的結論，才扼要地說出整個研究的所得，才點明整篇論文想要說出的成果。即使在小論文裡，「結論」的部分也通常不只一句話，它也會再綜合說出前面提過的重點，然後才提出最後的、總結性的說辭。其實，一篇論文的結論並不必然只有一項或一點，結論是可以有兩個或兩個以上。因此，有些英文的論文，其「結論」部分是標示為"Conclusions"，而非"Conclusion"。

　　在英文的論文裡，要提原先研究的目標或目的時，可能會說到類似下面的話語：

　　a. The objective of this study was to ...（本研究的目標是要 ...）

　　b. The purpose of this survey was to ...（本綜合調查的目的是要 ...）

請注意："objective/ purpose"前可加"original"（原先的）一字，但可以不加，用了過去式動詞"was"便表示是「當初的」。

　　可是，當初研究時的問題仍舊是現在寫論文時的問題，就因為這樣，所以在結論中提到那問題時，所說的英文可能會類似這樣，動詞用現在式：

　　a. Our problem is ...（我們的問題是 ...）

　　b. The question we ask is: ...?（我們問的問題是： ...？）

　　c. The issue we are confronted with is: ...（我們面對的議題是： ...）

　　同理，在結論中重提假說時，也是"Our hypothesis is: ..."。

另請注意：這裡的"we/ our"指整個研究團隊，如果研究者只有一人（撰寫論文者本人），則"we/ our"當然會變成"I/ my"。如果不喜歡用"we/ our"或"I/ my"，也可以這麼說：

a. The problem this study has to solve is: ...（本研究必須解決的問題是：...）

b. The question for this investigation is: ...?（本調查要回答的問題是：...？）

c. The issue/ hypothesis that goes with this research is: ...（跟隨本研究的議題／假說是...）

要說出這次研究的結果或發現時，可能的英文說法類似這樣：

a. We found that A is B.（我們發現A就是B）

b. We found that X increased as Y decreased.（我們發現：當Y減少時，X增加了）

c. A major finding of this research is ...（這次研究的一個主要發現是 ...）

d. As shown in Table 1, the result [of this study] is: no significant difference can be found between A and B.（如表1所示，[本研究的]結果是：A與B之間，無法看到重大的差異）

　　請注意：因為發現（discover或find）的時間是在過去的研究過程中，所以通常用found/ discovered。但發現的事情可以視為永恆的事實而用現在簡單式（如a句裡的A is B），也可以視為當初一時的現象而用過去簡單式（如b句）。

　　在指出研究的發現或結果之後，如果要講這個結果／發現是否合乎研究前的期望或假定、是否合乎一般的理論或想法、是否應驗了某種機制、或是否跟前人的研究結果一致，就可能寫到類似下面的英文：

a. As [originally] expected/ supposed, X comes/ came close to ...（如[原先]所料／所假定的，X接近於……）

b. The result/ finding is *in complete accord with/ in direct contradiction to* the hypothesis/ theory that ...（這結果／發現完全符合／直接牴觸……的假說／理論）

c. Obviously, the result *falls short of/ is broadly in line with/ has exceeded/ has met* our expectations.（顯然這結果不如／大致有如／已經超過／有達到我們的預期）

d. This finding can explain the mechanism by which A protects B against/ from C.（這發現能說明A保護B對抗／免於C所依靠的機制）

e. The result/ finding supports/ contradicts/ echoes the idea that ...（這結果／發現支撐／牴觸／呼應……的想法）

f. This result/ finding *agrees very well with/ does not quite agree with* that reported by James Miller.（這個結果／發現與James Miller所報導的那個 非常一致／並不很一致）

在引述別人的想法或研究的結果／發現時，有可能用到如下的英文：

a. James Miller, et al. (1992) found that ...（James Miller等人[在1992年]發現……）

b. In an essay, Johnson observes that ... (293). （在一篇論說中，Johnson評說……[其作品293頁]）

In an essay, it is observed that ... (Johnson 293) （在一篇論說中，有人評說……[Johnson作品293頁]）

c. It is believed that the theory of x will soon supersede the theory of y (Taylor & Shaw 2005). （有人相信x的理論會很快取代y的理論[見Tailor與Shaw 2005年著作]）

d. We cannot but agree that "Language is a habit formation" (Turner 28). （我們不能不同意說：「語言是一種習慣的養成。」[Turner著作第28頁]）

這裡**請注意**幾點：

(1) 在小論文中或在大論文的同一章節中，被引述的人，除非（在學門之內）很有名（如Shakespeare, Einstein等），否則第一次在文句中被提到時，應該用全名（如James Miller）。第二次以後被提到時，或者被用在文句後的括弧中來標示作者時，就只提其姓（如Miller）而不提其名。

(2) 有些學門的論文，在引述他人時，常在他人的姓名之後加年代，或加括弧及年代，例如Taylor & Shaw 2005或James Miller, et al. (1992)，用以表示引自哪一年分的著作。不過，有些學門的論文則在引述的人名及其話語之後用括弧標示著作的頁碼，或在引述的話語之後用括弧標示作者及著作的頁碼。如上頭b兩句中的(293)或(Johnson 293)。

(3) 當說到某人「發現」什麼時，英文還是discovered/ found，因為發現總在過去的某時候。可是，當說到某人在某文章中「說」什麼或「寫」什麼時，就要用says/ writes，因為在那文章裡，過去、現在、未來他都在說或寫那些話。跟says/ writes類似的字眼是observes（評說）、suggests（提示）、asserts（主張）等等。（見上頭b例句）

(4) 當直接引他人話語時，要加括號，如上頭d句中的"Language is a habit formation"。當間接引述（用自己的話來說別人的意思）時，則不加括號，如上頭c句中的the theory of x will soon supersede the theory of y。

　　在英文的論文中，要說本研究是否受到了某種限制、是否有特色或缺點、是否有應用的價值、是否有特殊的意義、是否有進一步研究的必要等事項時，可參考如下的模式：

　　a. Owing to the limitation on our budget/ space/ material supply/ time for work, we were unable to ...（由於我們預算／空間／材料供應／工作時間的限制，我們[當時]無法……）

　　b. Limited by ..., we could only ...（受限於……，我們[當時]只能……）

　　c. The strength/ advantage of this study is its ...（本研究的長處／優點是其……）

　　d. The weakness/ disadvantage of this method lies in ...（這方法的弱點／短處存在於……）

e. ... can be considered (to be) a special feature of this investigation.（……可視為本調查的一大特色）

f. The result shows/ proves that the theory/ idea of ... can be applied in the field of ...（這結果表示／證明……的理論／想法 能應用於……的領域）

g. With this finding, we may suggest that this new technique (should) be applied to the making/ production of ...（有了這發現，我們可以建議：這種新技術[應該]要應用於製造／生產……）

h. It is *significant/ noteworthy/ remarkable* that the ... has such a result.（本……有此結果，實在很有意義／值得注意／可大說特說）

i. *No less significant/ Equally remarkable* is the fact that ...（同樣有意義的／同樣值得注意的是……的事實）

j. The most important implication of these results is: ...（這些結果的最重要含意就是：……）

k. It may be necessary to *do further research for/ carry out one more research into* the causes of ...（或許需要進一步做研究／再進行一次研究以瞭解……的原因）

l. To understand its underlying mechanism, we have decided to conduct another experiment.（為了瞭解它的根本機制，我們已決定進行另一次實驗）

m.It may be suggested that A (should) collaborate with B for further exploration of ... （也許可以建議：A[應]與B合作進一步探索……）

在下結論時，可能會寫出類似這種模式的英文：

a. Our / My conclusion is: ...（我們／我的結論是：）

b. It can be concluded that ...（可能下結論說……）

c. In conclusion, ...（總之，……）

d. So far, we have *arrived at/ come to/ reached* the conclusion that ...（到此，我們已經來到了結論說……）

e. From the discussion above, two conclusions can be drawn: first, ...; second, ...（從以上討論，可以下兩個結論：第一、……；第二、……）

f. These results/ findings lead us easily to the conclusion that ...（這些結果／發現 很容易地帶我們來下結論說……）

g. Now, we must conclude this discussion by saying that ...（好，我們必須結束這次討論而說……）

講述「結果」或「發現」的句子，其動詞通常是過去式，因為那是研究過程中（在過去）一時看到的現象。相對的，講述「結論」的句子，其動詞通常用現在式，因為要把那結論當成恆常的事實。舉個例說，在報告研究過程時，可能講：

We found that vitamin B3-supplemented mice lived longer

than the control mice.

（我們發現補充維他命B3的老鼠比控制組的老鼠活得久）

句中用found和lived，表示「發現是在過去某時候」而「補充維他命B3的老鼠比控制組的老鼠活得久，也是那時候發現的現象」。可是，在寫結論時，句子可能是：

It can be concluded that mice live longer with supplementation of vitamin B3.

（可以下結論說：有補充維他命B3，老鼠會活得久一點）

句中用live不用lived，因為把那事實視為過去、現在、未來都會如此的事實。也就是說：補充維他命B3會讓老鼠活得久一點這件事，不只是在過去某時候被發現的現象，而是恆常的事實。

　　本章的題目是進行討論和下結論。不同的學門當然有不同的討論方式與下結論的手法，而論文的大小也會影響討論和結論的長短。用英文和用中文來寫論文都一樣，討論的方式與多寡要恰當合宜，結論要清晰有意義。只是英文不好的人，如果要用英文來討論和下結論，必然會有些困難。本章只提到一些可學習的模式與一些注意事項而已，更多的東西還需要從別人的好論文中去學習。

作業

1. 請找出一期屬於你們學門的（紙本的或電子的）英文學術期刊
   來看其中的一篇論文，據此回答下列問題：

   a. 該篇論文有沒有標示「討論」（Discussion）的部分？

   b. 該篇論文有沒有標示「結論」（Conclusion）的部分？如果
      有，是Conclusion或Conclusions？

   c. 該篇論文是把討論和結論合成「討論與結論」（Discussion
      and Conclusion）嗎？或有其他的組合方式？

   d. 該篇論文的討論有沒有離題？

   e. 該篇論文的討論是不是為了下它的結論？

   f. 該篇論文的討論有沒有下列的內容？
      (1)提當初研究的目標或問題

      (2)說出這次研究的結果或發現

      (3)講這個結果或發現是否合乎研究前的期望或假定

(4)講這個結果或發現是否合乎一般的理論或想法

(5)講這個結果或發現是否應驗了某種機制（mechanism）

(6)講這個結果或發現是否跟前人的研究結果一致

(7)講這個研究是否受到了某種（材料、方法、或其他的）限制（limitation）

(8)講這個研究是否有特色或缺點、是否有應用的價值

(9)講這個研究是否有特殊的意義、是否有進一步研究的必要

g. 該篇論文所做的結論是哪一句或哪幾句話？其中的動詞用現在式嗎？

2. 請找出一篇屬於你們學門的（紙本的或電子的）英文的學位論文來看，據此回答下列問題：

a. 那是碩士或博士論文？

b. 那論文有多長？（總共幾頁？）

c. 裡頭有某章（或某節）標示「討論」（Discussion）的部分

嗎？如果沒有，「討論」是不是等於分散在別的章節裡？

d. 裡頭最後有一專章（或節）標示「結論」（Conclusion或 Conclusions）嗎？如果沒有，結論在哪裡？

e. 該論文的討論有沒有離題？是不是為了下結論？

f. 該論文的討論內容有上題那九項嗎？

g. 該論文的結論是什麼？話中的動詞用現在式嗎？

3. 在一篇談野放蝙蝠的論文裡，「討論」（Discussion）的部分可能有好幾段，其中有兩段的部分文字可能如下：

The availability of insects for food *depends* very much on the temperature of the season (Taylor 1963); therefore, choosing the right season for releasing the bats *may be* crucial to their survival (Fleming & Eby 2003; Wang *et al* 2010). ...

Like hawks in the air, those bats usually *foraged* in certain restricted areas during the first 4 or 5 hours of the night (Barak & Yom-Tov 1989). ... *It is not unlikely* that our bats *directed* the suitable sites for their foraging by eavesdropping on their conspecies (Balcombe & Fenton 1988; Fenton 2003).

（註：這兩段英文經過虛擬、改寫，非真正取自該篇原文）

請理解：

a. 為何第一段第一句前半句的第一個動詞用現在式（*depends*）而第二段第一、二句的動詞卻用過去式（*foraged, directed*）？

b. 第一段第一句後半句的may be若改為might be，語氣（mood）有差別嗎？

c. 第二段第二句的It is not unlikely可改為It was not unlikely嗎？

d. 第一段第一句前半句、後半句的後面與第二段第一、二句的後面，都有括弧加上專有名詞及數字。專有名詞是作者的名或姓？為何不連名帶姓？數字是著作年分嗎？*et al*就是and others（等人）嗎？Fleming & Eby就是Fleming and Eby兩人嗎？Yom-Tov是一個姓或兩個姓？

4. 在一篇研究種族歧異與組織作為（ethnic diversity and organizational performance）的論文裡，「討論」（Discussion）的部分也可能有好幾段，其中有兩段的部分文字可能如下：

Two *primary contributions* have emerged from this significant research. ... Aside from the contributions, these results have several *implications* for further practical as well as theoretical consideration regarding organizational diversity.

After examining all the factors involved, we found that the ethnic diversity among the employees seemed to get in the way of their civility towards the service recipients and it seemed to have negatively affected the organizational performance. These findings should be *interpreted* in contrast with those previous findings which suggest the positive effects of ethnic diversity on organizational performance [e.g., Richard et al., 2004, 2007] ... Our findings certainly suggest that demographic diversity among employees might create or deplete resources for civility and ultimately influence the performance of organizations.

（註：這兩段英文也經過虛擬、改寫，非真正取自該篇原文）

請理解：

a. 第一段談到研究的primary contributions（主要貢獻），算離題（digression）嗎？

b. 第一段也談到研究結果的implications（意涵），算離題嗎？

c. 第二段第二句講到的These findings是指前一句中所說的這兩件事嗎？

　(1)雇員的種族歧異，似乎妨礙到給予服務對象的禮節。

　(2)雇員的種族歧異，似乎妨礙到組織的作為。

d. 第二段談到「應該如何interpreted（詮釋）發現的事實」，這算離題嗎？

e. 第二段提到前人的認定：他們認為種族歧異對組織作為有正面效用。像這樣在討論中提前人的結論，很正當嗎？

f. 這裡最後一句"Our findings certainly suggest that"這幾個字後面的那句話說：「雇員中人口分布的歧異會創造或用盡 助長禮節的資源而最終影響到組織的作為。」這句話是不是這篇論文的結論？這結論是不是牴觸前人的結論？

g. 在這兩段話中：
(1)Have emerged可改成had emerged嗎？

(2)seemed to get in the way可改成seem to get in the way嗎？

(3)把might create or deplete改為may create or deplete語氣更肯定嗎？會更好嗎？

h. 這裡用中括弧[ ]取代小括弧( )，有關係嗎？像這種格式的細節，是不是跟刊物的體例一致就好，不必太計較？

5. 有一篇英文論文["Bodies That Matter: How Does a Performer Make Himself/ Herself a Dilated Body?" in *Tamkang Review* (42:1, December 2011, 103-126)]討論演員（performers）如何使自己成為「膨脹的身體」（"dilated body"）。在那論文裡，並沒有

標示「引言」（Introduction）的部分，也沒有標示「討論」（Discussion）的部分。不過，卻有「結論」（Conclusion）的部分。其實，那篇論文從頭到尾都是在討論。論文一開始，討論的是「身體」（body）的定義，中間討論到「無器官的身體」（the Body without Organs）以及其他相關題目，最後才討論到「膨脹的身體在劇場中的功能」。文中有一句話說：

For Eugenio Barba, ... the body is a network of energy and the "whole body thinks/ acts, with another quality of energy"(*Paper Canoe* 52).

（註：此段及下面兩段英文，作者蘇子中[Su Tsu-Chung]允許直接引自該篇原文，在此特予誌謝）

這裡請問：

a. 為何把Eugenio Barba的名與姓一起寫出（而不僅僅寫其姓Barba）？是因為文中第一次提到他嗎？

b. 引言後的(*Paper Canoe* 52)是表示什麼？是表示*Paper Canoe*那著作的第52頁嗎？

c. 這裡可以把(*Paper Canoe* 52)改為(Barba 52)嗎？如果不可以，是因為什麼？這裡有兩個事實：(1)同一句中前頭已經提到Eugenio Barba。(2)文中引用到的Barba的著作不只*Paper Canoe*那一本（從「引用書目」中，可知文中總共引用到Barba三個著作）。這兩個事實是否就是原因？

這篇論文後來說到「無器官的身體」時，有一句話說：

In *A Thousand Plateaus*, Deleuze and Guattari *stretch* the image even further and *describe* the Body without Organs as a "worldwide intensity map"(165) and they *argue* that "... The BwO is opposed not to the organs but to that organization of the organs called the organism"(158).

請理解：

a. Deleuze and Guattari是指Gilles Deleuze and Felix Guattari這兩人。但文中為何不用全名呢？是因為這裡並非文中第一次提到他們兩人嗎？（文中前面確實已經提過他們）

b. 這裡的(165)和(158)是指著作第165頁和第158頁嗎？是誰的著作？就是句中提到的Deleuze and Guattari嗎？是哪一個著作？就是句前提到的*A Thousand Plateaus*嗎？如果句前沒有提到*A Thousand Plateaus*這著作，是不是(165)和(158)就必須改寫成(*A Thousand Plateaus* 165)和(*A Thousand Plateaus* 158)呢？（「引用書目」告知：在文中，那兩人被引用的著作有兩本，其一為*A Thousand Plateaus: Capitalism and Schizophrenia*，其二為*Anti-Oedipus: Capitalism and Schizophrenia*）。

c. 在這段話中，為何用stretch, describe和argue而不用stretched, described和argued呢？是因為兩作者在那著作中確實永遠（過去、現在、及未來）都會stretch, describe和argue嗎？

這篇論文的結論說到：

The performance of the dilated body is indeed the mystery of theatre. ... In this sense, to make a dilated body is both the foundation and the possibility of performance. It is an act to create a "secular sacrum" (Grotowski 49) in the theater ...

請理解：

a. 文中(Grotowski 49)為何不放在句後，而放在"secular sacrum"之後？是因為應該放在直接引用的話語後（不管一句或一詞）嗎？

b. 「引用書目」告知：在文中，Grotowski就是Jerzy Grotowski這個人。那麼這裡怎麼不寫(Jerzy Grotowski 49)呢？是因為括弧中只需引作者姓氏來告知出處嗎？

c. 「引用書目」也告知：Grotowski在文中被引用的著作只有 *Towards a Poor Theatre* 這一本。就是因為只有這一本，所以寫(Grotowski 49)就好，不必寫(Grotowski, *Towards a Poor Theatre*, 49)，是嗎？

d. 如果文中沒提到Grotowski，光在引言後寫(*Towards a Poor Theatre*, 49)可以嗎？那樣如何知道書的作者？

6. 有一篇研究某種罌粟花（*Cysticapnos*）的英文論文，它的「結論」寫成"Conclusions"，可見結論不只一點。我們仔細看，發現結論雖然只有一段，裡頭卻有好幾句話。

第一句話說：「我們已顯示（"We have demonstrated"）*Cysticapnos*是可以實驗栽培而對基因研究不會有困難的。」這種話是「研究的結果／發現」或「研究的結論」？或兩者皆是？

第二句話推測取得某種資料會便利（will facilitate）對*Cysticapnos*基因的研究，像這種推測（surmise）可以放在結論中嗎？

第三句話說*Cysticapnos*是第一個有基因功能研究資料的花種（species），這等於說出該研究的意義／重要性。這種定位的話也可以放在結論中嗎？

第四句話說：「我們當初發展（we developed）這套研究系統是為了進行有關*Cysticapnos*的比較研究。」第五句話說：「可是，這套系統也可以用來（can be used to）研究別的東西。」這兩句話合起來也可當結論的一部分嗎？附帶問：在這裡"developed"可以改成"develop"嗎？"can be used"可以改成"could be used"嗎？

最後一句話說：「比較各種罌粟花（poppies）的基因結構有了見地之後，未來的研究可以延伸到（may extend to）更基礎的延胡索的種類（basal fumitory species）。」這顯然是一個建議（suggestion）。建議可以當結論的一部分嗎？附帶問："may extend to"若改為"might extend to"，好嗎？會不會語氣太假設、太沒自信了？

第六章

摘要及其他副文

講解

　　學術論文通常會有摘要，但論文中不一定有「摘要」（Abstract）這個標題（heading）。不管有無那個標題，摘要的文字通常被印在論文的標題（title）之後，主文（main text）之前。不過，在寫論文的次序上，通常是寫完主文（從引言到結論）之後，才寫摘要。而且，摘要中的文句也可能會重複用主文中的文句。總之，摘要是主文的濃縮，通常濃縮到一頁或半頁以內，不管那論文是大論文或小論文。那一頁或半頁以內的摘要，通常不分段落，但要分成若干小段也未嘗不可。像某英文期刊的一篇論文，其摘要分四段而下四個標題，分別簡述研究的 Background and Aims, Methods, Key Results, 和 Conclusions 等。另一期刊的一篇論文則將摘要分五段而下五個標題，分別簡述研究的 Background, Purpose, Methods, Results, 和 Conclusion 等。

　　「摘要」就是「摘取」論文的「要點」，寫成那麼一段或幾段，好讓讀者「未讀全文，便知大概」的工夫。這工夫當然不容易，要有簡潔的文筆才辦得到。大體而言，一篇完整的摘要應該把研究的主題／問題、對象／範圍、動機／目的、方法／手法、材料／資料、假說／理論、經過／步驟、結果／發現、結論／建議等等，都用最簡短的話來概述一下。不過，有許多論文的摘要並不完整，有的缺動機／目的，有的缺經過／步驟或其他部分。

一般來說，研究的主題／問題、方法／手法、材料／資料、結果／發現、與結論，是不可或缺的。只是，有些從頭到尾都在討論的論文（通常是人文社會科學類的），可能就連方法／手法、材料／資料、結果／發現等都沒有，因此那種論文的摘要可能就是各章或各節論點的集合而已。

　　舉個例子最清楚。有某篇英文論文，它報告的是"The Anti-oxidative and Anti-atherosclerotic Effects of *Morus alba L.* Leaf Extract"（「白桑葉精的抗氧化與抗動脈硬化功效」）。它的摘要分四段：

　　　　第一段說cardiovascular disease（心血管疾病）是人類致命的主因之一，hyperlipidemia（高脂血症）會造成動脈硬化，oxidated LDL（氧化的低密度脂蛋白）會傷害血管內皮細胞、引起內皮功能失調、進而引發動脈硬化。第二段說該研究要透過a model of in vitro cell culture and anti-oxidation experiment（在試管中培養細胞與做抗氧化實驗的模式）來evaluate（評估）白桑葉精的抗氧化與抗動脈化功能。第三段說白桑葉精富含抗氧化的pigments（色素），該研究就在measure（計量）白桑葉精對氧化低密度脂蛋白之效用與抗動脈硬化之功能。研究發現白桑葉精有DPPH radical scavenging（清除DPPH自由基）之能力，研究中用了apoB fragmentation（脫輔基蛋白裂解），relative electrophoretic mobility（REM相對電泳移動量）以及thiobarbituric acid reactive substances（TBARS硫代巴比妥酸反應物質）之assay（測試）。結果顯示白桑葉精能保護apoB，能減少REM，也能抑制TBARS。同時發現：低濃度的白桑葉精就能顯著減少細胞內cholesterol（膽固醇）和triglycerides（三酸甘油脂）的積聚，而抑制foam cells（泡沫細胞）的形成。最後一段說「我們的研究展示：白桑葉精可能抑制低密度脂蛋白的氧化而有抗氧化與抗動脈硬化的效用。」

這樣的摘要有引言（第一段），有目標與手法（第二段），有材料、方法、結果、發現（第三段），也有結論（第四段），可以說是很完整的摘要。

　　再舉個例子來說吧。有一篇從頭到尾都在討論的論文，標題叫"Why Literature in a Language Department?"（「為何要文學在語言學系裡？」）。那篇論文的摘要如下：

This paper aims to explain why literature is taught in a language department. Three strong reasons are given in it. First, a literature course is "practical" in a language department, since the language used in literature is usually not quite different from the language used in our daily life. Literary fictionality is not equal to impracticality; the speech acts in literature resemble the speech acts in real life. Second, a literature course is pleasurable as well as practical, since literature is to delight and instruct at the same time. A literary work can indeed help teach a language through its delightful form and content. Third, a literature course can be more holistic than a linguistics course or a language-training course, since it provides not only literary knowledge but also general knowledge in life and for life. A literary text can be used to teach grammar, rhetoric, and pragmatics at once. It contains truth, beauty, and goodness. It can help develop the students' linguistic competence, literary competence, and communicative competence. Confucius knew the importance of literature to language education a long time ago. Modern language teachers will be following Confucius if they stress the importance of literature and use literary texts as language-teaching material.

（註：這是本書作者該篇論文的摘要）

　　這樣的摘要把討論的目標與各節的重點都扼要說出了（包括：文學也是實用語言、能悅人、內容含蓋比較全面。文本可用以教語法、修辭、語用，可提升語言智能、文學智能、溝通智能。孔子早就認知文學對語言教育的重要性。）。像這樣的摘要，也算很完整。

　　學術論文的摘要底下，通常還會附「關鍵詞」（Keywords）。所謂「關鍵詞」就是論文中討論（discuss）或指涉（refer to）的重要詞語（terms）或想法（ideas or concepts）。讀者看到你的「關鍵詞」，便約略知道你的論文是有關什麼了。其實，「關鍵詞」能方便（電腦）搜尋到你的文章，因此那是論文引人參考的重要指標（guide）。像上頭研究白桑葉的那篇論文，其「關鍵詞」就包括*Morus alba L.*（白桑葉），anti-oxidation（抗氧化），anti-atherosclerosis（抗動脈硬化）等詞語。而那篇談文學課的論文就以literature, language-teaching, holistic, linguistic competence, literary competence, communicative competence等為「關鍵詞」。一般而言，一篇論文的「關鍵詞」不必列太多，三、五個就可以，超過十個就太多了。

在撰寫論文的主文（main text）時，有時會覺得有些話應該順便說出來讓讀者知道，可是感覺起來那些話並沒有重要到必須放在主文中。另外，如果把它硬塞在主文中，讀起來也覺得有點離題或不順暢。遇到這種情形，把那些話用附注（note）的方式說出來，便是最好的方法。以前，很多註記（notes）都在告訴讀者引言的出處（sources of quotes），今天則通常把作者、著作名稱、出版年分、頁碼等訊息直接用某種方式寫在主文中告知讀者，而不採取另外註記的方式。今日學術論文中的注，確實是只保留給「想順便說一下而有助讀者額外瞭解」的話語。

註記或注釋（notes）有兩種方式，一種把全部的注釋都放在整篇主文之後的叫「尾注」（endnotes），另一種按頁把該頁中個別出現的注釋標寫在該頁下方的叫「腳註」（footnotes）。通常尾注要有「注釋」（"Notes"）這個標題（heading），腳註則沒有標題。如果尾注只有一條注釋，那「注釋」的英文標題，當然就是"Note"而非"Notes"。

不管是尾注或腳註，要標數碼和寫注文時，在各學術領域或各期刊中，都有其特別的格式與規定。MLA或APA或IEEE或其他學術組織都訂有這方面的寫作規範，寫論文的人應該留意遵行。如果你不熟悉，反正模仿你們本行的期刊格式便是。

做學術研究時，常常會參考別人的見解。在寫學術論文時，常常會引別人的話語或用別人的想法。引用他人的觀念或話語，一定要註明出處，否則便是嚴重違反學術倫理的抄襲或剽竊（plagiarism）。其實，學術論文的主文之後，除了可能有「注釋」（Note或Notes）之外，也通常會有「參考書目」（Bibliography）或「參考資料」（References）。這一部分也有稱為「引用著作」（Works Cited）或「引用文獻」（Literature Cited）之類的。有時候，如果參考的書目／資料太多而有大區別，也有將之分類的（如分成Primary Sources與Secondary Sources）。總而言之，在這一部分，要把參考到的作者姓名、著作名稱、出版資料（年分、城市、公司）等列在一起。在英文的論文裡，每筆資料通常都按作者的姓氏，以英文字母排列的順序來編列。不過，作者姓名之後，有的格式是先寫著作年分，再寫著作名稱以及出版資料，有的則先寫著作名稱以及出版資料，再寫著作年分。如果你不知道怎麼寫，還是同樣一句話：模仿你們本行的期刊格式便是。

在此附帶**請注意**：如果在英文的論文裡，你只列一筆資料或一本著作，這時References/ Works Cited便要改成Reference/ Work Cited（表示單數）。另外附帶說：參考的書目／資料有非常多的種類，如何寫「參考書目」或「參考資料」是非常複雜的問題。針對這方面，MLA或APA或IEEE或其他學術組織也都訂有寫作規範，撰寫論文時應依學門的適用對象選用一套來參考。

學術論文除了主文（main text）之外，常見的副文（sub-texts）是上面提到的摘要、關鍵詞、注釋、參考書目／資料等。其他可能有的副文包括「謝詞」、「宣告」、「前言」、「附錄」等。「謝詞」翻成英文通常叫"Acknowledgements"（也可拼成"Acknowledgments"）。這個英文字通常用複數，不用單數。「謝詞」當然是用以感謝所有幫助完成此研究與寫成此論文的團體、組織或個人（通常感謝不只一件，故Acknowledgements）。在成書的大論文（如碩士或博士論文）裡，「謝詞」會寫成一大段而用單獨的一頁放在整篇論文之前。在期刊論文中，「謝詞」則通常只用一小段文字附在「主文之後、注釋之前」。英文的「謝詞」免不了有類似下面的客套話：

I/ We would like to thank John Casey for ...

The authors *are grateful to / thank* Professor Miller for ...

Special thanks are due to ...

I/ We thank ... for ...   I/ We also thank ... for ...

I/ We particularly appreciate my friend Tony Brown's kind

help and encouragement.

I am/ We are deeply indebted to the NSC for its financial support.

Thanks go to ... for ..., and special thanks go to ... for ...

　　有時候「謝詞」裡會說到「資助」（Funding）的訊息。例如，會說出類似"This study was sponsored/ funded by ..."（本研究由……贊助／資助）或"The authors were supported by a grant from ..."（本文作者受助於……的贈與）的話。但有時候「資助」（Funding）的訊息沒有放在謝詞裡，而是單獨出現在主文之後。有時候，「謝詞」或「資助」也會用「作者註」（The Author's Note或The Authors' Note）的標題，來說出謝意或資助者。

　　期刊論文的主文之後，除了可能有「謝詞」或「資助」這個部分之外，有時候也會有"Declaration of Conflicting Interests"（有關利益衝突之宣告）。在這部分，論文的作者要宣告發表此論文或進行此研究有沒有跟任何團體、組織或個人產生何種利益衝突。而最常見的宣稱是：The author(s) declared no potential conflicts of interest with respect to the research, authorship, and/ or publication of this article（作者宣告：關於本研究與本文章之著作權和／或出版權並無潛在任何利益衝突）。

　　在成書的大論文裡，有的作者會在主文前（以另一頁或幾頁）寫一篇「前言」（Preface 或 Foreword）。那種前言通常是「額外的話」（extra words）：可以廣泛地說研究或寫作的背景，可以講到某種時勢人情，也可以述說一樁趣事軼聞。但無論如何，所說所講的還是多少要跟該著作或該研究有關。其實，有些作者也會在「前言」裡寫謝詞或提供資助訊息。不過，在小論文裡（尤其是期刊論文裡），不可能有空間讓人寫那種「前言」。

　　不管是大論文或小論文，有些論文會在篇後加上「附錄」（Appendix）。有時附錄不只一個（單數的Appendix變成複數的Appendices）。這時，便需要把附錄加以編號（如中文的「附錄一」、「附錄二」、「附錄三」……或英文的Appendix A, Appendix B, Appendix C, ...）。附錄雖然是「附屬的紀錄」（accessory records），卻常常提供額外的、有趣的、有助益的訊息（extra, interesting, helpful information），可讓讀者進一步瞭解那研究或那論文。例如，如果一個研究用了問卷調查（questionnaire）的方法去進行研究，論文裡可能就要附上那問卷的全貌。又如，如果某研究講到某地的考古發現，或許論文中會附上該地出土的文物照片。當然了，大部分的期刊並沒有太多空間可以讓投稿者放進太多附錄，但必要的「做證據用的文件」（evidential documents）還是會以附錄來呈現的。

　　本章講的都是論文中的副文，包括摘要、關鍵詞、注釋、參考書目／資料、謝詞、資助訊息、利益衝突宣告、前言、附錄等諸多項目。副文的重要性或許不如主文，但也是論文的重要環節。每一項副文當然都有寫作的成規，不過成規是死的，不一定要死死板板地依循。寫英文學術論文的人，最好還是多看別人發表出來的論文，拿一些好的樣本來參考，甚至於當範例，既模仿人家或變通其格式，也學會人家的詞語，那樣才會寫出好的英文論文。

作業

1. 請找出一期屬於你們學門的（紙本的或電子的）英文學術期刊來看其中的一篇論文，據此回答下列問題：

   a. 這篇論文中有沒有摘要、關鍵詞、注釋、參考書目／資料、謝詞、資助訊息、利益衝突宣告、前言、附錄等部分？有缺什麼部分？

   b. 這篇論文中有用Abstract, Keywords, Notes, Bibliography/ References, Acknowledgements, Funding, Declaration of Conflicting Interests, Foreword/ Preface, Appendix這些字當標題（headings）嗎？有哪個標題不是用同樣這個英文字？例如，Notes變Note嗎？References變Reference或Literature Cited嗎？Acknowledgements變Acknowledgement嗎？Appendix變Appendices嗎？

   c. 這篇論文的摘要有多長？接近一頁或半頁？有分段落嗎？有段落的標題嗎？內容很完整嗎？

   d. 這篇論文的關鍵詞有幾個？不夠或太多？是真正關鍵的詞語嗎？

e. 這篇論文的注釋（如果有的話）是尾注或腳注？總共幾個？有標數碼嗎？如何標？用「上標」嗎？

f. 這篇論文的參考書目／資料（如果有的話）總共有幾筆？有加以分類嗎？有按作者姓氏排列嗎？出版年分放在著作名稱前或出版訊息後？有漏列主文中提到的著作嗎？列出的著作都真的被參考到嗎？

g. 這篇論文的謝詞（如果有的話）感謝多少團體／組織或個人？包含資助訊息嗎？

h. 這篇論文的前言（如果有的話）包含利益衝突宣告嗎？

i. 這篇論文的附錄（如果有的話）有幾個？有編號嗎？真的值得附在那裡嗎？

2. 有一篇學生寫的，研究有關「*K-ras* 基因突變與直腸癌」的英文論文，它的摘要經過改寫後如下：

Recent advances in molecular genetics have revealed that multiple genetic alterations, including activation of oncogenes and inactivation of tumor suppressor genes, are required for tumor development and progression. *K-ras* is frequently mutated in colorectal cancer. Previous studies have shown that prostaglandin

E$_2$ (PGE$_2$) is involved in intestinal carcinogenesis through its binding to the PGE$_2$ receptor subtypes EP1 and EP4 and its activation of downstream pathways. But the molecular mechanisms by which *K-ras* is linked to PGE$_2$ receptors are currently undefined.

The aim of this study is to associate K-ras with PGE$_2$ receptors. We transferred pcDNA3. 1 and pcDNA-*K-ras* into HT29 colon cancer cells. The transfected cells and the control cells were analyzed by MTT assay and Western blot. Our data showed that over-expression of Ras protein led to cell proliferation with activation of the phosphatidylinositol-3 kinase (PI-3K)/ Akt pathway, an effect likely to be due to inhibition of GSD3ß activity. We also used COX-2 and EP4 inhibitors to confirm this pathway and collected colorectal tumor tissues to confirm the over-expression of Ras, pAkt and EP1/ EP4 protein. Our result indicates that colorectal cancer causes K-ras mutation, suggesting that the use of EP1/ EP4 inhibitor may be considered for prevention from colorectal cancer.

請理解：

a. 這摘要寫成兩段，可以嗎？可以合成一段嗎？

b. 這摘要的第一段就是告訴研究背景的「引言」（Introduction），這一段在摘要中是不必要（可以刪除）的部分嗎？應該是吧？

c. 這摘要的第二段講出研究的目標（aim）、研究的過程
（transferred ... analyzed ... used ... collected ...）、研究的材料
（pcDNA3.1，pcDNA-*K-ras*, HT29 colon cancer cells, COX-2
and EP4 inhibitors, colorectal tumor tissues）、研究的方法
（MTT assay and Western blot）、研究的發現（Our data
showed that ...）、研究的結論（Our result indicates that ...）、
以及研究的意涵（suggesting that ...）。講了這些，可說很完
整了，但仍有遺漏嗎？

d. 其實，這摘要裡並沒有說出*K-ras*與PGE_2 receptors如何關
聯，沒有說出兩者之間的molecular mechanisms（分子機
制）。這等於忘了寫研究的核心點。這是整篇摘要的一大缺
失，不是嗎？

3. 有一篇碩士學位的英文論文，它的謝詞經過稍微改寫後有如下
的文字：

Acknowledgements

I am grateful to my thesis advisor, Professor So and So.
Without his advice and guidance, I cannot have completed this
thesis. *I appreciate* Professor A and Professor B, who gave me
valuable comments and suggestions when they served as my oral
examiners. *I am also obliged to* my parents for their continuous
support during these years. *I would like to express my indebtedness,*

too, *to* my friends Mr. So and So and Miss So and So. They often encouraged me to go on with my research. *I owe special gratitude to* my roommate, Amy, who helped me collect some material. Finally, *my sincere thanks are due to* Steve, who read a large part of the first draft of this thesis and gave me some suggestions for revision.（註：斜體字原本為正體，人名已經隱略或係杜撰）

請理解：

a. 可以把Acknowledgements改成Acknowledgment嗎？

b. 文中的I（我）為何不改成We（我們）？是因為研究者／論文撰寫人都僅自己一人嗎？

c. 如果把I（我）改成The author/ researcher（作者／研究者），感覺起來會不會欠親切？期刊論文中常用the authors來取代we，那又為什麼？

d. 感謝這麼多人，每次都用不同的感謝用詞（見斜體字部分），有這種變化，是不是比較好？如果從頭到尾都用"I thank So and So for ..."的模式，好嗎？

e. 這些感謝用詞中（見斜體字部分），有一個用得不妥當，是哪一個？

f. 英文"appreciate"常被譯成「重視」或「感激」。其實，appreciate的受詞應該是事、物，不是人。中文可以說「我感激你」，英文卻不能說"I appreciate you"，除非你的意思是「我重視你，認為你有價值」。因此，這段謝詞的第三句應該改為"I appreciate the valuable comments and suggestions which Professor A and Professor B gave me when they served as my oral examiners"，不是嗎？

g. 感謝時，為何用複數的thanks (are due to ...)而不用單數的thank (is due to ...)？為何用gratitude而不用gratitudes？

第七章

論文中的名詞與代名詞

講解

　　英文學術論文中，無論在主文或副文的部分，經常都會用到名詞（nouns），而名詞也經常被代名詞（pronouns）所取代。論文中的名詞通常有些是學術用語（academic terms）或專門術語（technical terms），但大部分還是非專門術語的一般用語。不管是什麼用語，英文的名詞都遵守同一套的英文文法（grammar），字面上同樣可能有數（number）、性（gender）、格（case）的變化，造句時同樣要依數、性、格的不同而與不同的動詞（verbs）或代名詞連動。

　　英文的文法書裡，常把名詞分成五類：普通名詞（common nouns）、物質名詞（material nouns）、抽象名詞（abstract nouns）、集合名詞（collective nouns）、和專有名詞（proper nouns）。專門術語裡的名詞，一樣有這五類。例如，"generation gap"（代溝）裡的"generation"和"gap"都是普通名詞。"diesel oil"（柴油）裡的"diesel"，可能是指「內燃機」的普通名詞；但"oil"則是指「油」的物質名詞。"petit larceny"（小偷竊）裡的"petit"是形容詞，"larceny"（偷竊）則是抽象名詞。而"Oedipus complex"（戀母情結）裡的"Oedipus"是人名的專有名詞，"complex"則是集合名詞，指一群糾結的情思。

　　其實，英文的名詞在文法上最重要的分類是「可數」（countable, C）或「不可數」（uncountable, U）。字典上通常不會告知某字是普通名詞或物質名詞，是抽象名詞或集合名詞。但是，有許多好的字典，都把列入的名詞直接點出[C]或[U]。我們都知道：可數的名詞還進一步分成「單數」（singular, *s.*）與「複數」（plural, *pl.*）。句子的主詞（subject）是單數的名詞或複數的名詞，其動詞的現在式就有不同："*A* generation gap *is* found/ *has* been found/ *lies* there."；但"Three generation gap*s* *are* found/ *have* been found/ *lie* there."。我們也知道，可數的單數名詞前面會有冠詞a或an，不可數的名詞或複數的名詞前面則不能有a或an："I need *a* boy/ *an* ox."但"I need information/ water/ books/ libraries."

在英文裡，可數的名詞通常是普通名詞或集合名詞：a listener（一個聽者）, ten listeners（十個聽者）；a large audience（一大群聽眾），two different audiences（兩群不同的聽眾）。不可數的名詞則是物質名詞、抽象名詞、和專有名詞：air, meat, fire; beauty, wisdom, anger; Confucius, Edison, Berlin, Taipei.不過，在特殊的文句裡，有改變含義時，U也會變C。例如：He has *a cheerful air*（"air"是「形色、容貌」，不是「空氣」）；She is *a great beauty*（"beauty"是「美人」，不是「美麗」）；We have many Edisons in this class（"Edisons"是指「發明家」，不是「愛迪生」那個人）。

寫學術論文的人應特別注意一點：許多英文名詞確實都是C & U，到底何時為C何時為U，要視使用的場合與所指的含義而定（如上一段的例子所示）。但有一個很普遍的通則，那就是：許多原本是U的（抽象或物質）名詞，可以在其前面加上adj.成為C，而表示「某種……」或「某個……」。例如："You need consideration"裡的"consideration"是不可數的（抽象）名詞，指「考慮」的行為。但"You need *a political consideration* and *some other considerations*"裡的"consideration"和"considerations"則是可數的（普通）名詞，指某（幾）種／個「考慮」。又如：在"I like *meat*, but I don't eat *cold meats*"中，前一個"meat"（「肉」）是不可數的（物質）名詞，後一個"meats"是可數的（普通）名詞，指某幾種肉。其他類似的例子如："It is *under investigation*; it needs *a thorough investigation*"（它在調查之中；它需要一個澈底的調查）。"*Gas* is used as a fuel, but helium, *a very light gas*, is not used as a fuel"（瓦斯用為燃料，但氦[一種很輕的瓦斯]不用為燃料）。

但**請注意**：正確的英文說"He has *knowledge*. He has *a good knowledge* of history."但卻說"They have *made progress*. They have *made rapid progress*."可見：名詞前有adj.不一定就必然會變成可數的名詞。習慣的說法最要緊。

一個英文的名詞是C或U，確實完全是依使用的習慣，而不能以字的含義來判斷。同為一粒一粒的bean和rice，卻前者為C，後者為U：I often *eat beans*; I seldom *eat rice*.同樣指「訊息」的information和message，卻一為U，一為C：We lack *information*; we need *messages* from everywhere.

有些可數的英文名詞，雖然有單數形和複數形，卻常以*pl.*出現來表示某含義，如greetings（祝賀）、thanks（謝意）、regards（問候）、tidings（消息）、embers（餘燼）、ashes（灰燼、骨灰）、dregs（汁渣）、depths（深處）、heights

（高處）、precincts（界域、範圍）、whereabouts（下落、住處）、suburbs（郊區）、circumstances（境遇）、surroundings（環境）、manners（禮節）、pains（辛勞）、proceeds（所得）、belongings（所有物）、proceedings（年報）、contents（目錄）、goods（貨物）、riches（財富）等等。奇怪的是：clothes = clothing，前者為複數，但可說"many clothes"卻不可說"three clothes"，而要說"three suits of clothes"（三套衣服）或"three pieces of clothing"（三件衣物）。同樣怪的是：有兩條褲管的「一件褲子」要用複數a pair of trousers或pants，有兩條袖子的「一件襯衫」卻直接用單數a shirt。學英文的人一定要注意像這類的怪現象。

寫學術論文時，常會提到某物種／某類東西，或為某事物下定義。英文名詞用以泛指某物種或當某事物之「種類指稱」（generics）的方法，有如下幾種：

a. 如果U時，用n本身就好，如*Ether* is colorless. *Instinct* is a person's natural tendency. *Water* covers three fourths of the earth.

b. 如果C時，通常用a (n) + s. n，如：*A rose* is a pretty flower. *A cart* was used there for transporting goods. *An agent* is a doer. *An elephant* has a long trunk.

c. 如果C時，也可用pl. n，如：*Prairie dogs* live underground. *Apricots* are edible. *Computers* are becoming more and more important to us.

d. 如果C時，還可用the + s. n，如：*The wasp* has a painful sting. *The elephant* never forgets. *The computer* is a modern invention.

注意：平常the elephant是指「這隻象」。不過，有時候 the elephant 是指「象（這種動物）」，而非「這隻象」。從本義來說，the elephant 是說「象這種動物」，an elephant是「任何一隻象」，elephants是「所有的象」。但翻成中文時，the elephant, an elephant, elephants都是「象」。其他，the rose/ a rose/ roses, the wasp/ a wasp/ wasps等的區別與翻譯也是一樣。

另注意：身體的部位／器官以及各種儀器／器械，通常都用 the + s. n來表示通稱（generics）。如："It is in the brain/ the heart/ the leg/ the liver"。"They invented the airplane/ the laser/ the optical scanner/ the watch"。

大家都知道：單數的英文名詞，通常在字尾加(e)s就變成複數（girl/ girls, church/ churches），但有時還帶一點變化（如duty/ duties, shelf/ shelves等）。不過，這條規則也有不少例外：如woman/ women, mouse/ mice, goose/ geese, ox/ oxen等。有些字的單、複數同形：如deer/ deer, sheep/ sheep, species/ species, series/ series, means/ means等。

其實，寫學術論文的人最應注意的是：有不少源自外來語（希臘文、拉丁文等）的英文名詞，至今還保留原來的單、複數形：如criterion/ criteria, analysis/ analyses, axis/ axes等。不過，那種外來語的複數形已經漸漸被英文的複數形所取代，所以在focuses/ foci, radiuses/ radii, pupas/ pupae, formulas/ formulae, memorandums/ memoranda, indexes/ indices, apparatuses/ apparatus, bureaus/ bureaux, seraphs/ seraphim等這些複數形中，每一雙的前者都漸漸比後者用得平常（尤其在美式英語中）。

有趣的是：data原為datum的複數形，但今天很多人把它用做U，雖然有時也當*pl.*，所以人們會說類似"The data is not available"和"We must deal with these data"這種句子。另外，也漸漸有人不知phenomena是phenomenon的複數，結果把phenomena當單數，而另創phenomenas為複數。然而，這種趨勢還沒有被接受。很奇特的一個字是昆蟲學家所說的imago（成蟲），它的複數可為imagines或imagoes，而當然後者會勝過前者。

除了有「數」的變化，英文的名詞也有「性」的變化。許多原本陽性的英文名詞，語尾若接有-ess就變成陰性，如poet/ poetess, lion/ lioness, god/ goddess, emperor/ empress, duke/ duchess, actor/ actress, master/ mistress等。但有不少陽性的英文名詞，其陰性名詞是完全另一字，如nephew/ niece, lord/ lady, bachelor/ spinster, widower/ widow, bridegroom/ bride, hero/ heroine, wizard/ witch, horse/ mare, bull/ cow, gander/ goose, drake/ duck, stag/ hind, ram/ ewe, drone/ bee, he-goat/ she goat, cock-sparrow/ hen-sparrow, peacock/ peahen, jack-ass/ she-ass, tom-cat (he-cat)/ she-cat, man-servant/ woman-servant (maid-servant), orphan-boy/ orphan girl等。

寫論文若牽涉及性別，就要特別注意用字。動物學家當然不會把「馬／蜜蜂」都說成horse/ bee，有需要說「母馬／雄蜂」

時就會用mare/ drone。不過，在女性主義逐漸抬頭的今天，有許多女詩人會希望你說"She is a poet"，而非"She is a poetess"。也有許多woman writers或women writers會希望你說"They are good authors"，而非"They are good authoresses"。

英文名詞的「格」有三種：當主詞的主格（nominative case），當受詞的受格（objective case），和表示所有的所有格（possessive case）。主格與受格都不改變字形。代表人或動物的名詞，其所有格則通常在字後加's來表示，如John's, the fox's。但字尾已有複數的s時，就只加 ' 就好，如the ladies', the birds'。人名之後有-sas, -ses, -sis, -sos,或-sus時，也只加 ' 就好，如Moses', Jesus'。如果人名之後只有一個s時，通常還是加's才好，如Dickens's, Keats's。

通常，不是代表人或動物的名詞不能用's來表示所有格，而要用the ... of ...的方式，如the purpose of this study, the leaves of those trees。但有些表示時間、距離、重量、價格的字眼，有些人格化的抽象名詞和特別加以尊重的對象，以及有些固定的成語，也都會用's的方式，如today's world, three months' payment, forty miles' journey, ten pounds' weight, two dollars' worth; Duty's call, Fortune's smile; nature's work, our country's welfare; at his wit's end, at arm's length, for convenience' sake, for goodness' sake 等等。

其實，為了方便起見，今日的英語也常有破格用's而不用 the ... of ...的例子，如the city's tallest building, the story's theme, the world's most famous statesman等。不過，寫學術論文的人，還是不要隨便破格才好。把the influences of the theory on the value of the product說成the theory's influences on the product's value總是不合文法。

英文名詞和代名詞的所有格，有個特殊的用法。那就是：當名詞片詞（nominal phrase）或動名詞片語（gerundive phrase）的主詞。例如：We have heard of *Paul's/ his* marriage with Jane. We have also heard of *Paul and Jane's/ their* leaving for Hong Kong. We regret *the death/ the running away of the horse.*這種語法跟中文很不一樣。

撰寫英文論文時，為了簡省起見，有些一再使用的字詞或字群常常會被縮寫（abbreviated），使之成為簡略的「略語」（abbreviation）。一篇論文中，如果「略語」只有少數幾個，通常會在行文中用括號的方式來告知略語。可是，如果整篇論文中有好多個「略語」，就有必要在文章前面先列出「略語清單」（List of Abbreviations）來告訴讀者。例如，一篇研究Charles Dickens的論文，可能會把引用到的眾多小說名稱統統用來編列出「略語清單」，像BH（*The Bleak House*）、DC（*David Copperfield*）、HT（*Hard Times*）、OT（*Oliver Twist*）、TTC（*A Tale of Two Cities*）等等。

英文的「略語」不見得都是來自名詞或等於名詞的字群，像I.O.U.就是句子"I owe you"的略語，雖然它是「借據」的意思。不過，大多數的「略語」確實是既等於名詞，也來自名詞或名詞片語。在各行各業中，都有許多等於名詞的現成的「略語」。例如，在商業術語中，a/ c＝account（帳）、B.D.＝bank draft（銀行匯票）、c.i.f.＝cost, insurance, & freight（含運費、保費價；起岸價）、d/ d＝days after date（發票日後……天）、F.O.B.＝free on board（船上交貨價；離岸價）、L/ C＝letter of credit（信用狀）、P.O.D.＝pay on delivery（交貨付款）。其實，在一般英文字典裡，都查得到大家常用的「略語」。例如，e.g.＝for example, et al.＝and other authors, etc.＝*et cetera*（and others）, ibid.＝the same as the previous reference, i.e.＝that is, *sic*＝thus（the error is in the original quote）, viz.＝namely,等等。有時，英文字典也會有附錄列出某行業的「略語」，如果不知某略語，用Google等加以搜尋也會得知。

　　寫學術論文最常用的度量衡單位名稱（units of measurements）也常會縮寫成「略語」。例如，cc＝cubic centimeter(s), g＝gram(s), h.＝hour(s), he.＝hectare(s), l.＝liter(s), lb.＝pound(s), mm＝millimeter(s), oz.＝ounce(s)等等。寫這種略語要注意有沒有加句點(.)，有沒有別種寫法。例如，cc＝c.c.，h.＝hr.及hrs.，l.＝lit.，而ounces＝oz.或ozs.等等。如果對這種單位名稱及其縮寫不明白，也可查字典或進行線上搜尋。

　　在這裡我們要說明一點：撰寫英文論文時，為了簡省起見，作者對某一些一再使用的字詞、字群，可以隨「本行內的慣例」加以縮寫；如無慣例可循，也可自行加以縮寫。通常縮寫時，會取原來字詞、字群的首字母，用大寫而不加句點。例如：the

International Bar Association會變成the IBA，the platelet-derived growth factor receptor會變成the PDGFR，oxidative stress會變成OS，endoplasmic reticulum會變成ER，而selective laser sintering會變成SLS。在縮寫和使用略語時，**請注意**：

a. 通常在論文的正文裡第一次出現那字詞、字群時，就要用括號把代表的字母交代清楚。從此以後，在論文中就全用那「略語」以求方便，不要再用那「全名」了。如：在 "The International Bar Association (IBA) identified ..."這句中，第一次在括號裡告知用"IBA"來代表"International Bar Association"之後，後面每次提到那國際律師協會，就要用那縮寫，不要用全名。

b. 如果那縮寫有複數，還是要加-s為宜。如：human umbilical vein endothelial cells縮寫成HUVECs，而mulberry leaf extracts縮寫成MLEs。

c. 使用那縮寫時，也要合乎前後文的語法。如some representatives of the IBA這詞語中仍保有the，不把the去掉。又如Some HUVECs are used to ...這句子中用are不用is當動詞。

名詞的略語是代表名詞的用語。其實，最常代替名詞的字是代名詞。英文的代名詞有四種：人稱代名詞（personal pronouns）、指示代名詞（demonstrative pronouns）、疑問代名詞（interrogative pronouns）、和關係代名詞（relative pronouns）。這些代名詞的用法請參看一般文法書。在這裡我們要提的，是一些跟論文寫作特別有關或比較容易弄錯的事項。

撰寫論文的人或做研究的人，有可能只有一人，但也有可能不只一人。不管大論文或小論文，只要不是單一作者的，行文通常用"we"來代表整個研究團隊，就像報社寫稿時也常用"we"來指整個編寫群一樣。所以在論文中，會說"We aim to ...," "we adopted the method of ...," "we used ... as our material," "we found that ...," "we suggest that ...,"這種話。在謝詞裡也會說"We thank ...," "we appreciate ...,"之類的話。可是，撰寫論文的人或做研究的人如果只是單獨一人，當然"we"就要改成"I"了。

在此附帶**請注意**：有時"we"是泛指「我們人類」或「人們」。如：*We* are apt to look down on the poor people.這種"we"有時改用"you"也可以，如：Whenever *you* see a bee, *you* will find it seemingly busy all the time.有時"they"也可用來指某些「人們」，如：When you come to the bridge, you will find that *they* are repairing it. *They* say that Mary is married to Smith.

寫英文論文時，最常用到的人稱代名詞應該是"it"。其用法有下面幾點必須說：

　　a. 用以指前頭提到的某字（word）、某語（phrase）、某句（sentence）。如：I bought a gold *watch*, but *it* was soon lost. I had wanted *to get up earlier*, but *it* was impossible. *You have paid me the money*; I know *it* all too well.

b. 用做「虛字」（expletive）來指後頭的不定詞或分詞片語、或（that/ wh-）子句。如：*It* is stupid of you *to tell him the lie. It* is important *to tell the truth. It* is no use *crying over spilt milk. It* is no good *making fun of him. It* is suggested *that x should be replaced by y. It* depends on you *whether she can recover or not.* I thought *it* likely *that he has returned.* We consider *it* significant *where and when the criminal will be tried and sentenced.*

c. 用以指天氣、時間、距離或不明性別的人。如：*It* lightens and thunders before *it* rains. *It* is still early; *it* takes only 15 minutes. *It* is about two miles from here. Who is *it* at the door? Is *it* a he or a she?

指示代名詞this/ these和that/ those有幾個特殊用法如下：

a. 指前述兩者之「後者」和「前者」。如："Health is above wealth; *this* gives trouble while *that* gives happiness."（注意：this 是「後者」，that 是「前者」）。"Elephants and giraffes are both big; *these* impress you with long necks, *those* with long trunks."（these＝後者giraffes，those＝前者elephants）。

b. 用that/ those of代替前面的名詞，以免重複。如：The climate of Taiwan is warmer than *that* (= the climate) of Japan. The ears of a fox are not so long as *those* (= the ears) of a rabbit.

c. 用this或that來指前面那句話或那件事。如：Atoms contain protons, neutrons, and electrons. *This*（或 *That*）means: atoms are not the smallest things. He has apologized, but *this/ that* is not enough.

d. 用and that來指前述的那件事。如：You must come, *and that* quickly.（and譯成「而且」，that = you must come）。

指示代名詞 one/ ones 的幾個特殊用法如下：

a. 代替前述可數的名詞，以免重複。如：If you need *a test tube*, I can give you *one* (= a test tube). Talking of *compact disks*, there are several good *ones* (= compact disks) here.注意：說"If you need bread, I can give you one."是錯的，要說成"If you need bread, I can *give it to you/ give you some*."才對，因為"bread"是不可數的物質名詞（像water一樣）。但是，說"If you need loaves of bread, I can give you some big ones."則是對的，因為loaf/ loaves（塊）是可數的名詞。

b. 用one來指「任何人」，其功能有如we, you。如：*One* should love *one's* country. (= We/ You should love our/ your country.)。注意：one要跟one's連用，但*Everyone* must do *his* duty. *Someone* has neglected *his* duty. *No one* knows *his* own fate.這裡的his不能改成one's。

c. 用one和the other來表示「其一」和「另一」。如：We found two problems; *one* was financial, and *the other* technical.

d. 用the one和the other來表示「前者」和「後者」。如：We must solve the financial problem and the technical problem, *the one* (= the former) before June, and *the other* (= the latter) before October.

關係代名詞that常常引導子句來當動詞的受詞，如"We found that A is more effective than B"。除了這個用法之外，這裡要特別提幾個使用的場合。

a. 代替who/ whom或which引領子句來限定或修飾前面的先行詞（antecedent）。如：I met the man *that* (= who) worked with you. I met the man *that* (= whom) you worked with. We used an assay *that* (= which) they had never used before.

注意：當who/ whom或which前面有附加逗點時，也就是當它們用以「補充說明」而非「限定／修飾」前面的先行詞時，就不能用that來取代。如：I met *Dr. Lin, who* worked with you/ *whom* you worked with（這裡的who/ whom不能用that取代，因為不是限定「跟你工作的那個林博士／你跟他工作的那個林博士」，而是補充說「林博士跟你工作／林博士你跟他工作」）。We adopt *your method, which everybody adopts/ which is adopted by everybody*（這裡的which也不能用that取代，因為不是限定「每個人都採用的你的方法」，而是補充說「你的方法每個人都採用」）。

b. 當先行詞含有指人與非人之名詞時，不好用who/ whom 或which，只好用that來指涉。如：The car ran over *an old man and his dog that* were crossing the road.

c. 為避免"who ... who ..."或"which ... which ..."的重複時。 如：Who is the researcher *that*（不重複用*who*）has done the same research? Which is the finding *that*（不重複用 *which*）you consider the most significant?

注意：相對的，也要避免"that ... that ..."和"those ... that ..." 的重複。如：We refer to that species *which*（不重複用 *that*）is close to this. They design those styles *which*（不重 複用*that*）cater to most of the ladies.

d. 先行詞帶有最高級形容詞時。如：They found *the most* important evidence *that* concerned the case. He is *the best* man *that* can help you.

e. 先行詞有the only, the same, the very, all, any, no這種字詞 時。如：She is *the only* girl *that* is allowed to work here. We wantcd *the same* device *that* helped them succeed. This is *the very* idea *that* I had just now. *All* the materials *that* have been tried were bought there. He would not choose *any* agent *that* has worked with your company. *No* man *that* has common sense will do it.

f. 與it is/ was連用，以加強語氣時。如：*It was* John *that* came into my room last night. *It is* wisdom *that* you lack.

g. 用於A is that to B which X is to Y或What X is to Y, that is A to B的模式中，來表示「A與B的關係猶如X與Y的關係」。如Air is that to man which water is to fish. What water is to fish, that is air to man.注意：這句話也可說成"Air is to man as water is to fish"或"As water is to fish, so is air to man"或"Air is to man what water is to fish."

　　本章講解的是英文的名詞和代名詞在論文寫作時應特別瞭解的一些文法問題。由於篇幅的限制，我們無法講解所有細節。要精確把握文法，還是要靠平日閱讀文章時，養成留意文法的習慣。英文的句子（sentence）或子句（clause）通常都有主詞（subject）和動詞，動詞之後有時會再有受詞（object）或補語（complement）。動詞的主詞和受詞都是名詞或代名詞，補語有時也是名詞或代名詞。另外，介系詞的受詞也是名詞或代名詞。平時閱讀英文文章時，一定要留意那些名詞或代名詞是怎樣被使用的。尤其是名詞的U或C，以及它與冠詞連用的情形，更是大家非努力觀察不可的問題。

作業

1. 請找出一期屬於你們學門的（紙本的或電子的）英文學術期刊
   來看其中一篇論文的一段話，據此回答下列問題：

   a. 該段英文裡有幾個英文句子？

   b. 每個句子的主詞都是名詞嗎？有的是代名詞嗎？

   c. 有沒有句子中還有子句的？子句中有主詞嗎？主詞是名詞或
      代名詞？

   d. 每個句子或子句中有受詞嗎？受詞是名詞或代名詞？

   e. 每個句子或子句中有補語嗎？補語是名詞或代名詞？

   f. 每個名詞是哪一種名詞？是普通名詞（common nouns）、
      物質名詞（material nouns）、抽象名詞（abstract nouns）、
      集合名詞（collective nouns）、或專有名詞（proper
      nouns）？它是陽性或陰性？是所有格嗎？是C或U？如果是
      C，它是*s.*或*pl.*？

   g. 每個名詞前有冠詞嗎？如果有，冠詞是the或a(n)？

h. 每個名詞後有關係代名詞嗎？如果有，是who, whom, which 或什麼？

i. 每個代名詞代表哪個名詞？或代表哪個片語或句子？

j. 有沒有哪個複合名詞用縮寫字母來代表？

2. 為了參考起見，請到圖書館查看至少十本英文字典，瞭解裡頭是否有下面幾項，也瞭解其情形如何：

a. 在字典的entries（編入的字詞）中，在每個名詞的各個 definition（定義）之下，有沒有附帶告知是C或U？

b. 一般的abbreviations（縮寫或略語）是散在entries中或統合一起放在appendices（附錄）裡？

c. 有沒有附錄在告知某行某業technical terms（專用術語）的 abbreviations，如commercial terms（商用術語）的略語？

d. 有沒有Tables of Measures and Weights（度量衡表）的附錄？如果有，有包括你想知道的嗎？比方說，有長度的單位 Linear Measures嗎？有面積的Square Measures，體積的Cubic Measures，土地的Land Measures，容積的Volume Measures，容量的Capacity Measures，測量的Surveyor's Measures，航

海的Nautical Measures，乾貨的Dry Measures，液體的Liquid Measures，藥劑流體的Apothecaries' Fluid Measures，圓弧的Circular Measures，有表列這麼多「度量單位」（measures）嗎？還有，有表列各種「衡計單位」（weights）嗎？如常衡的Avoirdupois Weight，金衡的Troy Weight，藥衡的Apothecaries' Weight等。

3. 請仔細閱讀下面一段（經過改寫的）有關 berberine（黃連素）的英文，再回答後面的問題。

　　Lung cancer has become a major cause of cancer-related mortality all over the world. The high mortality of lung cancer is often traced to lack of effective methods for therapy. Now, berberine (an isoquinoline alkaloid) is known to have a number of biochemical and pharmacological effects. Recently we found that it certainly could reduce, in a dose-and-time-dependent manner, the proliferation and viability of several cell lines related to human non-small cell lung cancer (NSCLC)—such as A549, H460, H1299 and H1355. Meanwhile, we found the proliferation and viability of normal cells—such as MRC-5 and HUVEC—were not significantly affected by the use of berberine.

　　a. 從這段英文中，可知"cancer"是U或C？"mortality"呢？"cause"呢？

b. "The high mortality of lung cancer"可以改成"High mortality of the lung cancer"嗎？"lack of effective methods for therapy"可以改成"the lack of the effective methods for the therapy"嗎？

c. "Berberine"（黃連素）是物質名詞或抽象名詞？是U或C？"alkaloid"（生物鹼）呢？"... berberine (an isoquinoline alkaloid) is known to have ..."可以改成"A berberine (isoquinoline alkaloid) is known to have ..."嗎？

d. 第三句中"...a number of biochemical and pharmacological effects"這些字裡的"effects"為何用*pl.*？可改成"effect"嗎？

e. 第四句中"NSCLC"是哪些字的「略語」？"A549, H460, H1299 and H1355"是不是某些"cell lines"（細胞株）的代號？"MRC-5 and HUVEC"呢？

f. 英文"cell"（細胞）一字是C，所以會加-s，如"normal cells"。但在"human non-small cell lung cancer"一詞裡，為何用"cell"而不用"cells"？是因為該"cell"已經當形容詞（如her boy friends裡的"boy"）嗎？

4. 請仔細閱讀下面兩段有關美國總統之職權的英文說明，再回答後面的問題。

In the USA, the President acts as the nation's principal spokesman on foreign policy; therefore, the initiative in the conduct of foreign relations rests with the President. Normally, it is he who, either in his own utterances or through his Secretary of State, points the path to be followed. This is part of the leader's power that American presidents enjoy most.

There are certain areas of action which are reserved exclusively to the President. It is his constitutional prerogative, for example, to appoint the ambassadors, ministers and consular representatives of the United States, though his nominees have to be approved by the Senate.

a. 把USA寫成U.S.A.可以嗎？而the President和the Senate可以改成the president和the senate嗎？

b. 為何Congress不說成the Congress？為何the Senate不說成Senate？這都是習慣用法嗎？

c. "Normally, it is he who, either in his own utterances or through his Secretary of State, points the path to be followed."這句中的"who"可以改成"that"嗎？如果可以，是因為那是「強調語氣」的方法嗎？美國總統不一定是男的，因此這句中的he, his是不是改成he/ she, his/ her比較合理？其實，在女權高漲的今天，英文裡還是習慣用he, him, his來泛指每一個人，不是嗎？

1
4
1

d. "This is part of the leader's power that American presidents enjoy most."這句中的"This"是指什麼？是前一句"It is he who ..."（「是他指出路徑讓人跟隨」）這個事實嗎？that可以改成which或省略嗎？part of可以改成a part of嗎？

e. "It is his constitutional prerogative to appoint the ambassadors, ministers and consular representatives of the United States."這句中的"It"是「虛字」（expletive）嗎？它代替後面哪些字？是"constitutional prerogative"或"to appoint ... States"？

5. 請仔細閱讀下面兩段有關美國地理的英文，再回答後面的問題。

　　Like the Mississippi, all the waters east of the Rockies finally reach the Atlantic; all the waters to the west of the Rockies finally arrive at the Pacific. For this reason the Rocky Mountains are known as the Continental Divide. There are many places in the Rockies where a visitor may throw two snowballs in opposite directions and know that each will feed a different ocean.

　　Life in New England has always required clever, careful planning. It is still chiefly a place of carefully planned specialties. For instance, farms on the strip of good land along the Connecticut River specialize in the kind of tobacco in which cigars are wrapped. The tobacco is grown with great care, under acres (hectares) of thin cloth which shades the delicate leaves. The stony farms are devoted to dairy cattle. The farmers also tap the sweet juices from maple trees to make maple sugar.

a. 專有名詞像Mississippi, Atlantic, Rocky, Pacific, Continental Divide, Connecticut River等，為何前面都有the？英文是否習慣在河流、湖泊、山脈、海洋、群島等名稱前加the？

b. 文中waters一字是由U的物質名詞water（水）變成C的普通名詞而指「水流」嗎？The Rockies是指the Rocky Mountains嗎？

c. 動詞divide可當名詞指「分水嶺」嗎？落磯山做為the Continental Divide也叫the Great Divide，那大分水嶺分開的Continent叫the Continent of North America或the Continent of the Americas？

d. 在"... a visitor may throw two snowballs in opposite directions and know that each will feed a different ocean."一句中，"in opposite directions"可改成"in the opposite directions"或"in opposite direction"嗎？為何不能？另外，each指什麼？指snowball或visitor或direction？

e. 第二段開頭"Life in England"（英格蘭的生活）可改成"A life in England"（英格蘭的一條命）或"The life in England"（英格蘭的那種生活）嗎？動名詞"planning"是U或C？與C的

"plan"含意上有何不同？是否比較強調計劃的動作而非完成的某計劃？

f. 英文specialty一字是C嗎？Land（土地）一字是U嗎？而cigar呢？還有tobacco呢？請看第二段以瞭解其用法。

g. 在"The tobacco is grown with great care, under acres（hectares）of thin cloth which shades the delicate leaves."這句中，"The tobacco"是泛指「菸草」或「某種／棵菸草」？而care和cloth均為U是因為this（後者）is a material noun and that（前者）is an abstract noun嗎？至於"the delicate leaves"，那是指the delicate leaves of the tobacco (plants)嗎？

h. 英文cattle一字是*s.*或*pl.*或*s. & pl.*？在"The stony farms are devoted to dairy cattle."一句中，"cattle"是*pl.*嗎？

i. "The farmers also tap the sweet juices from maple trees to make maple sugar."這句可改成"Farmers also tap sweet juice from the maple tree to make maple sugars"嗎？為何不能？

第八章

論文中的動詞與句型

講解

　　寫英文的學術論文和寫一般的英文文章一樣，每句話除了用到名詞或代名詞之外，通常也都會用到動詞（verbs）。學過英文的人都知道：每一個英文動詞都有「原形」（root form）、「過去式」（past form）、「過去分詞」（past participle）和「現在分詞」（present participle）等不同的字形變化。絕大多數的英文動詞，其字形變化有規則可循（如deliver, delivered, delivered, delivering），但有些動詞的字形變化卻不合規則（如go, went, gone, going; be, am/ are/ is, was/ were, been, being）。這種有規則或不規則的變化在中文裡是沒有的。無論用在何種場合，中文的動詞都是不變的一個樣，英文卻要「隨機變形」，這就是華人學習英文時最為困難之一項。英文動詞是隨時態（tense）、語態（voice）、語氣（mood）、和句法（syntax）的變化而改變形狀的。其基本法則在文法書裡都會講得很清楚。在這裡限於篇幅，只能再提醒一些比較重要也比較容易讓人犯錯的事項。

　　傳統的文法書都說英文的動詞有十二種時態：現在、過去、未來簡單式（如write/ writes, wrote, will/ shall write），現在、過去、未來進行式（如am/ are/ is writing, was/ were writing, will/ shall be writing），現在、過去、未來完成式（如has/ have written, had written, will/ shall have written），和現在、過去、未

來完成進行式（如has/ have been writing, had been writing, will/ shall have been writing）。沒錯，英文是有the twelve tenses。但是，說英語或寫英文的人，腦筋裡並沒有十二種時間觀念（time notions）。按照A. S. Hornby在*A Guide to Patterns and Usage in English*一書中的說法，說、寫英文的人腦筋裡也不是只有現在、過去、未來三種時間。他說英文的時間觀念有如下七種：

a. The (immediate) present ------------^--------- now

b. The past time ------*-----^-------- yesterday

c. The future time ----------^----*---- tomorrow

d. The all-inclusive time <------------------→ every year

e. The inclusive past ---→*-----^-------- by 1930

f. The inclusive present --------→^---------- so far

g. The inclusive future ---------^---→*---- by 2050

十二種「時態」是配合這七種「時間」來表達的。配合的情形大致如下：

a. The (immediate) present（此時此刻的現在）

am/ are/ is + V-ing　　　I *am cooking* right now.

V-s　　　I *know* it. Here he *comes*! The war *goes* on.

b. The past time（過去某時）

V-ed　　　He *studied* very hard last week.

was/ were + V-ing   She *was cleaning* the house when I went in.

c. The future time（未來某時）

will/ shall + V   We *shall start* at five tomorrow.

will/ shall + be + V-ing   They *will be practicing* all week.

d. The all-inclusive time（統括過去、現在、與未來）

V-s   The sun *rises* in the east. We *go* there every day.

e. The inclusive past（從以前到過去某時）

had + V-en   I *had finished* it when he came back.

had + been + V-ing   I *had been working* before he arrived.

f. The inclusive present（從以前到現在此時）

has/ have + V-en   She *has had* three sons by now.

has/ have + been + V-ing   She *has been living* in peace up to the present time.

g. The inclusive future（從以前到未來某時）

will/ shall + have + V-en   We *shall have won* the prize when she comes.

will/ shall + have + been + V-ing   He *will have been writing* it for 3 years if he continues till June.

（註：V-s為現在式，V-ed為過去式，V-en為過去分詞，

V-ing為現在分詞。）

　　的確，英文的時間與時態是這樣配合的。針對撰寫英文學術論文的人，要特別提醒的有下面幾點：

a. 理論上，真正此時此刻的時間很短，也許只是一秒鐘，但實際上可以延長不少。或許"right now"或"at this very moment"是真正的此時此刻，但"now"（現在）和"at present"（目前）可能指合起來幾天幾月或幾年的「這段期間」。當你告訴朋友"I am writing a novel now"時，有可能此時真正在寫（某一本）小說。但當你告訴朋友"I am writing novels now"時，你此時可能沒有在寫小說，而是說近來這段期間都在寫（幾本）小說。

b. 英文的進行式（progressive tense）用be + V-ing來表達，中文的進行式則用動詞加「（正）在」、「著」、或「在……著」來表達。如：I am writing a letter（我正在寫信），When I entered, she was singing（當我進來時，她唱著歌），When you come, she will be still waiting for you（你來時，她將還在等著你）。

c. 有些動詞通常不會有「正在進行此動作」的說法，這時就算時間在此時此刻，也不用進行式來說「正在……」。如："I know French"（我懂法文），不能說成"I am knowing French"（我正在懂法文）。"It did not matter"（它沒關係），不能說成"It was not mattering"（它正在沒關係）。這一類的動詞包括許多種，像表達情感的 love, like, hate, fear；表達感官覺知的see, hear, smell, taste, notice；表達心智活動的understand, remember, realize, recognize；和其他有持續狀態的resemble, possess, belong, continue等等。

d. 在許多句子中，動詞的動作或狀態若同時發生或存在於過去、現在和未來，則通常用現在簡單式來表達。如：The earth is round. It moves round the sun. I get up at six every morning. I work eight hours a day.。就是因為這樣，寫科技文章時會說：This paper aims to ... This compound has the effect of ... This result suggests that ...。

e. 可是，如果動作或狀態只在過去某時發生或存在，就要用過去式。例如：We made an experiment. We added A to B. We found they mixed easily.同理，如果動作或狀態只在未來某時發生或存在，就要用未來式。例如：I will make an experiment. I will add A to B. I shall find the result.

f. 英文的完成式（perfect tense）用have + V-en來表達，中文的完成式則用動詞加「已（經）……（完）（了）」或「曾（經）……（過）」來表達。例如：Previous studies have shown that ...（以前的研究已經顯示……），No one has ever done the same research（沒人曾經做過同樣的研究），By that time, Einstein had found that ...（到那時候，愛因斯坦已發現……），By this time next year, we shall have made five experiments of the same nature（到下一年這時候，我們將已做完了五次同性質的實驗）。

g. 英文的完成進行式翻譯成中文常有「一直」的含義。例如：They have been trying to solve the problem（他們一直想要解決此問題），They had been probing into the problem before they understood it（在瞭解之前，他們一直深入探究此問題），We shall have been supporting them for ten years by 2020（到2020年，我們將一直支持著他們十年）。

英文的時態在「間接陳述」（indirect statement）中，要注意「關聯」（sequence）。像原本為"He said, 'I will come'"的句子，若間接陳述為"He said that he would come"時，"I will"就變成了"he would"。在此，要提醒大家的是：在間接陳述時，雖然現在式通常會改為過去式，但如果陳述的事實是過去、現在、未來都可能不變的事實（如真理、定律），則那個事實依然要用現在的時態來陳述。如"He said that the earth *is* round and it *moves* round the sun"便是一例。就是因為這個緣故，所以在學術論文中，引述他人所講的恆常事實時，也會用現在式：Professor Chang concluded that X *plays* an important role in Y and A *has* the effect of ... on B.

寫學術論文時，報告研究的過程通常用過去的時態，因為事情是在過去某時段進行的。所以會有像"We used ..., we adopted ..., we found ..."或像"An experiment was conducted to ..., X was used as a material to ..., two results were found ..."這樣的句法。不過，在論文中講述小說或劇本的情節時，會把那些情節視為在作品中恆常存在的事實，因而用現在的時態來講述。例如：Hamlet *grieves* over his mother's speedy remarriage. He *is told* that his father's ghost *has appeared* to his friends. He *rails* against women and *urges* Ophelia to go to a nunnery. He finally *kills* Ophelia's father and her brother before he *kills* Claudius, his stepfather.

英文有主動語態（active voice）與被動語態（passive voice）。被動語態由be + V-en形成。被動語態配上時態也有多種變化。以"write"為例，被動語態就有下面幾種變化：

簡單式：am/ are/ is/ was/ were/ will be/ shall be written

進行式：am/ are/ is/ was/ were being written

完成式：has/ have/ had / will have/ shall have been written

關於被動語態，**請注意**下面幾點：

a. 由be + *v-en* + prep.形成的被動語態，不要忘了保留那介系詞。如：The lab must be well taken care *of*. All unnecessary ceremony has been done away *with*. We do not know the theory it is based *on*. This crime is being looked *into*. The new equipment had been set *up* when he arrived.

b. 要強調動作者就用主動語態；不強調動作者或動作者不明時，就用被動語態。如：Dr. Wang believes that ...（強調Dr. Wang相信……）。It is believed that ...（不明誰相信……或不想說出誰相信……）。因此，感謝別人時要說"I/ We appreciate Dr. Wang's support."，不要說"Dr. Wang's support is appreciated."。可是，報告研究過程時會說"Newcastle Disease vaccination was carried out on the first day."，不會說"Some people carried out Newcastle Disease vaccination on the first day."。

c. 並非被動語態的句子中，都有by +動作者。既然不強調動作者，根本就不需要講「by誰」，反而更常用其他介系詞來講別的事情。如：說"Two experiments were conducted in the lab."而不說"Two experiments were conducted by us in the lab."。文中已經知道做實驗的人是「我們」，故不必說by us，反而要告知做實驗的地點為in the lab。

d. 有不少表示身心狀態（喜怒哀樂等）的英文動詞都常用被動，而且有時會加特定的介系詞。如：I *have been interested in* music. We *were disappointed at* not finding him there. I *am pleased* to see you. We *were* all *excited by* the news. She *will be disgusted with* him.

說、寫英文的人要陳述事實或發問時，用的是「直說語氣」（indicative mood），要命令或請求時，用的是「命令語氣」（imperative mood），而要假定事實或祈求願望時，則用「假設語氣」（subjunctive mood）。前面講的時態和語態變化都是就「直說語氣」而言的。如果是「命令語氣」，就只用動詞原形，如"Be honest."和"Please lend me your pen."等。至於「假設語氣」或「假設法」，則可以分成如下四類：

a. 針對現在或未來，做有可能（疑信參半）的假設時，用現在的時態，和can/ may/ must/ will/ shall等連用。如：If it *rains* tomorrow, I *will* not go. If you *have finished* the work, you *can* leave. If she *is coming* now, you *must* keep waiting.

b. 針對現在或未來，做極不可能（只有萬一）的假設時，用were to V或should V而和could/ would/ should/ might等連用。如：If her parents *were to die* next week, she *would* cancel the plan. If he *should appear* right now, what *might* you do?

c. 針對現在，做違反事實的假設時，be動詞用were，其他動詞用過去式，再與could/ would/ should/ might等連用。如：If I *were* a bird, I *would* fly to you now. If I *had* more than two hands, I *could* lend you one at once. If the blind beggar *could* see, he *might* hate you.

d. 針對過去，做違反事實的假設時，用had V-en，而和could/ would/ should/ might have V-en連用。如：If we had adopted a different method, we might have finished the experiment earlier. If you had told me the truth yesterday, I would have forgiven you then.

針對假設法的使用，有下面幾點**請注意**：

a. 並非用"if"才能有假設語氣，不少其他字眼也有可能。如：

I will not come *unless* you give me a formal invitation.

Suppose he should quit, who might take the position?

This can be finished by June, *provided that* the plan is approved in time.

Even though I asked him a thousand times, he would not answer me.

He stepped in and looked *as if* he had seen a ghost.

Would that money grew on trees!

We *wish that* we could visit the moon soon.

But for his idleness, he would be a good student.

O that I had a wealthy father as she does!

Your heart will not stop beating *so long as* you are alive.

b. 使用有命令、建議、或主張之含義的動詞時，其所陳事項尚未成為事實，所以常用should V的假設法，而行文時此should可以省略。如：The court ordered that he (should) leave the city within three days. They suggest that the new method (should) be adopted. He insists that the data (should) be analyzed carefully.

c. 用"It is/ was proper/ natural that ..."這一類句子來表達意見時，因所陳事項也尚未成為事實，所以也常用(should) V的假設法。如：*It is fitting and proper* that the briefing (should) be done as soon as the visitors come. *It is only natural* that they (should) speak for their team. *It was crucial that the catalyst (should) be put in at the right time when the experiment was being made.*

d. 假設所針對的時間如有變動,假設的方法也會跟著變動。像"If it had rained yesterday, I might have stayed home"這句話的時間都是昨天,所以前後用had rained和might have stayed這種假設法。如果改成"If it had rained yesterday, I would not water the flowers now."這時,後半句的時間變成現在,其假設法也就隨之改為would not water而不是would not have watered的形式。

e. 因為用would/ could/ might的假設法比較客氣,所以許多人反而不敢用can/ may/ will來說話。其實,寫科學文章時不需太客氣,反而要多用can/ may/ will來表示「有可能性」。例如,做完實驗之後,你的結論是「X能怎樣」,你就說"X can ..."而不要說"X could ..."。

　　大家都知道英文的「不定詞」(infinitive)就是to V(動詞原形加to)的形式。使用不定詞的場合很多,下面幾點請特別注意:

a. 除了有簡單式之外,不定詞也有完成式、進行式、與完成進行式,除了主動語態之外也有被動語態。所以如下的句子都是有可能的:

I expect you to study the plan.

I expect you to be studying the plan when she finds you.

I expect you to have studied the plan before June.

I expect you to have been studying the plan when she finds you.

I expect the plan to be studied by all of you.

I expect the plan to have been studied before June.

b. 含有「推定含義」的動詞（seem, appear, be thought等）加完成式的不定詞，表示動作已發生在前。如"He *seems/ appears/ is thought* to have lost his ambition"這句話表示：他喪失野心是在「此時似乎／顯得／被以為」之前已經發生。同理，"Sorry *to have kept* you waiting"這句話是「讓人一直等著之後」說的。如果人家還沒等，而你要先說「抱歉，要讓你們持續等著」，英文便是"Sorry to keep you waiting"。

c. 有些表示願望或意向的動詞（如hope, wish, want, intend, expect等），用其過去式+ to have V-en，或用其過去完成式＋ to V，都有「過去的願望或意向沒有實現」的含義。如：

I hoped to have succeeded. I had hoped to succeed.

I wished to have pleased her. I had wished to please her.

I wanted to have invested the money. I had wanted to invest the money.

I intended to have finished it. I had intended to finish it.

I expected to have seen him. I had expected to see him.

在這些句子中，succeeded, pleased her, invested the money, finished it, saw him都只是過去未實現的願望或意向。

d. 不定詞可以像名詞一樣當主詞或受詞，也可以像形容詞一樣當（主格或受格）補語。例如：

To know is one thing; *to do* is quite another. （主詞）

For him to lie is harder than *for him to die*. （隨含義主詞for him當主詞）

It is hard *to know him*; it is harder *to get along with him*. （等同主詞it）

It is difficult *for us to know him*. （隨含義主詞for us當主詞，等同It）

We want *to know him* and (*to*) *get along with him*. （當want之受詞）

We are studying *how to know him*. （隨同how當studying之受詞）

We found it difficult *to know him*. （等同受詞it當found之受詞）

They found it difficult *for us to know him*. （隨for us當found之受詞＝ it）

They expect *us to get along well with him*. （隨us當expect之受詞）

We seemed *to get along well with him*. （當主格We之補語）

They believe us *to be honest*. （當受格us之補語，to be可省略）

註：含義主詞（sense subject）只是含義上的主詞，不是文法的主詞。

e. 英文be + to V可視為be supposed/ expected/ arranged to V的省略，其含義往往等於can/ may/ will/ must之意。如："We are (supposed/ expected/ arranged) to meet every other week." = "We will/ may/ must meet every other week." "Not a single soul was (expected/ supposed) to be seen there." = "Not a single soul could be seen there."

f. 英文不定詞省略"to"的情況有三：在某些「知覺動詞」（verbs of perception）之後，在某些「使役動詞」（verbs of causation）之後，與在某些特定詞語之後。例子如下：

I *saw* the dog *run* and *heard* it *bark*.

I *felt* the house *shake* violently and *observed* the clock *fall* down.

I *watched* him *leave* but *noticed* no others *come* in.

We *let* them *stay* in the cell and *made* them *cling* to one another.

We will *bid* them *wait* for us and *have* one of them *show* us the way.

You *had better take* a rest and they *had best work* on.

I *cannot (choose) but laugh* and she *can do nothing but cry*.

All I could do and *the best I could do* was *leave* the city.

He came to *help* me *pack* clothes into a trunk.

注意一：cannot (choose) but, can do nothing but, all somebody can/ could do is/ was, the best/ only thing somebody can/ could do is/ was, help (somebody)等詞語後也可以保留"to"。如：I *cannot choose but to stay*, and *all she can do is to leave*. *The best thing I could do was to ask* for help. They *helped to control* the fire and we *helped them to get* water.

注意二：被動語態中要還原"to"。如：The dog *was seen to run* and *heard to bark* all the way. They *were made to stay* and one of them *was bidden to show* the way.

注意三：order, command, get, cause不列入省略"to"的使役動詞。所以像下面三句都有"to"："They ordered/commanded him *to* fire." "They got some boys *to* paint the wall." "Bad hygiene caused the disease *to* spread."

g. 不定詞片語可像形容詞一樣修飾名詞，也可像副詞一樣修飾動詞、形容詞、和副詞。例如：

We are seeking a catalyst *to react with these compounds*.（修飾catalyst）

If you come to Taiwan, you will find many sights *to see*.（修飾sights）

He gave me no money *to buy it with*.（修飾money）

We eat *to live*, not live *to eat*.（修飾動詞，表示目的）

Byron awoke *to find the house on fire*.（修飾動詞，表示結果）

We all rejoice *to hear the good news*.（修飾動詞，表示原因）

Is this water good *to drink*?（表目的，修飾形容詞good）

I am terribly sorry *to hear that*.（表原因，修飾形容詞sorry）

She is rich enough *to allure him*.（表程度，修飾副詞enough）

But she is too foolish *to marry him*.（表程度，修飾副詞too）

h. 有些不定詞的成語，要學會使用。如：*To tell the truth*, it is a good method for our purpose, *to be sure*. *To make matters worse*, he turned into a wise fool, *so to speak*. He is frugal, *not to say* stingy. He knows French, *not to speak of* English.

英文動詞的「現在分詞」（present participle, V-ing）通常有「主動與進行」的意味；「過去分詞」（past participle, V-en）則有「被動與完成」的意味。所以，a moving story是一個令人感動的故事，a moved listener是一個被感動的聽者。a flying bird是一隻在飛行（中）的鳥，a killed bird是一隻已被殺死（了）的鳥。不過，這原則也有少數幾個例外。像a wanting volume是a volume that is wanted（缺少的一冊），a missing paper是a paper that is being missed（遺失的文件）。a learned man是a man that has learned a lot（有學問的人），a well-read man是a man that has read a lot（讀很多書的人），a well-spoken man是a man that speaks very well（能言善道者）。

有些不及物動詞的V-en因為不可能表示「被動」，所以只有「完成」的意味。像a retired professor（已退休的教授）、a well-behaved citizen（行為好的公民）、an escaped convict（逃跑的犯人）、a returned emigrant（回來的移民）、a decayed tooth（朽壞的牙齒）、a grown-up son（長大的兒子）、a rotten egg（壞掉的蛋）、a withered flower（凋萎的花）等。

請注意：像a hot-tempered man, a kind-hearted lady, a long-armed monkey, a one-eyed monster, a four-footed beast, a three-legged stool, a V-shaped structure, a multicolored material等都不是

V-en的字，而是N-ed的字。

　　英文的動詞變成分詞之後，其功能通常等於形容詞，可以修飾名詞，也可以當主格或受格補語。請看下面的例句：

　　a. We know the man *cheerful/ complaining/ taunted* all day long.

　　b. She sat there *seemingly thoughtful/ thinking of her past/ lost in thought.*

　　c. We found the house *empty/ standing on a hill/ painted in white.*

　　請注意：像b例句一樣，常常會接分詞當補語的動詞有sit, stand, lie; come, go; become, get, grow等，而get + V-en往往類似be + V-en是被動語態。

　　另注意：可接原形動詞的覺知動詞（see, hear,等）均可像c例句一樣接現在分詞與過去分詞，用以強調「進行」或「被動」。如"I saw the rabbit run into a hole"只說看到兔子跑進洞裡，若說"I saw the rabbit running into a hole"便是強調看到兔子正在跑進洞裡。

　　再注意：可接原形動詞的使役動詞"have"可在受詞後接V-en來表示「被動」或「經驗」。如"I shall have the house painted"是「我將讓房子被粉刷」，而"I had my arm broken last year"則是「我去年有手臂被折斷的經驗」（不是故意讓手臂被折斷）。

　　英文的分詞常常用於「分詞構造」（participial construction）中。一個「分詞構造」等於一個「從屬子句」（subordinate clause），其功能像是在補述「主要子句」（principal clause）的主詞，又像在修飾其動詞，可以說兼有形容詞與副詞的功能。例如：

a. *Having finished* (= As/ After I had finished) my work, I went home.

b. *Engaged* (= Since they are engaged) to be married, they live together now.

c. *Going* (= When he went) down town, he met an old friend.

d. *Frightened* (= Though he is frightened) by the news, he still keeps his head.

請注意：分詞構造的「含義主詞」（sense subject）就是主要子句的主詞，所以像"Walking to the beach, many boulders were found"這種句子是錯的，因為many boulders（許多鵝卵石）不會walked to the beach，而要改成"Walking to the beach, we found many boulders"才對。不過，有些變為成語的分詞構造，是不用管主詞為何的，這包括如下例子中的成語：

a. *Generally speaking,/ Judging from their behavior*, women are more nervous than men.

b. *Granting that/ Provided that* you get the allowance in time, will you keep your promise?

c. *Talking of* ghosts, some ghosts are lovable rather than horrible.

d. *Considering* her age, she is still too young to understand this situation.

另注意：分詞構造不一定要放在句首，有時也可放在句中或句後。如：

a. The suspect, *watching TV*, knew that he was already suspected of the crime. （嫌疑犯，看電視時，知道他已被懷疑犯罪）。

b. The milkman, *pleased to see me*, waved to me happily. （賣牛奶的人，因高興看到我，快樂地對我揮手）

c. The rich man threw the beggar a coin, *looking at him with distaste*. （有錢人丟給乞丐一個硬幣，不屑地看著他）

d. The thief ran out of the house, *chased by a pack of dogs*. （小偷跑出房子，被一群狗追著）

　　再注意：分詞構造的「含義主詞」如果跟主要子句的主詞不同，也要呈現出來，造成所謂「獨立片語」（absolute phrase）。如：

a. *The men having left*, the women began to talk of them.

b. He sat dreaming in a sofa, *his legs quivering*.

c. *The hares all caught*, the hunter decided to kill the hound.

d. He shouted and shouted, *his arms folded across his chest*.

　　最後補充說：近來在科技的文章中，我們常常看到句子後面加上"using ..."或加上"..., suggesting ..."，那用法很像「獨立片語」。例如："Deficiency of cytochrome c oxidase was induced *using morpholinos to reduce ...*"（用嗎琳基去減少……時，就會

引起細胞色素c氧化酵素之缺乏）。"Calcium levels were found to be increased by retinoic acid when ..., *suggesting that calcium levels decrease during myeloid differentiation*"（當……的時候，鈣量被發現因外用A酸而減少，這表示 在脊椎細胞的分化中，鈣量是減少了）。

英文的「動名詞」（gerund）跟動詞的現在分詞一樣，都是V-ing的形式。不過，分詞是動詞兼有形容詞的功能，動名詞則是動詞兼有名詞的功能。動名詞像動詞一樣，可以有完成式與被動語態，本身可以接受詞或補語，也可以被副詞修飾，如"having arrived punctually," "being repeatedly ridiculed," "selling books," "breaking loose"等。動名詞片語也像名詞一樣，可以當主詞，也可以當動詞或介系詞的受詞。例如：

a. *Selling books* is his way of living.（當主詞）

b. It's now no good *selling books as a way of living*.（＝It當主詞）

c. He wants to avoid *being repeatedly ridiculed*.（當avoid之受詞）

d. You must prevent the horse from *breaking loose*.（當from之受詞）

e. I found it worth while *having arrived punctually*.（＝it當found之受詞）

一般動詞的主詞用名詞或代名詞的「主格」（nominative case），動名詞的「含義主詞」則用名詞或代名詞的「所有格」

（possessive case）。其對照如下：

a. *He sells* many books. I envy *his selling* many books.

b. *The horse broke* loose. They talked about *the horse's breaking* loose.

c. *She has arrived* on time. *Her having arrived* on time is praiseworthy.

d. *Paul was ridiculed. Paul's being ridiculed* seemed unnoticed.

可是，動名詞在當受詞的場合，其「含義主詞」漸漸有將「所有格」變成「受格」（objective case）的趨勢。例如：

a. I can't imagine *him/ his being* so stupid.

b. How can you blame me for my *brother/ brother's* neglecting his duty?

c. They want to stop *it/ its* being turned into a regular activity.

d. We cannot bear *these garbage cans* lying so near to our houses.

在上面d句中，因為these garbage cans是物不是人，所以把它改成these garbage cans'當然是不可能的。

有些英文的動詞只會接不定詞為受詞，有些只會接動名詞，有些則接兩者皆可。學英文的人應隨時留意這一點。例如下面這些動詞只接V-ing，不接to V：

a. I enjoyed/ finished/ avoided/ resented *watching* that movie.

b. I *cannot help/ do not mind/ can't stand/ won't give up doing* it.

c. He would advise/ consider/ prevent/ suggest *meeting* her.

可是，像下面這些動詞只接to V為受詞，不接V-ing：

a. Please don't bother/ hesitate/ agree/ consent *to come.*

b. They want/ expect/ hope/ intend/ wish/ long *to see* you.

而像下面這些動詞則接to V或接V-ing為受詞都有可能：

a. I like/ dislike/ love/ hate/ prefer *joining* / *to join* such clubs.

b. They have begun/ started/ commenced/ ceased *mending*/ *to mend* it.

請特別注意：有些動詞加to V和加V-ing的場合不同，其含義也不一樣。例如：

a. Please *remember*/ *don't forget to* come tomorrow.（記得要／不忘要……）

I *can remember*/ *have forgotten seeing* you before.（能記得／已忘記……）

b. I *regret to* tell you that she has left.（抱歉要……）

I *regret* hav*ing* told you the bad news.（抱歉已經……）

c. They then *stopped to* eat lunch and take a rest.（停下來要……）

They then *stopped* eat*ing* lunch and began to work again.（停止……）

d. I *try to* win my boss' confidence.（努力要……）

Do *try* add*ing* some salt to it.（嘗試……）

e. He *went on to talk* about his personal history. （接著談到……）

He *went on talking* about his personal history. （繼續談論……）

f. The house *needs repairing* = The house *needs to be repaired*.

They may *require looking* after = They may *require to be looked* after.

The killer *deserves hanging* = The killer *deserves to be hanged*.

英文"to"可能是不定詞to v的"to"，也可能是介系詞的"to"。如果是介系詞，通常有「於」或「對」之意，而後面接的是名詞、代名詞、或動名詞。例如：

a. *With a view to helping* the poor, he donated a lot of money. （有意於……）

b. *Owing to/ Due to/ Thanks to his reminding* me, I did not forget it. （由於……）

c. This can be *applied to nursing* children at home. （應用於……）

d. Her life was henceforth *devoted to rearing* her grandson. （奉獻於……）

e. We all *object to their building* a factory there. （反對……）

f. He is *used to/ addicted to stealing* money. （習慣於／沈溺於……）

g. My parents cannot *consent to my leaving* school. （對……表示同意）

英文的動詞如果有同系的名詞，通常就用該名詞而不用其動名詞。例如，我們通常說"I know his arrival"而不說"I know his arriving"；說"We need their agreement"而不說"We need their agreeing"。但如果強調動作（過程）本身而非該動作的結果，則可能用動名詞取代同系的名詞。如"I enjoy the conquering"是樂於那征服的過程，而"I enjoy the conquest"則是樂於那征服的結果。

英文 *v.t.* 的動名詞可以直接加受詞，其同系的名詞則要加介系詞"of"才可接受詞。例如，我們可以說"I appreciate *your suggesting it*"，卻不能說"I appreciate your suggestion it"，而要說"I appreciate *your suggestion of it*"。同理，我們說"His *robbing the bank* is astonishing"，卻說"His *robbery of the bank* is astonishing"。我們說"We are waiting for their *confirming the report*"或"We are waiting for their *confirmation of the report*"。說"I am surprised at her *promoting him*"或"I am surprised at her *promotion of him*"。

有關助動詞（can, may, must, will, shall 等）的用法，下面幾點**請注意**：

　　a. 說話者說"I/ We will ..."時，是說話者「（我／我們）有意志要……」；如果說"I/ we shall ..."，則是說話者「無意志」，只是說「我／我們將……」。如："I/ We will fight on"（我／我們（決心）要繼續打下去），"I/ We shall fight in a forest"（我／我們將在森林中打鬥）。

　　注意：如果說話者說"Shall I/ we ... ?"，那是要問對方的意志「要我／我們……嗎？」。

如"Shall I/ we come again tomorrow?"（要我／我們明天再來嗎？）。

另外注意：通常說話者不會說"Will I/ we ...?"來問自己「有意志要……嗎？」，除非人家先問你"Will you ... ?"而你重複說"Will I/ we?"。例如：A問B："Will you help us?"（你／你們要幫我們嗎？）。B回說："Will I/ we? Of course, I/ we will."（我／我們要嗎？當然我／我們要）。

b. 當說話者說"You/ he/ it/ they shall ..."時，就是說話者有意志要人家怎麼樣，如"You/ he/ it/ they shall be killed"就是「（我決心）你／他／牠／他們要被殺死」。但當說話者說"You/ he/ it/ they will ..."時，說話者並沒有意志，只是說人家「要／將……」而已。如"You/ he/ it/ they will live very long"（你／他／牠／他們要／將活得很長）。

c. 助動詞could/ would/ should/ must/ might/ ought to + have + V-en是表示「過去有能力／要或會／應該／必定／或許／有義務怎樣，但沒怎樣」。例如：You could/ would/ should/ must/ might/ ought to have succeeded last time, but you did not（你上次能／會／應／必定會／或許會／該成功的，但你沒有）。

d. 助動詞should在疑問或惋惜的語氣中，有驚訝的意涵，譯成中文是「會」。如"I wonder *how* he *should* come to know the secret"（我詫異他怎麼會得知那祕密），*"Who should* say that except that gossip?"（除了那愛說閒話的人，誰會說那個？），"It is a great pity that she *should* lose her only child"（她會失去獨子，真是一大遺憾）。

e. 英文need和dare兩字，在否定句或疑問句中常當助動詞（用法如can, may, must等），但在肯定句中則當普通動詞。例如：You need not tell me the reason. She dare not tell me the reason. Need I tell you the reason? Dare she tell you the reason? I need to tell him the reason and she needs to as well. I dare to tell him the reason and she dares to as well. 不過，像這樣的句子也是對的：I did not need/ dare to tell him the reason.

從句法結構方面來看，一個英文句子（sentence）通常分成主語（subject）和述語（predicate）兩部分。主語由名詞／代名詞來當核心，述語則由動詞來當核心。每一個核心至少有一個字：除了核心的字眼之外，可能加上其他若干字。那些另加的字有可能也是名詞、代名詞或動詞，但更可能是其他詞類。例如，在"Black tea can protect low-density lipoprotein from oxidation"（紅茶能保護低密度脂蛋白，使之免於氧化）這句英文中，主語為"Black tea"兩字，其中"tea"一字為核心，"Black"是另加的字，它是形容詞。而"can protect low-density lipoprotein from oxidation"這些字是述語，其中"protect"一字是當核心的動詞，另加的"can"是助動詞，另加的"low-density lipoprotein"是由形容詞"low"與兩名詞"density"和"lipoprotein"組成的受詞，而另加的"from oxidation"是由介系詞"from"和名詞"oxidation"組成的副詞片語。

一般文法書都把英文句型由"主語加述語"（S＋P）擴充為下列五種基本句型：

S V（主詞＋動詞）如"I know."

S V C（主詞＋動詞＋補語）如"I am right/ here/ a boy."

S V O（主詞＋動詞＋受詞）如"I know him/ the secret."

S V O O（主詞＋動詞＋受詞＋受詞）如"I gave him a book."

S V O C（主詞＋動詞＋受詞＋補語）如"We elected him president."

其實，這五種基本句型可以再擴充。像A. S. Hornby就把它們擴充為25種，名為VP1~VP25。不過，不管多少種，英文的句型（sentence patterns）確實就是動詞的前後接續型態，是VP（verb patterns）。而每一個英文動詞會使用什麼pattern(s)，往往跟它的屬性有關。

英文的動詞通常被粗分為「及物動詞」（transitive verb, *v.t.*）與「不及物動詞」（intransitive verb, *v.i.*）兩種。「及物動詞」後面可以直接加名詞或代名詞當它的受詞，「不及物動詞」則不可以。許多英文字典會把動詞標示*v.t.*或*v.i.*後才給定義、例子。例如："resemble：（*v.t.*像）She resembles her mother."。"differ：（*v.i.*不同）She differs from him"。

其實，純及物或不及物的英文動詞並不多。大多數的英文動詞都既是*v.t.*也是*v.i.*，只是有的較常當*v.t.*或*v.i.*而已。像

differentiate, discriminate, distinguish這些字都常用於differentiate/ discriminate/ distinguish A from B的語句中，那是及物動詞，但如果用於differentiate/ discriminate/ distinguish between A and B的語句中，則是不及物動詞。

學英文的人一定要隨時注意：動詞後面有直接加受詞嗎？到底是及物或不及物呢？「及物或不及物」往往不是由字義來決定的。例如：laugh, ridicule, scoff, taunt都是「笑」或「嘲笑」，但通常只說laugh at him/ scoff at him或ridicule him/ taunt him，不說laugh him/ scoff him或ridicule at him/ taunt at him，因為laugh和scoff在那場合是*v.i.*而ridicule和taunt則是*v.t.*。又如：depend和rely都是「依賴、依靠」，但你不能說depend/ rely him，而要說I can depend/ rely on him，因為兩字都是*v.i.*。

英文「及物動詞」後面不能沒有受詞，所以當人家問你"Do you want the book?"時，你不能說"Yes, I want."而要說"Yes, I want it."。如果人家問"Do you want a book?"時，你也要回說"Yes, I want one."。

英文「及物動詞」後面的受詞，除了可能是名詞或代名詞之外，也可能是等於名詞的不定詞（片語）、動名詞（片語）、that-子句、或wh-子句。如：

I like *to sing at night.*

I like *singing songs.*

I know *that he is married.*

I know *when he will come.*

有時受詞後面還有補語（complement），而補語可能是名詞或形容詞、或等於形容詞的現在分詞或過去分詞、或兼有形容詞與副詞功能的質詞（particle）。如："I think her *a liar/ clever enough for it.*" "We found him *lying on a sofa/ bound to a chair.*" "We must *think it over/ set it up.*"等。

有時受詞有兩個，一為直接受詞，一為間接受詞，而直接受詞可能是字詞或wh-子句。如："I gave him *a book.*" "He granted me *what I needed.*"。

英文的「知覺動詞」中，有些通常不用進行式，例如：不會有"I am seeing/ hearing/ noticing/ recognizing the bird"（我正在看見／聽見／注意到／認得那隻鳥）這種句子。但"I am seeing my doctor this afternoon"（我下午去看醫生）和"The judge is hearing a case"（法官在聽審案件）則是可能的。

有些「知覺動詞」像smell, taste, feel等，當*v.t.*時可以用進行式，例如：I am smelling the flower / tasting the food/ feeling his pulse（我在聞那朵花／嚐那食物／摸他的脈搏）。不過，這些動詞當*v.i.*時通常不用進行式，但可接補語。例如：It smells/ tastes/ feels good/ like onion（它聞／嚐／摸起來很好／像洋蔥）。其實，look和sound也算這種*v.i.*的「知覺動詞」，所以也會說：It looks/ sounds good/ like a bird（它看／聽起來很好／像鳥）。

英文有一類動詞叫「非即結束的動詞」（non-conclusive verbs）。那一類動詞常常表示一種不會立即結束的狀態，如表喜惡的love, like, hate, dislike等，表知悉的know, understand, realize等，表疑信的believe, doubt, suppose等，表同異的differ, resemble, agree, seem等，以及表其他含義的remember/ forget, contain/ consist, hope/ wish, belong, depend等。這些動詞通常用簡單式，不用進行式。但如果加"always"這種字來表示「老是／總是……」時，也可以用進行式。例如：He is always loving a young girl, knowing our secret, doubting others, differing with me, forgetting decency, and depending on his wealth（他老是愛著年輕的女孩，知道我們的祕密，懷疑別人，跟我意見不一，忘掉莊重，而依靠他的財富）。這句中"always"可換成"constantly," "continuously," "forever"等類似字眼。

英文也有一類動詞叫「進入狀態的動詞」（inchoative verbs）。那一類動詞常常帶有「變成、轉成」的含義，包括get, become, grow, come, go, turn, fall, run, wear等。這些動詞都可接形容詞或名詞當補語，例如：

a. He *got angry* immediately.（他立刻生氣）

b. Peter has *become a pauper*.（彼得已變成窮人）

c. You'll know it when you *grow old*.（你老了就知道）

d. Her dream has come true.（她的夢已成真）

e. He went mad at last.（到最後他發瘋了）

f. The leaves are turning yellow.（樹葉正在轉黃）

g. They all suddenly fell ill.（他們都突然生了病）

h. The boy has run wild as expected.（那男孩如預料的變野了）

i. The material is wearing thin, you see.（你看到了，那布料在

變薄）

還有一類動詞是「表示意見的動詞」（opinionative verbs），這一類動詞常常加that-子句，來說出主張或認定的事實。這一類的動詞是寫學術論文時經常會用到的，所以大家一定要學會使用。下面是一些例句：

a. We *think/ believe/ suppose that* A equals B in such a case.（我們認為／相信／假定在如此場合A等於B）

b. It may be *suggested/ proposed/ stipulated that* X (should) be canceled.（可以建議／提議／明定的是：X要加以取消）

c. The author holds/ asserts/ affirms/ maintains that it is impractical.（作者堅持／主張／斷言／堅持說那是不實際的）

d. This result suggests/ implies that we need one more experiment.（這結果提示／暗示說我們需要再一次實驗）

以上有關英文的動詞和句型，我們好像講了很多，其實仍然有很多還沒有講到。學英文的人每碰到一個動詞時，一定要留意它的用法，尤其要留意它以什麼（人或事物）為主詞，它接著是什麼：是受詞或補語，是名詞、形容詞或介系詞，是等於名詞的不定詞、動名詞、that-子句、wh-子句或等於形容詞的分詞、介系詞片語等。要知道：每一個動詞都有其特殊用法以及使用的句型。你知道嗎？我們可以說"I wish you to come"，卻不可以說"I hope you to come"。我們用「直說法」說"I hope (that) you can come"，卻用「假設法」說"I wish (that) you could come"。許多人會依中文的句法說"We suggest to use ..."與"We suggest you to use ..."，但那是不合英文句法的，要說"We suggest using ..."與"We suggest that you (should) use ..."才對。

作業

1. 請到圖書館查看至少十本英文字典，瞭解裡頭是否有下面幾項，也瞭解其情形如何：

   a. 在字典的entries（編入的字詞）中，每一個動詞有沒有告知其過去式、過去分詞、現在分詞的拼字（spelling）？

   b. 每一個動詞有沒有告知是*v.t.*或*v.i.*？

   c. 每一個動詞有沒有告知可用在什麼VP（句型）？

   d. 有沒有例句來佐證使用的句型？

2. 請找出一期屬於你們學門的（紙本的或電子的）英文學術期刊來看其中一篇論文的一段話，據此回答下列問題：

   a. 該段話裡有沒有一句話沒動詞的？

   b. 每句話的動詞是用什麼時態（tense）？現在、過去、或未來？簡單、進行、完成、或完成進行？

   c. 有什麼表示時間的詞語用來配合那時態？

d. 有幾句話是用主動語態（active voice）？幾句是in passive voice？

e. 用被動語態的句子，是基於何種原因？

f. 有沒有帶subjunctive mood的句子？是什麼字詞表示有假設法？

g. 如果有帶假設語氣，是疑信參半或萬一的假設？是違反現在事實或過去事實的假設？

h. 有「間接陳述」的句子嗎？如果有，有「時態的關聯」（tense sequence）嗎？

i. 有多少句子帶有功能像形容詞的分詞？是現在分詞或過去分詞？

j. 有多少句子帶有功能像名詞的動名詞？有「含義主詞」嗎？如果有，是什麼？用「所有格」嗎？

k. 每一個句子是屬於五種基本句型的哪一種？

3. 請仔細閱讀下面一段統計學方面設想有關error rate（錯誤率）所寫出的英文報告，然後回答接著的問題。

In recent years, some scholars were invited to investigate the error rate of Type I in doing the one-sample *t*-test, given that each time the used sample had already passed the necessary, preliminary, goodness-of-fit (GOF) test. The data collected for their investigation were, as we know, sampled carefully from certain normal, uniform, and exponential populations. After analyzing the collected data, they almost unanimously agreed that screening of samples by a pretest for normality results in a more conservative, conditional, Type-I error rate than application of the one-sample *t*-test without doing any preliminary GOF test.

請問：

a. 這段話的第一句裡，"were invited"是因為"in recent years"（最近幾年）而用過去式嗎？可否改成"have been invited"以表示一些學者在最近幾年「已經被邀請」去調查？

b. 第一句的後半"given that ... test"這個子句，是不是「分詞構造」（participial construction）？如果是，它的「含義主詞」也就是主要子句裡的"some scholars"嗎？也就是這子句等於" as some scholars were given (the fact) that each time the used sample had already passed the ... test"這意思嗎？

c. 其實，這個"given that"是個成語。它等於"on condition that"或"if"。它就像出現在數學裡的"Given that A equals B, then C equals D"（設若A等於B，則C等於D）。它是表示條件的假設法，在這裡是一種「有可能」的假設。既然如此，句中"had passed"是表示違反過去的事實（也就是其實沒通過）嗎？如果不是，那句話是否只是說「最近幾年，一些學者受邀調查進行單一樣本*t*-test之第一型錯誤率，而其條件是每次那使用的樣本都已經通過必要的、先期的、適合度的檢定」？而"had passed"表示"passed"的時間是在調查之前，不是嗎？

d. 第二句（"The data ... populations."）裡，"collected"一字是"collect"的過去式或過去分詞？它的意思是「收集」或「被收集的」？其實，"The data collected for their investigation"這句話等於"The data which were collected for their investigation"（「為他們之調查所收集的資料」），它是整句話的主語，不是嗎？而這句話的述語是"were, as we know, sampled carefully from certain normal, uniform, and exponential populations"（「是（如我們所知）仔細地由某些正常的、一致的、指明的口數來形成樣本」）這句話，不是嗎？句中"were ... sampled"可改成"was ... sampled"嗎？可改成"are ... sampled"嗎？

e. 第三句（"After analyzing ... GOF test."）裡，"analyzing"一字是現在分詞或動名詞？它是"After"的受詞嗎？它後面的"the collected data"又是它自己的受詞嗎？

f. 第三句中"they ... agreed"可改成"they ... agree"嗎？他們當時同意「A導致B」，英文說成"they ... agreed that A *results* in B"，可以嗎？為什麼不改成"they ... agreed that A *resulted* in B"呢？是因為要表示那是恆常的事實嗎？

g. 第三句中，在"A results in B"的句型裡，A是"screening of samples by a pretest for normality"（為常態而藉前測來篩選樣本），這裡的"screening"是名詞或動名詞？

如果剛好"screen"的名詞是"screening"而其動名詞也是"screening"（就像swim的名詞和動名詞都是swimming一樣），我們如何判斷這裡的"screening"是名詞或動名詞？把"screening of samples"改成"screening samples"可以嗎？如果可以，前者的screening為名詞，後者的screening為動名詞，不是嗎？

h. 第三句中，在"A results in B"的句型裡，B是"a more conservative, conditional, Type-I error rate ..."（一個更保守而有條件的第一型錯誤率……），這句話的核心是哪一個字？是"rate"嗎？"error rate"是名詞修飾名詞嗎？"Type-I error rate"是複合名詞"Type-I"修飾複合名詞"error rate"嗎？

i. 第三句中，在"A results in B"的句型裡，B其實是"a more conservative, conditional, Type-I error rate than application of the one-sample *t*-test without doing any preliminary GOF test"

（比起應用無任何先期合適檢測的單樣本t測試，有一個更保守而有條件的第一型錯誤率）。在這裡，"application of the one-sample *t*-test"可改為"applying the one-sample *t*-test"，不是嗎？

4. 下面的文字取自達爾文（Darwin）的名著 *The Origin of Species* 的第一章前三段。請仔細閱讀，然後回答接著的問題。

　　When we reflect on the vast diversity of the plants and animals which have been cultivated, and which have varied during all ages under the most different climates and treatment, I think we are driven to conclude that this greater variability is simply due to our domestic productions having been raised under conditions of life not so uniform as, and somewhat different from, those to which the parent-species have been exposed under nature. ... No case is on record of a variable being ceasing to be variable under cultivation.

It has been disputed at what period of life the causes of variability, whatever they may be, generally act; whether during the early or late period of development of the embryo, or at the instant of conception.

　　Sterility has been said to be the bane of horticulture; but on this view we owe variability to the same cause which produces sterility; and variability is the source of all the choicest productions of the garden. I may add that as some organisms will breed most freely under the most unnatural conditions (for instance, the rabbit and ferret kept in hutches), showing that their reproductive system has not been thus affected; so will some animals and plants withstand domestication or cultivation, and vary very slightly— perhaps hardly more than in a state of nature.

請問：

a. 在"It reflects heat/ his thought"的句子中，reflect後面不加on/ upon，但在"When we reflect on the vast diversity of the plants and animals which ..."的句子中，卻有on，為什麼？是不是因為：當「反射、反映」之意時，reflect是*v.t.*，而當「省思」之意時是*v.i.*？

b. 在"the plants and animals which have been cultivated, and which have varied during all ages"這句話中，為何不說成"... which have cultivated, and which have been varied ..."？是因為plants and animals是「被（人）栽培／培養」而自己「變種／變異」嗎？是因為"cultivate"是*v.t.*而"vary"是*v.i.*嗎？如果把這句話譯成中文，應該是「那些已被培養（了）而在各年齡中已產生（了）變化的動植物」或「那些曾被培養（過）而在各年齡中曾產生（過）變化的動植物」？

c. 在"I think we are driven to conclude that ..."這句中，"think"之後是可加"that"。但加了以後變成"I think that we are driven to conclude that ...", 一下子來了兩個"that"好嗎?另外,句中只說「我們被驅使去下結論」,沒說「我們被什麼驅使去下結論」,那是因為「其實很難說出被什麼驅使」嗎?

d. 在"this greater variability is simply due to our domestic productions having been raised under conditions of life"這句中,"having been raised"是完成又被動的分詞或動名詞?如果是due to的受詞,那就是動名詞,不是嗎?其實,our domestic productions就是它的「含義主詞」。但動名詞的主詞不是應該用「所有格」嗎?怎麼不寫成our domestic productions'呢?是因為「我們家裡的產物」不是人,本來就不能加(')嗎?如果改成代名詞,是不是應該用"their"(due to their having been raised)?

e. 在"those to which the parent-species have been exposed under nature"這句中,"those"就是"those conditions of life"。這句話等於"those (conditions of life) which the parent-species have been exposed to under nature"。講的是「在自然之下,為父為母那些物種已被暴露到的那些(生活環境)」。在這句中,用的是"A is exposed to B"(A暴露於B)的句法,只是不僅被動,還是完成的時態。請問:為什麼要用被動語態呢?不能說"The parent-species have exposed to those conditions of life"嗎?如果不能,那是因為"expose"這字是*v.t.*嗎?

f. 在"No case is on record of a variable being ceasing to be variable under cultivation"這句中，講的是「記錄上沒有案例說：在（動植物）還在培養之下，一個變數會處於不再是可變動之（過程）中」。這句話的基礎結構是"No case of something is on record"，只是這個something就是"the fact that a variable is ceasing to be variable under cultivation"。如果原句寫成"No case is on record that a variable is ceasing to be variable under cultivation"這樣子，也是對的。不過，達爾文把that-子句變成動名詞片語，所以"is ceasing"變成"being ceasing"。這時，"a variable"跟著變成"being ceasing"的含義主詞，不是嗎？

附帶說：cease（停止）用進行式的頻率不高，說"They have ceased to be nobles"（他們已不再是貴族）比說"They are ceasing to be nobles"（他們正在變成不是貴族）的機會多。另外，cease to V和cease V-ing都可以，"They have ceased to be nobles"="They have ceased being nobles"。可是，把達爾文的"a variable being ceasing to be variable"改成"a variable being ceasing being variable"好嗎？

g. 在"It has been disputed at what period of life the causes of variability, whatever they may be, generally act"這句中，It是代替"at what period ... act."這子句，而講的是：「不管會是什麼（原因），通常變異的原因在生命的什麼時期來發生作用這個問題，已經被爭執過。」針對這爭執，有人可能說

"They generally act at the early/ late period of life"。這種"act"是*v.t.*或*v.i.*呢？

在"whatever they may be"這句中，they是指"the causes of variability"。那麼，為何不說"whatever they are"呢？用may來跟whatever, however, whoever, wherever, whenever, whichever這種字，是不是一種「有可能的假設」？如果把may改成might，文法也對。可是，那是不是變成一種比較「不可能的假設」？

h. 可以把"during the early or late period of development of the embryo"這片語改成"during the early or late period of/ in developing the embryo"嗎？如果可以，可見"develop"可當*v.t.*，不是嗎？

i. 在"Sterility has been said to be the bane of horticulture"這句中，"has been said to be"應譯成「曾經被說是」或「已經被說是」？如果把本句改為"Sterility is said to have been the bane of horticulture"可以嗎？如果可以，意思變成「不結果實被說成一直是園藝的致命傷」，是嗎？

j. 在"I may add that ..."這句中，"add that ..."是「增加那個」或「補充說」的意思？在此，"I may add"等於"I may say additionally"，不是嗎？

k. 在"as some organisms will breed ...; so will some animals and plants withstand ..."這句中,用的是"As A will ..., so will B..." 的句法,意思是「就像有些有機體會孕育...,同樣的有些動植物也會抗拒……」。而"as some organisms will breed most freely under the most unnatural conditions (for instance, the rabbit and ferret kept in hutches), showing that their reproductive system has not been thus affected"這一句,在說完「就像有些生物體在最不自然的情況下(比如,被養在圈欄裡的兔子和白鼬)會很自由的孕育」這句話之後,補了「顯示牠們的生殖系統還沒有如此的被影響到」這句話。在這一句中,"showing that ..."是個分詞構造,但它的「含義主詞」是什麼?是什麼在showing that ...?是some organisms嗎?是the most unnatural conditions嗎?是the rabbit and ferret嗎?或是整句話所說的「這件事」?這句法是不是就像"He comes to see her every day, indicating that he is in love with her"一樣?(他每天來看她,這件事indicates他愛上了她)

l. 在"so will some animals and plants withstand domestication or cultivation, and vary very slightly"這句中,"withstand"(抗拒)後面有受詞"domestication or cultivation"(馴養或培養),"vary"(變異)後面只有修飾語"very slightly"。可見"withstand"是v.t.而"vary"是v.i.,不是嗎?如果把"withstand"後的"domestication or cultivation"改成"domesticating or cultivating"好嗎？同理，要把「所有生物體都抗拒死亡」譯成"All organisms withstand death"或"All organisms withstand dying"？

5. 請模仿下面各句的用字與句型各造一句屬於你們學門的話語：例句的劃底線部分，要保留在你的造句中，句型要合乎所提示的。（S = subject, O = object, C = complement, V = verb, V-en = past participle, V-ing = present participle）

   a. The rain caused the weeds to grow fast. (S cause O to V)

   b. This finding leads me to the conclusion. (S lead O to O)

   c. They have reported it (to be) the best book. (S report O [to be] C)

   d. We all consider it unwise to insult him. (S consider it adj. to V)

   e. We count it a disgrace to hurt the animal. (S count it N to V)

   f. Did you notice any dog run into the gate? (S notice O V)

   g. George will help you carry the box upstairs. (S help O V)

   h. My wife likes to have the house look clean. (S have O V)

i. We decide to <u>keep</u> the machine work<u>ing</u>. (S keep O V-ing)

j. The president <u>nominated</u> him ambassador to Japan. (S nominate O C)

k. He tried to <u>make</u> his influence felt everywhere. (S make O V-en)

l. The government <u>has brought</u> <u>about</u> great reforms. (S bring about O)

m. We <u>hypothesized</u> <u>that</u> opium can induce sleep. (S hypothesize that ...)

n. I <u>explained</u> <u>to</u> them <u>that</u> my delay was inevitable. (S explain to O that ...)

o. You must <u>inform</u> them <u>that</u> you are here. (S inform O that ...)

p. Have you <u>decided</u> <u>where</u> <u>to</u> spend the weekend? (S decide wh- to V)

q. Will someone <u>show</u> them <u>how</u> <u>to</u> operate the machine? (S show O wh- to V)

r. We cannot but <u>wonder</u> <u>why</u> she left so quickly. (S wonder wh-clause)

s. She is advised to <u>practice</u> play<u>ing</u> the piano regularly. (S practice V-ing)

t. She has to <u>provide</u> her son <u>with</u> daily necessaries. (S provide O with O)

u. He <u>owes</u> <u>it to</u> them <u>that</u> he can succeed at last. (S owe it to O that ...)

v. I <u>would</u> like to lend you the money <u>if</u> you <u>could</u> save me the trouble. (S would V to V O if S could V O O)

w. <u>It</u> <u>does not</u> <u>matter</u> <u>whether</u> the theory is right <u>or not</u>. (It V wh-clause)

x. <u>It</u> wouldn't <u>be</u> any good your talk<u>ing</u> to him. (It be C one's V-ing)

y. <u>It</u> <u>was</u> the rule <u>for</u> men and women <u>to</u> sit apart. (It be C for ... to V)

z. <u>It</u> looks <u>as if</u> there were going to be a snowstorm. (It V as if clause)

第九章

論文中的形容詞、
副詞、介系詞

講解

在英文的句子中，名詞／代名詞（或其對等語）以及動詞是說話的主幹，其他詞類（包括形容詞、副詞、介系詞、連接詞、和感嘆詞）則是枝葉：主幹不能沒有，枝葉則可有可無、可多可少。這個道理並不僅僅存在於一般的言語或文章中，也存在於嚴謹的學術論文中。

寫學術論文時，當然也可以感嘆，有時也會引用別人感嘆的話語，但畢竟論文是要論說與論斷，不是要抒情感嘆，所以極少會用到ah, oh, hurrah, ouch, my goodness, shame on you這一類的感嘆詞語。至於比較常用到的形容詞、副詞、介系詞、和連接詞等，在一般文法書中都有不少一般原則性的講解，在此不便一一贅述，我們只能就一些與論文寫作比較相關的重點，提請特別注意而已。

英文的形容詞，廣義來說，包括冠詞。冠詞中的a或an有下面幾種特殊用法值得注意：

a. 在"of a(n) N"的詞語中，等於"the same"之意。如：They are *of a mind*（他們同心）；We are *of an age*（我們同齡）；birds *of a feather*（同羽之鳥）；two *of a trade*（同業之兩人）。

b. 有時等於a certain之意。如：*A* Miss Liu（某一劉小姐），once upon *a time*（有一次在某時），*A man* came to call on you（某人來拜訪你）。

c. 有時等於per（每一）之意。如：60 miles an hour（每小時60哩）；twice a week（每週兩次）；10 dollars a dozen（每打十元）。

　　英文the本來就是用以指特定的人、事、物，所以在家中說the servant就是指特定的那一位僕人，在學校說the teachers就是指學校裡特定的那些老師，在任何地點說the world, the sky, the north等，就是指你我皆知的這個世界、那個天空、那個往北的方向。因此，在論文中講the paper, the experiment, the materials, the conclusions等，也是指特定的這篇論文、這個實驗、那些材料、那些結論。除了這種「表示特定」的用法之外，**請注意**：

a. 用the加單數名詞，有時指該種類的動、植物、器械、發明或某身體部位、器官。如："The whale is a mammal"（鯨魚是一種哺乳動物），"The orchid has a great variety of colors and shapes"（蘭花有很多樣的顏色和形狀），"The laser disc is a new invention"（雷射光碟是一種新發明），"He was shot through the heart"（他被射穿心臟）。由此類推，the pen, the sword不僅指筆、劍之物類，還可指文、武之才；而the heart vs. the head不僅是心與頭兩器官之對照，也是感性（sensibility）和理性（sense）的對照。

b. 用by the加量詞，表示「以……計」。如：sold by the pound, by the yard, by the gallon（以磅、以碼、以加侖

賣），rented by the month（按月租），hired by the hour（按小時租用）。

c. 用the加adj.等於那一類的人或事物。如：the rich = the rich people, the wise = the wise people 而the impossible = the impossible thing, the sublime = the sublime object。因此，Even the poor love the beautiful 是說「即使窮人也愛美的（人或事物）」。

關於用或不用冠詞，**請注意**下面幾點：

a. 說"such a great man"或"so great a man"。但只說"such pure water"而不說"so pure water"。這用法與名詞是C或U有關。同理，"What a good time it is"="How good a time it is"。但只說"What pure water it is"，而不說"How pure water it is"。

b. 表示人的職位、身分時，常省去冠詞。如："He is chairman of the committee, son of President Wang, author of the book, and cousin to him." "As commander of the army/ editor-in-chief of the magazine/ professor of poetry, I must ..." "She was made duchess/ elected vice-president/ appointed premier."同理，稱呼人的身分時也不用冠詞。如："Come, general." "Boys, fetch chairs."

c. 兩名詞用連接詞或介系詞連在一起，表示成雙、共同、對照、連續之含義時，常會省去冠詞。如：man and wife

（夫婦）, mother and child（母子）, master and man（主僕）, knife and fork（刀叉）, pen and ink（筆墨）, cart and horse（車馬）, hand in hand（手牽手）, pipe in mouth（口啣煙斗）, face to face（面對面）, night after day（夜以繼日）, from top to toe（從頭到腳）。

d. 說"at school, at church, at table, at work, at play, at breakfast" 是說「在上學、在做禮拜、在吃飯、在工作、在玩耍、在吃早餐」，如說"at the school/ the church/ the table"則是說「在那學校／那教堂／那桌邊」。同理，"go to school/ church"是「去上學／上教堂」，而"go to the school/ the church"則是「去那個學校／那個教堂」。

e. 說the bread and butter是指「那（塗）奶油（的）麵包」，說the bread and the butter是指「那麵包與那奶油」。同理，說a watch and chain是指「一個加鏈的錶」，而a watch and a chain是指「一只錶和一條鏈」。因此，說"A lady and gentleman is coming"是笑話，說"A lady and a gentleman are coming"才對。

f. 有很多成語有冠詞，也有很多成語無冠詞，或有無皆可。這只能隨時留意了。如："He lives *in the country*. He went *to town* last week." "*In view of* this/ *In regard to* that/ *With a view to* helping her/ *In (the) light of* morality/ *At (the) sight of* the ship, I ..."。

由代名詞產生的形容詞叫「代名形容詞」（pronominal adjectives），它包括my, our, your, his, her, its, their; this, that, these, those; what, which, whose等來自人稱代名詞、指示代名詞、與疑問／關係代名詞的字詞。關於這些字請**特別注意**：

a. 中文不用「我的、你的、他的……」的句子，譯成英文卻往往要有my, your, his, ...的字眼。如：中文說「我舉起手來」，英文卻說"I raised *my* hand"，不說"I raised hand/ a hand/ the hand"。同樣的，中文說「他們在回家的路上」，英文卻說"They are on *their* way home"。

b. 指示形容詞（this, that, these, those）有承續句意的功能。如："It is *suggested* that we should do some further research. *This/ That suggestion* is reasonable, but impractical."又如："We *found* that A is equal to B, C is less than D, and E is much more than F. *These/ Those findings* show that ..."。

c. "What man is he?"是問「他是什麼樣的人？」，"What a man he is!"則是感嘆「他是什麼樣的一個人啊！」這種區別同樣存在於"What price have you offered?"與"What a price you have offered!"這兩句間。

d. 關係形容詞（which, whose）的用法有如："She spoke to me in Chinese, *which language* I do not speak." "We used A as a catalyst for the reaction, *which method* had never been adopted before." "They came to seek the support of Allen Brown, *whose foundation* has helped many institutes."

表示數量或程度的「數量形容詞」（quantitative adjectives），像數字（one, two, hundred, ...）或不定數／量的many/ much, (a) few/ (a) little, several, enough, some, any, no, all等，其用法應特別注意：

a. 有時one有「某一、同一、一致」之意。如：*One*（某一）Mr. Chen asked to see you. They held *one*（同一）opinion. The team was *one*（一致）in spirit.

b. 表示「許多量」用"much"，接的是不可數名詞，如："*Much evidence is* needed."表示「許多數」用"many"或"many a"，但前者接複數名詞，後者語法上卻視為單數。如："*Many a* method *has* been tried (= *Many methods have been tried*)."

c. 含義上，"few"是數目方面「很少」（＝ not many），"a few"則是數目方面「有些」（＝ some）。相對的，"little"是量方面「很少」（＝ not much），而"a little"則是量方面「有些」。用法如："Few people came and few things did they do." "Few people came but they did a few things." "A few people came and they did a few things." "A few people came but they did few things." "They gained little knowledge and left disappointed." "They had gained a little knowledge before they left."

d. 含義上，"several"只指數目方面「有若干」（＝ some），"some"指數或量「有一些」，"enough"則指數或量「有足夠多」。用法如："He gave several pieces of advice." "We need some advice." "He advised us on some important points." "He gave us enough advice." "He advised us on enough points."

e. 通常"any"可接C或U的名詞，而用於問句、否定句或條件句中。如：Do you need any advice/ book(s)? We do not need any advice/ book(s). If you need any advice/ book(s), just let me know.

f. 通常"no"和"all"都可接C或U的名詞。如："No evidence is found." "No clues are found." "All required evidence is found." "All important clues are found."

寫科學文章常要報告數據。關於數目的說法，不能不知。在此提供下面的例子，請參考學習：

the twelfth volume（第12冊），the twenty-second day（第22日），the one hundred and third person（第103人），the ten thousand four hundred and fifty-sixth gallon（第10,456加侖）。

Charles II (Charles the second), Henry IV (Henry the fourth)。chapter two = the second chapter, room five = the fifth room。

A/ One half of the quantity（那數量的一半），a/ one third of the amount（那數額的三分之一），two thirds of the number（那數目的三分之二），three fourths/ quarters of your money（你錢財的四分之三），nine tenths of their territory（他們版圖的十分之九），

two and seven eighths of this area（這個面積的二又八分之七倍），twenty-seven *over/ by* one hundred and eight（108分之27）。

Half the usual price（尋常價格之半），double/ twice/ two times the fare you paid（你所付車費之雙倍），treble/ three times the sum（價額之三倍），four and a half times the size（那大小的四倍半），half a mile = one half of a mile, two miles and a half = two and a half miles。

The third power of three（3的三次方）, the ninth power of ten（10的九次方）。Ten square kilometers（十平方公里）, one cubic foot（一立方呎）, two point eight five pints（二點八五品脫）。

絕大多數的形容詞都是「性質形容詞」（qualifying adjectives）。像courageous, wonderful, diligent; wooden, earthen, silken; Platonic, Victorian, Florentine; idealist, humanist, romantic; exciting, learned; one-eyed, womanly, lady-like, well-off, well-to-do等等都是。有不少名詞也可當形容詞用，像a *steel* pen, a *straw* hat, *silk* umbrellas, *guest* houses, *women* novelists, *savings* banks等等。

其實，很多形容詞來自名詞，像courage/ courageous, wonder/ wonderful, wood/ wooden, Plato/ Platonic, ideal/ idealist, woman/ womanly, trouble/ troublesome等等。也有很多形容詞來自動詞，像oppose/ opposite, differ/ different, distress/ distressing, miss/ missing, move/ movable, mention/ mentionable等等。學英文一定要懂得名詞、動詞、形容詞、乃至副詞之間的詞類變化，一定要隨時留意字形、字意方面的異同關係，才能詞彙廣博而用字精確。

通常形容詞都是放在所形容的名詞之前，但有下面幾種例外的情形：

a. 形容something, anything, nothing, everything時，放其後。如：There seems to be *nothing/ something peculiar* about him. Is there *anything great* to be done? You can experience *everything fashionable* there.

b. 形容詞引導的片語放在所修飾的字之後面。如：a man *fond of music*, the people *eager to see you*, the beverage *good to drink*等。

c. 已有最高級形容詞或有all, every來形容時，-able/ -ible的形容詞常放後面。如：He is *the best doctor knowable*. She created *the most* mysterious *character imaginable*. We have tried *every/ all* means *permissible*.

d. 有些a-開頭的形容詞，只當補語，也只放在所形容的名詞之後。如：All men alive have weaknesses alike. A man (who is) afraid is a man (who is) ashamed. Don't wake the child asleep (= the sleeping child = the child who is asleep).

e. 有些固定的成語。如：a knight errant（遊俠武士）, a poet laureate（桂冠詩人）, the body politic（政治團體）, the sum total（總計）, from time immemorial（自遠古以來）, rhyme royal（皇韻）。

f. 習慣說"the drunken man"或"the man is drunk"，不說"the drunk man"或"the man is drunken"。

g. 要知道："the present women"是「當今的女人」，"the women present"是「在場／出席的女人」。"the proper study"是「那妥當的研究」，"the study proper"是「那研究本身」。

性質形容詞有時用以形容人，有時用以形容事、物，如a kind/ generous person會有a kind/ generous act。但在說話或行文時，到底是對人或對事物，一定要弄清楚而精確的表達。中文說：「你方便來嗎？」英文卻不說"Are you convenient to come?"而說"Is it convenient for you to come?"因為convenient的不是人，而是事。同樣的，英文也不說"You are impossible to succeed"，而要說"It is impossible for you to succeed"。不過，奇怪的是：英文也說"You are likely/ unlikely to succeed"。

形容詞是指人或指事的區別，會有如下的對照：

a. It is kind/ generous *of* you to give me the money.（指人用of）

It is necessary/ important *for* you to thank him at once.（指事用for）

b. How considerate/ thoughtful *of* her to do that!（指人用of）

How difficult/ cumbersome *for* her to do that!（指事用for）

關於形容詞的比較級與最高級以及如何說出比較的句子，有下面幾點請特別注意：

a. 家族中的排行大小用elder, eldest，一般年齡的大小用older, oldest。時間上的先後用later, latest，順序上的先後用latter, last。真正距離的遠用farther, farthest，程度上的深遠用further, furthest。

b. 用"all the比較級"表示「反而更……」，如："She is *all the more beautiful* after giving birth to a child." 用"none the比較級"表示「倒也不更……」，如："I am *none the happier* for being promoted to a higher position." 用"the比較級 ... the比較級"表示「越……越……」，如："The more careful you are, the fewer mistakes you will make."

c. 可用"more/ less adj.1 than adj.2"來表示「兩性質中1多於／少於2」，如：We all know that he is more clever than honest, and less sincere than courteous（我們都知道他聰明多於誠實，而真心少於客氣）。

d. 注意下面有無the的對照：

They set off *last night*.（說話時／現在的昨晚）

They set off on *the last day*.（當時的最後一天）

We will depart *next Saturday*.（說話時／現在的下星期六）

They then departed *the next Saturday*.（當時的下星期六）

e. 在superior, inferior, prior, anterior, posterior等字後用"to"代替"than"。如：A is *superior/ inferior to* B in quality. (= better/ worse than)

I intend to do this *prior to* (= before) that.

It happened *anterior to* (= earlier than) World War II.

It was known *posterior to* (= later than) the 20ᵗʰ century.

　　副詞（adverbs）用以修飾動詞、形容詞、或整個句子。有的副詞表示時間，有的表示地點，有的表示方法、手段、程度、原因、理由等等各種含義。其實，許多副詞在許多場合都可化成介系詞片語而明確表示含義。例如：

a. There was no other expedient *then*. (=at that time)

b. We must store it *here/ there*. (= at this/ that place)

c. *When* are you about to leave? (= At what time)

d. *Where* is she to live? (=At what place)

e. *How* did he finish it? (= In what manner/ way 或 By what means)

f. *How* is your uncle? (= In what state of health)

g. *How* do you like the movie? (= To what degree)

h. *How* is it that you always make the same mistake? (= From what cause)

i. *Why* dare you not tell the truth? (= For what reason)

j. Come *whenever* you like. (= at any time)

k. Sleep *wherever* you feel comfortable. (= in any place)

　　請注意關係副詞when, where, why, how前面的「先行詞／介系詞片語」若是用time, place, reason, way這種字眼，往往會被省略掉，尤其用到how當關係副詞時。如：

a. She came (at a/ the time) when I least expected her.

b. Better leave it (in the place) where it was before.

c. Can you tell me (the reason) why I cannot retire?

d. Please teach me (the way) how I can succeed.

但**注意**：She came *on a day when* I least expected her. Better leave it *in the basement where* no one can easily find it.類似這種句子中，要保留「先行詞」（即前面的介系詞片語），免得不知道講的是某天、某地下室。

關係副詞跟關係代名詞一樣，有限定用法，也有補述用法。在書寫時，前者不加逗點，後者要加。例如：

a. She came *on a day when* I least expected her.（限定用法）

（她在「我最沒料到她的那一天」來）

She came *on October 10, when* I was in Taipei.（補述用法）

（她十月十日來，[補充說]那時我在台北）

b. Leave it *in the basement where* it cannot be seen.（限定用法）

（把它留在「它不會被看到的地下室」裡）

Leave it *in Room 4, where* we will have a meeting.（補述用法）

（把它留在四號房間，[補充說]在那裡我們將開會）

複合關係副詞whenever, wherever, however等，有表示「無論……」的用法。例如：

a. *Whenever* (= No matter when) you may realize it, you will respect him.

b. You would not answer, *whenever* (= no matter when) I asked you a question.

c. *Wherever* (=No matter where) she may go, I will remember her kindness.

d. *However* (= No matter how) hard we may try, we cannot win the goal.

許多副詞都是形容詞加 -ly變成的,如greatly, honestly, humbly, publicly, specifically, tediously等。但許多副詞並沒有 -ly,像long, soon, seldom, forever, well, ill等。有些副詞有兩個字,一有-ly,一無-ly,而含義有別。如:

a. *Lately* he seldom came *late*.(lately:最近。late:遲到)

b. I am *deeply* in debt. It is buried *deep*.(deeply:抽象的深。 deep:實際的深)

c. He is highly respected. It flies fly.(highly:高度地。high: 實際很高)

d. I bought it cheap. I won it cheaply.(便宜買,輕易贏得)

e. I sold it dear. I pay dearly for it.(賣得貴,付很大代價)

許多原本為介系詞的字,有時後面卻沒有受詞,而實際上變成副詞。例如eat it *up*, eat *up* the food, put it *on*, put *on* the garment, take it *off*, take *off* the hat, come *in*, get *out*, stand *by*, come *to*（蘇醒過來）, he was done *for*（他完蛋了）, it is *over*（結束了）等等都是。在唸這種字時，也要重如副詞，而非輕如介系詞。

請參看下面各句，學會使用那些拿來修飾比較話語的用詞：

a. The sediment in Cup 1 is *much/ little/ no* more than that in Cup 2.

b. This reaction is *far/ much/ little/ no* better than that.

c. A is *almost/ hardly/ never* as valuable as B.

d. It is a *good/ great deal* more useful to me than to him.

e. It is *by far* the better of the two/ the best of them all.

f. It comes *a little/ somewhat* higher than expected.

g. This amount is *three times* as big as/ bigger than that.

h. This animal runs *twice/ two times* as fast as/ faster than that.

i. I am *ten years* older than she. (= I am older than she by ten years.)

j. This well is *200 feet* deeper than that. (= This well is deeper than that by 200 feet.)

據說，對講中文的人而言，英文有三大難：動詞的時態、冠詞、和介系詞。英文的介系詞／前置詞（prepositions）共約五十字，每字都有若干特殊含義與用法，其詳情可看字典或文法書。其實，英文的每一個介系詞幾乎都有其習慣的用法：常跟某類或某個字詞連用。在此，僅就最需要再解說的一些事項，整理出一些或許可以幫助寫作的重點，供大家參考。底下 sth. = something 而 sb. = somebody。

首先，介系詞一定有受詞。介系詞的受詞通常跟在後面，但也有在前面的可能。在 "I laughed at the man" 這句裡，受詞 "the man" 跟在 "at" 之後。在 "There was no man (for you) to laugh at" 這句裡，受詞 "no man" 就在 "at" 之前。不管如何，介系詞的受詞可能是名詞或代名詞，也可能是等於名詞的動名詞或名詞片語／名詞子句。例如：

a. I look up *to Mary* but she looks down *on me*.（名詞、代名詞）

b. They found the dog *by watching* a TV news report.（動名詞）

c. You must think *about how to finish it*.（名詞片語）

d. He cannot decide *on whether they should come or not*.（名詞子句）

不過，**請注意**：介系詞通常不接 "that- 子句"。所以，我們說 "She informed me of the news" 和 "We are certain of it"，卻說 "She informed me that he had arrived" 和 "We are certain that the price has risen"。

表達「談論……」「書寫……」或「研究……」之意時，應該知道：

a. "talk / speak/ write *about* sb. or sth."="talk/ speak/ write *of* sb. or sth."，前者比較口語，後者比較正式，都是「談／講／寫 有關某人／事物」。

b. "speak/ write *on* sth."是「以某事物為題來講／寫」。

c. "a study *of* sb. or sth."是「一個對某人或某事物之研究」，"a study *on* sth."是「以sth.為題之研究」，"a study *in* physics"則是「在物理方面的研究」。

d. "a research into sth."是「對某事物的探索研究」而"a research for sth."則是「為某事物所進行的探索研究」。

在位置上，above是「高於」，如above sea level（高於海平面）。below是「低於」，如below the horizon（低於地平線）。over是「在（正）上方」，如over the head（在頭上）。under是「在（正）下方」，如under the table（在桌子下）。on是「（貼）在上面」，如on the surface（在表面上）。beneath是「（貼）在下面」，如beneath his coat（在他外衣下）。across是「橫過」，如across the street（橫過街道）。through是「穿過」，如through the tunnel（穿過隧道）。其他有before, behind, beside, beyond表示「在前、在後、在旁、越過」。

請學會下面這些詞語與用法：

"above/ below the average"（在平均之上／下），"above all"（尤其是），"described/ mentioned above"（上頭敘述／提到的），"see below"（請看下文），"temperatures at zero or below"（零或以下之溫度）。

"over 1,000"（超過一千），"ten times over"（連續十次），"under six years of age"（年齡在六歲之下），"the topic under discussion"（在討論中的題目）,"the road under repair"（在修理中的路）。

"less than two miles across in some places"（在某些地方不到兩哩寬）,"through/ by the mechanism"（經由／藉那機制）,"through carelessness"（由於不小心）。

"before long"（不久）,"night before last"（前晚）,"leave sth. behind"（留 sth. 在後頭）,"beside the point/ question"（離題）,"thirty years old and beyond"（三十歲以上）,"beyond compare/ control/ measure"（無法比較、控制、度量）。

介系詞"at"除了指某時（at the moment/ beginning/ start/ end; at present, at night/ noon）或某地（at the station/ crossroads/ door/ gate; at Tom's/ the dentist's/ the hairdresser's）之外，**請注意**這幾種用法：

a. At work（在工作）, at play（在玩耍）, at leisure（在休閒）, at rest（在休息）, at war（在戰爭）, at peace（在和平）, at school（在上學）, at church（在上教堂）, at college（在上大學）, at table（在吃飯）, at breakfast/ lunch/ dinner（在吃早／午／晚餐）。

b. At a party/ dance/ meeting/ concert/ soirée（在[參加]某個派對／舞會／會議／音樂會／晚會 時）。At the news/ sight/ sound of ...（一得到……消息／看到／聽到……時）。

c. At 10 dollars each（以每一個[價格]10元）, at 110 kilometers per hour（以每小時110公里）, at high/ low temperatures（在高／低溫時）。

d. To look/ stare/ gaze/ aim/ shoot/ catch/ grab/ hit at sb. or sth. （看向／注視／凝視／標向／射向／抓向／緊抓向／打向某人或某事物）。

e. An expert at cooking（烹飪行家）, good/ bad at sports/ gardening（對運動／園藝很行／很差）。

f. At his best/ worst/ strongest（在他最好／最壞／最強時）。

g. At his request/ suggestion/ invitation/ beck and call（在他要求／提議／邀請／招手示意之下）。

h. Call me/ reach us at (04) 24587442（以……號碼打給我／找我們）。注意：在這種場合，英式英語會用on取代at。

　　介系詞"by"除了表示被動之「被」以外，常有「藉、用、以、靠」之意，如by bus, by email, by the traditional method, by means of sth., by a route, by doing sth.等。另外**請注意**：

a. By five o'clock, by the first of May, by the time you learned it, by the time she comes back之"by"指「到了……之時／前」。

b. Prices rose by 10%, broke the record by 1.7 seconds, older than she by 3 years, higher by 5 degrees之"by"表「差距」。

c. Take sb. by the arm, pick up a CD by the outer edge, catch her by the skirt之"by"表示「以……部位」。

d. By nature, by name, by birth, by profession, by the standard之"by"表「以……來說」。

e. Priced by the yard, sold by the dozen, paid by the week,之“by”表「以……計」。

f. Multiply by, divide by, three feet by five之“by”表「乘／除以」。

g. Little by little, one by one, day by day, stage by stage之“by”表次序上「接著」。

介系詞“in”除了指「在某物之內」（in a room, a container, a vehicle, a pocket）或「某段時間、某地方裡頭」（in the morning, in spring, in 1980, in the past/ future, in the war, in my life, in Chicago, in China, in the sky, in the world）之外，**請注意**這幾種用法：

a. In the center/ middle/ south of ...（在……之中心／中部／南方）。

b. Will be back in a minute/ two days/ three months（一分鐘／兩天／三個月之後會回來）。

c. In the past year/ the last few days（在過去那年／過去那幾天）。

d. The first speech in years/ five months（幾年內／五個月內之第一次演講）。

e. In pairs, groups, circles, twos and threes（成雙，成群，成圈，成為三三兩兩）。

f. In length/ width/ height/ area/ volume/ shape/ color/ meaning/ sense（在長度、寬度、高度、面積、體積、形狀、顏

色、意義、含義方面）。

g. Temperatures in the upper/ lower 30s（在三十好幾／三十不多的溫度）, get marks in the seventies or eighties（得七十幾分或八十幾分）, lived in the 1970s（住在1970年代）, be in one's teens/ forties（在十來歲／四十來歲）。

h. In medical science/ farming/ engineering/ history/ economics（在醫學、農作、工程、歷史、經濟學 方面）。

i. In love/ danger/ agreement/ competition/ confusion/ trouble/ good health/ a mess（處於戀愛、危險、同意、競爭、混亂、麻煩、健康、一團亂之中）。

j. In a hat, an evening gown, a black skirt, red shoes（戴帽、穿晚服、黑裙、紅鞋）。

k. In ink, pencil, chalk, oils（用墨水、鉛筆、粉筆、油彩 來寫、畫）。

l. In English, in a style, in a way, in the tradition, in cash, in order（用英文、以某風格、以某方法、以那傳統、以現金、按次序）。

介系詞"on"除了指「在……之上」（如on the floor/ wall/ ceiling/ moon/ hook/ list/ agenda/ computer/ radio/ train/ plane/ bus/ team/ committee）之外，**請注意**這幾種用法：

a. On Sunday, on November 2, on a rainy day, on a farm, on an island, on the outskirts,（指某特殊時間、地點）。

b. On an elbow, on one's knees, on one leg, on the back（指支撐身體「靠……」）。live on fish, run on batteries, travel on a grant（也指「靠……」）。

c. A report on sth., a conference on sth., on the topic/ subject of ...（表示「有關」）

d. Talk on, read on, stay on, walk on, move on; from now/ then/ that moment on; go on doing sth., keep on doing sth.（表示「繼續」）。

e. On a tour, a cruise, a trip, an expedition, a journey（表示「進行」）。

f. On a diet, on drugs, on antibiotics（表示「在吃……」）。

g. On doing sth.（= immediately after doing sth.表示「一……」），如"On finishing the work, he went home"（一完成那工作，他就回家）。此用法有別於 *in* doing sth.（= in the course of doing sth.「在……時」）。如"In working, he seldom talked"（在工作時，他很少講話）。

　　另外**注意**：在許多場合，"on"都可用"upon"來取代。如：depend on/ upon, rely on/ upon, on/ upon doing sth., look down on/ upon sb., fall on/ upon the ground, fix one's eyes on/ upon sth, on/ upon arrival, his attacks on/ upon me等等。

　　介系詞"of"除了在各種A of B的場合表示「B的A」之含義以外，**請注意**下面幾點：

a. 像a glass of water, a box of chocolates, a swarm of bees, two years of war, several weeks of problems裡之"of"，不必譯出「的」。若要譯出，也是「一杯的水……幾週的問題」，而不是「水的一杯……問題的幾週」。

b. 像be proud of, tired of, ashamed of,和die of之"of"為「（由）於」之意。

c. 而stand clear of the ground之'of'為「離開」之意。

d. "It is stupid/ clever of you to do so"之"of"也沒「的」之意。

e. 片語of no use, of little value, of great significance, of special interest = useless, not very valuable, very significant, specially interesting。

f. 句式rob/ rid/ deprive/ bereave/ clear A of B都有自A拿掉B之意。如"deprive him of his right"（剝奪掉他的權利），"clear the field of weeds"（清理掉田野的雜草）。

介系詞"to"在各種場合都常表示「到、向、往、對」之意。下面的用法請**特別注意**：

a. To the left/ right/ north/ west是「到左／右／北／西邊的方向」而on the left/ right和in the north/ west是「在左／右邊」和「在北／西面（或部）」。

b. To most of them, to me, to John之"to"是「對……（來說）」。To my mind, to the best of my knowledge,之"to"是「就……而言」。

c. To his surprise/ delight/ great horror/ great astonishment,表達「令他（大為）……的是」之意。如：To my joy, she appeared（令我歡喜的是，她出現了）。

d. March to the drum, dance to the music, cater to his appetite, agree to their plan, the keys to my desk, the answer to the question之"to"是「迎合、配合」之意。

e. Win by five goals to three是「以五分比三分而贏」。

介系詞"for"通常表示「為、替、給、供」之意，另外要注意的是：

a. For three months/ a while/ five miles/ 100 dollars之"for"表示時間、距離、價格「計、達……」。

b. To be for sth., vote for sth.,之"for"表「贊成」。

c. To be bound for a place, leave for a place之"for"表「前往」。

d. For me, for most Americans, for a child of six,之"for"表「對……來說」。

e. "She cried, for she had lost her purse"之"for"表「因為」。

介系詞"with"有時表「用」，如with a pen, with a spade等。有時表「跟、和、與、同」，如go with him, discuss sth. with her, argue with them, compete with us等。有時表「（具）有、（擁）有」，如a car with four doors, a worker with high wages等。有時

指「帶著」，如came with flowers, arrived with servants等。有時指「原因」，如shudder with cold, tremble with rage等。但請特別注意表示「附帶狀況」的"with"，如：

a. He spoke on, *with* his head *raised* high and his fists *clenched*.

b. The bird hopped in, *with* its wings all *wet*.

c. The actress appeared, *with* her costume *shining* in all directions.

英文介系詞"aboard, after, against, among, around"等的特殊用法，有下面幾點值得注意：

a. Aboard（在車、船上）可當prep.或adv.，如aboard the ship, get aboard。這字不要跟abroad（在國外）混淆。

b. After有「（在後）追逐、尋求」之意，如run after wealth, be after money。另外，"a street named after him"是「以他（之名字）來給街道命名」，"after all"是「畢竟」，而"day after day"是「一天接一天（的）」。

c. Against除了有「反對、對抗、違反、不利於」之意以外，有時有「觸及、依附、襯托」之意，如"It brushed against the leaves"（它掃到了葉子），"It was propped against the wall"（它依牆撐著），"I saw a white sail against the blue sky"（我看見襯托在藍天中的白帆）。有時有「以防、防備」之意，如"protect against frost"（防備霜害），"be vaccinated against smallpox and polio（注射疫

苗以防麻疹和小兒麻痺）。有時也有「對比」之意，如
"this year's rise of 20% against 26% last year"（今年升
20%，對比去年26%）。

d. Among指「在（多者）之中」，"from among ..."是
「從……之中」，如"Choose one from among the committee
members（從委員會成員中選一人）。成語"among other
things"是「除了別的（事項、東西）之外」，如"We
discussed, among other things, the oil crisis"（除了別的事項
之外，我們討論石油危機）。

e. Around除了有「圍著、繞著、在周圍」之意以外，有時
指「大約」，如"around ten million people"（大約一千萬
人）。

英文介系詞"besides"用法等於"in addition to"，是「除了……
之外（還有）」之意。如："Besides books, he gave me money"
（除了書，他還給我錢）。"Besides giving me money, she taught
me how to succeed"（除了給我錢，他還教我如何成功）。相對
的，介系詞"except"或等於"except"之"but"則是「除了……（沒
有）」之意。如："Except books, he gave me nothing"（除了書，
他沒給我什麼）。"He taught me nothing but how to earn money"
（他只教我如何賺錢）。

英文介系詞"despite"等於"in spite of"或"notwithstanding"（儘

管（有）……）。例如："Despite widespread opposition, they decided to build one more nuclear power station"（儘管有廣泛的反對，他們決定建另一座核能電廠）。

　　注意：許多人常把"despite"拿來接子句，那是錯的。如："*Despite* (that) there was widespread opposition, they decided to ..."是錯的，應改為"*Despite/ Notwithstanding/ In spite of* widespread opposition, they decided to ..."或"*Despite the fact* that there was widespread opposition, they decided ..."。

　　另外，"despite"後不加"of"，而"in spite"後要加"of"。所以，「不顧他生氣」只能說成"despite/ in spite of/ notwithstanding his anger"，不能說成"despite of his anger"或"in spite his anger"。

　　英文介系詞"down"在「向下、往下」的含義中，有時指距離說話者「越來越遠」，如："He rode down the road/ drove down the street/ sailed down the river"。相對的，"up"則有「越來越近」的含義，如："I saw him ride up the road/ drive up the street/ sail up the river"。因為這緣故，"move up and down"不一定是「上下移動」，也可能是「來來往往」。

　　另外，"down"與"up"常當adv.指「下降／上升」，如"The price is down/ up by about 10%"（價格下降／上升幅度大約10%）。還有，"down"與"up"有時也指「關了、完了」，如：The computer is down; the time is up.

英文介系詞"from"在「從／自……」的含義中，有時指「由於」，如die from starvation, suffer from hunger, be wet from walking in the rain等。有時指「離開、停止」，如"rise from table"（停止用餐而起身），"two miles from London"（離開倫敦兩哩）。有時指「免於」，如"prevent/ protect A from B"（避免／保護A使免於B）。有時則指「區別」，如differ from sth., know/ tell A from B, distinguish/ discriminate/ differentiate A from B等。

英文"like"一字，當動詞為「喜歡」之意，在若干成語中當形容詞為「同樣」之意，如"in like manner"（以同樣方式），"of like mind"（屬同樣的心）。當介系詞時，"like"是「像」的意思，如taste like sugar, act like mad。

注意："as"也有「像、如同」之含義，但用於"the same(...) as," "such(...)as," "as ... as," "so ... as," "as below/ above/ follows," "as if/ though"等成語中，或用於連接子句。例如："He cannot behave *like the others/ as the others do*"（他行為無法像其他人／如別人一樣）。近來在口語中，"like"也會接子句而等於"（looking）as if"，例如：She stared at the beggar, *like* she had seen a ghost."

其他介系詞，像between, into, near, off, past, round, since, throughout, toward(s)等，只要依其原有字義使用即可。其實，所有的介系詞都會固定地跟某些動詞、名詞、或形容詞連用。因此，學英文常常要把某些動詞、名詞、或形容詞跟其連用的介系詞一起背起來，變成習慣用法。下面便提供一些例子供參考：

    a. 與動詞連用：Abide by a promise, appeal to a person, ask for sth., break into a house, break through restraint, come across sb., communicate with sb., complain of/ about sth., excel in skill, glance at sth., revenge oneself on/ upon sb. for sth., run into debt, seek after/ for happiness, stand to one's opinion, take after one's father, think over a matter, wait on/ upon a person, work out an answer.

    注意：To provide sb. with sth. = to provide sth. for sb. A consists in B = B consists of A = B contains A. Distinguish/ differentiate/ discriminate between two things = Distinguish/ differentiate/ discriminate one thing from another.

    b. 與名詞連用：Acquaintance with sb. or sth., apology for some fault, caution against error, confidence in sb., dislike to sb. or sth., entrance into a place, failure in sth., indifference to sth., insistence on/ upon sth., preparation for sth., progress in sth., reputation for sth., request for sth., supremacy over a person/ country, sympathy with sb.

    c. 與形容詞連用：Be absorbed in sth., afraid of sth., angry at sth., anxious about sth., aware of sth., conscious of sth., convinced of sth., detrimental to sth., disgusted with sth., faithful to sb., fond of sth., free from sth., ignorant of sth., jealous of sth., necessary to sth., satisfied with sth., slow at sth., sure of sth., victorious over one's opponent, worthy of consideration.

注意：Somebody is familiar with something. = Something is familiar to somebody.

我們必須瞭解：有時在同一句中，用不同介系詞，含義便不一樣。例如："I gazed at her"是「我以她為目標而看她」，"I gazed on/ upon her"則是「我繼續盯著她看」。又如："I called for a policeman"是「我需要一個警察」，"I called on/ upon a policeman"是「我拜訪一個警察」，"I called up a policeman"是「我打電話給一個警察」，而"I called to a policeman"則是「我對一個警察叫喊」。

其實，在不同的場合就會用不同的介系詞。例如：This admits of no excuse（這不容藉口），This path admits to the garden（這條路通到花園）。又如：We deal in cotton and tea（我們經營棉花和茶的生意），We seldom deal with merchants（我們很少跟商人來往），We must deal out the property fairly（我們必須公平地分配此財產）。還有例如：his neglect of duty（他的怠忽職守），his neglect in taking measures（他採取措施時的疏忽）。

最後，我們必須知道：許多介系詞會跟某些字結合成固定的idioms（成語）。如at first, by means of, for the sake of, in regard to, in view of, on account of, without fail, beyond description等等。這種成語多到無法計數，平常聽到、看到時，就要學起來，而且要用看看。

作業

1. 請找出一期屬於你們學門的（紙本的或電子的）英文學術期刊來，選看其中一篇論文的一段話，據此做下面幾件事：

   a. 把那段英文中的冠詞和形容詞全部畫底線。

   b. 瞭解冠詞是a/ an或the，為何要有那個冠詞。

   c. 瞭解每一個形容詞的種類，是代名形容詞、指示形容詞、關係形容詞、數量形容詞、或性質形容詞。

   d. 瞭解放在形容的字詞之前或之後，為何如此。

   e. 瞭解所修飾、形容的是人或事物。

   f. 瞭解該形容詞是原級、比較級或最高級。

   g. 如果那是講數量的詞語，唸看看你會不會唸。

2. 請再找出一期屬於你們學門的（紙本的或電子的）英文學術期刊來，選看其中另一篇論文的一段話，據此做下面幾件事：

   a. 把那段英文中的副詞全部畫底線。

b. 瞭解那些副詞有加-ly或沒有，有沒有原本是介系詞變成的。

c. 瞭解那副詞用以修飾動詞、形容詞、或整個句子。

d. 瞭解那副詞是表示時間、地點、方法、手段、程度、原因、理由、或其他什麼含義。

e. 如果有關係副詞when, where, how, why等，查看那副詞前面有沒有先行詞（被省略掉），前面有沒有逗點（表示補述用法而非限定用法）。

f. 如果有複合關係副詞whenever, wherever, however等，瞭解那字有沒有帶著「無論」的含義。

g. 瞭解有沒有修飾比較級形容詞的副詞或副詞片語，如far better和a great deal more useful裡的far和a great deal。

3. 同樣請再找出一期屬於你們學門的（紙本的或電子的）英文學術期刊來，選看其中另一篇論文的一段話，據此做下面幾件事：
   a. 把那段英文中的介系詞全部畫底線。

   b. 瞭解那介系詞的受詞是在前或在後。

c. 瞭解那介系詞的受詞是名詞或代名詞，或等於名詞的動名詞或名詞片語／名詞子句。

d. 瞭解那介系詞的含義。

e. 瞭解那介系詞是跟哪一個字（某noun or verb or adj.）連用。

f. 瞭解那是不是固定的介系詞成語。

4. 下面一段英文是針對investment（投資）所提出的勸告，請仔細讀過，再研究後面的問題。

    Very few of us, even including clever speculators, are skilled at and fond of using crystal balls for investment. We know it is hardly possible to tell with any certainty whether prices will go up or go down between the time when we make an investment and the time when we want to use the money. Experience tells us that the key to true wisdom in personal investment is in the word *diversification*. That means: money, like eggs, should not be put in just one basket; it should be placed in a variety of channels with different attributes. For instance, against the funds placed in insurance, banks, and bonds, there should be some invested in corporate stocks or in real estate as a hedge against inflation. You know, when prices rise, the value of your corporate securities or of your real estate would rise as well (in some cases by larger amounts, on the average). When prices fall down, your money in insurance, banks, and bonds would then increase in value.

a. 在第一句（Very few of us, even including clever speculators, are skilled at and fond of using crystal balls for investment.）中，"even"是修飾"including ..."的副詞嗎？"skilled"是分詞轉成的形容詞嗎？"crystal"是名詞轉成的形容詞嗎？"at"和"of"的受詞都是動名詞"using ..."嗎？"at"是跟"skilled"連用而"of"是跟"fond"連用嗎？

b. 在第二句（We know it is hardly possible to tell with any certainty whether prices will go up or go down between the time when we make an investment and the time when we want to use the money.）中，"It is hardly possible ..."可以改成"We are hardly possible ..."嗎？"tell ... whether ..."可以改成"tell ... about/ of whether ..."嗎？"with any certainty"可以改成"in/ by any certainly"嗎？"the time *when* we make an investment and the time *when* we want to use the money"中的"when"可以省略嗎？

c. 在第三句（Experience tells us that the key to true wisdom in personal investment is in the word *diversification*.）中，"the key to ..."可以改成"the key of/ for ..."嗎？"in personal investment"可以改成"of personal investment"嗎？"in the word *diversification*"的"in"可以省略嗎？

d. 在第四句（That means: money, like eggs, should not be put in just one basket; it should be placed in a variety of channels with different attributes.）中，"like"是動詞或介系詞？"a variety of"是等於"various"的成語嗎？"with different attributes"是等於"having different attributes"而用以修飾"channels"的介系詞片語嗎？

e. 在第五句（For instance, against the funds placed in insurance, banks, and bonds, there should be some invested in corporate stocks or in real estate as a hedge against inflation.）中，"against the funds ..."的"against"是表示「對抗」、「對比」、「對照」、或「面對」的含義？"some ..."等於"some funds ..."嗎？"corporate"是"corporation"的形容詞嗎？它跟"corporal"有區別嗎？"a hedge against inflation"的"against"是表示「對抗」、「對比」、「對照」、或「面對」的含義？

f. 在第六句[You know, when prices rise, the value of your corporate securities or of your real estate would rise as well (in some cases by larger amounts, on the average)]中，"the value of your corporate securities or *of* your real estate"省去第二個"of"好嗎？用兩個"of"是不是更清楚地表示"the value of your corporate securities"or"the value of your real estate"呢？"rise by larger amounts"的"by"是表示「差距」嗎？"on the average"是成語嗎？它是什麼意思？

g. 在第七句（When prices fall down, your money in insurance, banks, and bonds would then increase in value.）中，"down"是由介系詞轉成的副詞嗎？

5. 下面一段英文指出：culture（文化）的意涵，在一般人心目中，比較狹隘。請仔細讀過，再研究後面的問題。

In anthropology the word"culture"is defined far more comprehensively than it is ordinarily understood. For many ordinary people culture is synonymous with development or improvement acquired by training or education. For them, accordingly, a"cultured,"or more properly,"cultivated,"individual is one who has acquired a certain command of knowledge or skill in certain specialized fields, usually such as literature, art, and music. Such cultivated individuals are expected and often found to have good manners as well. Consequently, those who are not so well educated in these fields, or those whose manners are considered"bad"as they were learned in the streets rather than in polite society, are often called uncultured people.

a. 在第一句（In anthropology the word"culture"is defined far more comprehensively than it is ordinarily understood.）中，"far"修飾"more"嗎？可換成"much"或"a great deal"嗎？"comprehensively"何不改為"comprehensive"？"ordinarily"修飾動詞"understood"嗎？

b. 在第二句（For many ordinary people culture is synonymous with development or improvement acquired by training or education.）中，"For many ordinary people"的"For"是「為了」或「就／對 ... 而言」？"is synonymous with"可以改成"is synonymous to"嗎？可以改成"has the same meaning as"嗎？"acquired by"之"by"等於"by means/ way of"嗎？

c. 在第三句（For them, accordingly, a"cultured,"or more properly,"cultivated,"individual is one who has acquired a certain command of knowledge or skill in certain specialized fields, usually such as literature, art, and music.）中，"cultured,""cultivated"和"specialized"都是分詞轉成的形容詞嗎？"more properly"可以改成"properlier"嗎？看得出"certain"可接單數或複數名詞嗎？"usually"可以改成"usual"嗎？

d. 在第四句（Such cultivated individuals are expected and often found to have good manners as well.）中，"manners"可以改成"manner"嗎？

e. 在第五句（Consequently, those who are not so well educated in these fields, or those whose manners are considered"bad"as they were learned in the streets rather than in polite society, are often called uncultured people.）中，"those who ..."和"those whose ..."的"those"都等於"those people"嗎？"as they were learned in the streets"的"they"是指"ordinary people"或"their manners"？"rather than"是成語嗎？等於"instead of"的意思嗎？"uncultured"像"uneducated"一樣，是否定而且是分詞形式的形容詞嗎？

6. 下面一段英文談到animals for experiment（實驗動物），請仔細讀過，再研究後面的問題。

According to statistics, by far the most common organisms used in the psychology laboratories are firstly the white rat and secondly the college sophomore. The underlying reasons are: first, both are readily available; second, both are inexpensive to use. Other animals are sometimes used, of course. The rhesus monkey and the chimpanzee also get their share of attention in many fields of study. Sometimes even the sow bug, cockroach, and the amoeba are used instead of the frog or the rabbit in learning experiments.

a. 在第一句（According to statistics, by far the most common organisms used in the psychology laboratories are firstly the white rat and secondly the college sophomore.）中，"by far" 是成語嗎？表示「差距很大」嗎？"by far the most common" 就是「（比起來）遠最為平常」的意思嗎？"the most common"可以改成"the commonest"嗎？"the psychology laboratories"（＝ the laboratories for psychology）可以改成

"the psychological laboratories"嗎？（同理，history teacher 等於 historical teacher嗎？）而"the white rat and the college sophomore"可以改成"white rat and college sophomore"嗎？用單數加the是代表全體嗎？"firstly"和"secondly"變成"first"和"second"可以嗎？

b. 在第二句（The underlying reasons are: first, both are readily available; second, both are inexpensive to use.）中，"underlying"是分詞的形容詞嗎？"first"和"second"可以改成"firstly"和"secondly"嗎？"readily available"可以改成"ready available"嗎？等於"ready and available"嗎？"inexpensive to use"的"to"是介系詞的"to"或不定詞的"to"？

c. 在第三句（Other animals are sometimes used, of course.）中，"Other animals"可以改成"The other animals"嗎？可以改成"Some/ Certain other animals"嗎？

d. 在第四句（The rhesus monkey and the chimpanzee also get their share of attention in many fields of study.）中，"The rhesus monkey and the chimpanzee"也是用單數加the來代表全體的物種嗎？"their share of attention"可以改成"their attention of share"嗎？"in many fields of study"可以改成"in many field of studies"嗎？

e. 在第五句（Sometimes even the sow bug, cockroach, and the amoeba are used instead of the frog or the rabbit in learning experiments.）中，"cockroach"為何不也說成"the cockroach"？是因為它是同位語，等於the sow bug嗎？"the amoeba"是哪一類的「動物」？"the frog"和"the rabbit"是指某一隻青蛙／兔子或指青蛙／兔子這一類動物？"in learning experiments"等於"in experiments for learning"或"in learning to make experiments"？

第十章

論文中的連接詞、
句子、段落

講解

在學術性的論文裡，跟在其他場合一樣，經常都會使用到連接詞。英文的連接詞（conjunctions）分為「對等連接詞」（coordinate conjunctions）和「從屬連接詞」（subordinate conjunctions）兩種。前者包括and, or, but, so等，後者包括that, which, whether, who, whom, whose, what, when, where, how, why, while, as, if, since, till, before, after, then, because, unless, though, yet等關係代名詞、關係形容詞、或關係副詞。在這兩種之中，as well as, as soon as, as long as, in order that等另稱為「連接詞片語」，而both ... and, not ... but, not only ... but also, either ... or, neither ... nor, hardly ... when, scarcely ... before, no sooner ... than, such ... that, so ... that等又另稱為「關聯連接詞」。

通常「對等連接詞」用以連接對等的單字、片語、或子句。例如：

a. *Jane and Jack* could come *by land or by sea.*（單字、片語）

b. Jane came by land, *but* Jack came by sea.（子句）

c. They did not come by air, *so* they saved some money.（子句）

d. He is healthy *as well as* wealthy, *but* she is often ill.（單字、子句）

e. It is *either* because he is poor *or* because he is ill.（子句）

f. I am here *not only* for your good *but also* for my own safety.

（片語）

因此，使用「對等連接詞」時，如果不對等，就是不對或不好。例如："She ran all the way and tired"應改為"She ran all the way and (she) was tired"才對等。"I want not only your obedience but also you love me"應改為"I want *not only* your obedience *but also* your love"才對等。"He is dissatisfied neither with you nor your friend"應改為"He is dissatisfied *neither* with you *nor* with your friend"或"He is dissatisfied with *neither* you *nor* your friend"才對等。

英文"and"譯成中文通常為「和、跟、同、與、及」，有時則為「而、而且」，如"He went north, and she went south"（他往北，而她往南）；"He became rich, and was elected mayor"（他變有錢，而且被選為市長）。

當"and"跟祈使句連用時，則是「那麼」，如"Come, and you'll have it"（來，那麼你就有它），"One more step, and you are a dead man"（再走一步，那麼你就沒命）。

有時在句首時，"and"有「接著」之意，如"He rose and left. And he said he would not come back"（他起身而離開，接著他說他不回來）。

另外，"and"還有特殊用法如下：

a. Come and see (= Come to see). Try and do it (= Try to do it). Go and buy one (= Go to buy one).

b. A carriage and four（四馬馬車）, brandy and water（摻水白蘭地）, a cup and saucer（一套杯碟）, man and wife（夫

妻）, two and four（二加四）.

c. "You must come to see him, *and that* quickly"（你必須來看他，而且快來）。

d. "He aimed straight, *and so* he hit the mark"（他瞄得準，於是他射中目標）。

e. They walked *for miles and miles by twos and threes*（他們三三兩兩走好多好多哩）。

英文"or"通常為「或」之意，但與祈使句連用時為「否則」，如"Get out, *or (else)* I'll beat you"（出去，否則我要打你）。

另外，"or"也有特殊用法如下：

a. You must *either* tell the truth *or* say nothing（你得或說實話或不說話）。

b. I want 20 dozens *or so*（我要二十打左右）。（= about 20 dozens）

c. We want to know *whether* she will stay *or* go（我們要知道她要留 抑或 要走）。

英文"but"通常為「可是、但、然而」之意，但有時是「除卻、除了」之意。例如："I can live anywhere, but here"（除了這裡，我可住任何地方）；"I want to save nothing but my face"（除了臉之外，我什麼都不保留）；"I cannot choose but leave"（除了離開，我別無選擇）。

在doubt/ deny but的句子中，"but"="that"，如："I do not doubt/ deny but he will support you"（我不懷疑／否認他會支持

你）。其他場合，"but"也有特殊用法如下：

a. They *never* played *but* a quarrel followed. *None* sought his aid *but* were helped.（but為「而不」之意）

b. Who *but* a fool would do that?（but為「除非」之意）

c. *But for* your help, I might have failed. We shoud come on time *but that* it is impossible.（此but為「要不是」之意）

d. After all, he is *but* a child.（but = only）

e. The child was *all but* drowned.（all but = almost）

f. "Sorry, *but* I have overslept myself."（but只接語句，沒有含義）

有關"as well as"和"not only ... but also"要注意的是：在A as well as B的句法中，強調的是A，就像A, along with/ together with B一樣。但在not only A but (also) B的句法中，強調的卻是B。因此，文法上有如下的差異：

a. <u>John,</u> *as well as/ along with/ together with* his brothers, <u>is</u> accused of theft.

b. *Not only* John *but* (*also*) <u>his brothers</u> <u>are</u> accused of theft.

有關"both ... and," "either ... or," "neither ... nor."和"not ... but"的文法現象，請看下面的例句：

a. Both Jack and Jill <u>are</u> here to welcome you.

b. Either you or I / Neither you nor I <u>am</u> to blame.

c. It is not I but <u>you</u> that <u>are</u> to be responsible for that.

另外注意："both ... not"是部分否定，"neither ... nor"才是全部否定。例如：

a. Both Jack and Jill are not here = Not both Jack and Jill are here（並非Jack和Jill都在此）。就像All of them are not here = Not all of them are here.

b. Neither Jack nor Jill is here.（Jack和Jill都不在此）。就像 None of them is/ are here（他們都不在此）。

有關"such ... that…"和"so ... that…"的文法現象，請看下面的例句：

a. He is <u>such a stupid man </u>that no one respects him.

b. He is <u>so stupid a man</u> that no one respects him.

c. It is <u>such pure water</u> that you can drink it for health.

d. The water is <u>so pure</u> that you can drink it for health.

關係代名詞、關係形容詞、和關係副詞都是引導「從屬子句」而連接「主要子句」的字詞，所以它們都是連接詞，只是另有代名詞、形容詞、和副詞的功能而已。像下面的句子都有兩子句，前為主要子句，後為從屬子句。

a. I wore a hat *that/ which* she bought for me.（關係代名詞 = it）

b. They found the child *whose* father was killed.（關係形容詞 = his）

c. It came *when* we had left.（關係副詞，修飾came，表示來的時間）

注意："I know that he is a liar"="I know the fact that he is a liar"。"I am certain that he is a liar"="I am certain of the fact that he is a liar"。

有不少字詞是引導子句而兼有副詞功能的連接詞，像表示時間的至少就有如下：

a. You may come *when/ while/ whenever/ as soon as/ as long as/ before / after* I need you.

b. You can stay *till/ until* you want to leave.

c. *Since* he came, we have had no peace.

d. She had *no sooner/ scarcely/ hardly* seen me *than/ before/ when* they took her away.

e. The dog ran off *the moment/ the minute/ the instant/ every time/ directly/ immediately/ once* it saw me.

表示地點的如："Leave it *where/ wherever* you think it right"。

表示方法、方式的例如：

a. Please treat him *as* you would treat your own child.

b. He does treat me *as if/ as though* I were his son.

c. *As* the desert is like a sea, *so* is the camel like a ship.

表示程度的如："John is *as/ not so* handsome as Paul (is)"和 "John is *more/ less* handsome *than* Paul (is)"。

表示原因或理由的例如：

a. He is beloved of all, *because* he is considerate.

b. He must be sociable, *for* many people love him.

c. *Since/ Now that* you say so, I must believe it.

d. *As* I am hard up myself, I cannot lend you the money.

e. I refused to lend him money *on the ground that* his credit was not good.

表示目的的如："We tried our best (*so/ in order*) *that* we might succeed"。

表示結果的如："He worked *so* hard *that* he earned a lot of money"和"He is *such* a diligent worker *that* he can soon finish the task"以及"We have said a thousand times, *so that* we will not repeat it again"。

表示條件的如："They will agree *if/ provided that/ in case/ on condition that* we agree first"。

表示讓步的例如：

a. *Though/ Although/ Despite the fact that* he is clever, he is not wise enough.

b. It does not concern me, *(no matter) whether* it is true or not.

c. They cannot help us *even if/ even though* they want to.

d. Hero *as* he is/ Brave *as* he is/ Courageously *as* he can act, he may be shocked at the sight.

英文的句子通常分為四種：簡單句（simple sentences），合句（compound sentences），複句（complex sentences），和合複句（compound complex sentences）。一個「簡單句」只有一個子句（clause），雖然它可能有使用到對等連接詞。例如：

a. It induces apoptosis.

b. Farnesol and other isoprenoid alcohols induce apoptosis.

c. Farnesol and other isoprenoid alcohols induce apoptosis in various carcinoma cells.

d. Farnesol *and* other isoprenoid alcohols induce apoptosis in various carcinoma cells *and* inhibit tumorigenesis in several in vivo models.

一個「合句」有兩個（以上的）子句，由對等連接詞加以連接。例如：

a. Such studies are important, *but* they are not known.

b. Studies on retinoblastoma have been at the heart, *but* advances in the laboratory have had little effect on it.

c. Studies on retinoblastoma have been at the heart of many of the landmark discoveries, *but* advances in the laboratory have had little effect on the treatment of children with retinoblastoma.

d. We know the fact *and* we want to deal with it, *but* we have not found the proper method *and* we have not gained enough support.

一個「複句」有兩個（以上的）子句，由從屬連接詞加以連接。例如：

a. It is encouraging *that* there is broad agreement among them.

b. *When* cells are treated with the regulator, signs of terminal differentiation will be found.

c. This result shows *that* we need to know *where* the fossil has been deposited.

d. This result shows *that* we need to know *where* the fossil has been deposited in such a way *as* we have noticed.

一個「合複句」有三個或三個以上的子句，那些子句既有對等連接詞也有從屬連接詞加以連接。例如：

a. We now know *that* studies on retinoblastoma have been at the heart of many of the landmark discoveries, *but* advances in the laboratory have had little effect on the treatment of children with retinoblastoma.

b. This result shows *that* we need to know *where* the fossil has been deposited in such a way *as* we have noticed, *and* that we must make some more experiments as soon as possible.

c. *Since* the mechanism by *which* such ants protect their territory is not yet fully understood, it is certainly necessary *that* one more investigation at least should be launched into the problem of *how* they react against invaders, *but* it will be futile if no consideration is given to where they live *or* how they build their nests.

有些作家，如海明威（Hemingway），喜歡用簡單句和合句，因而寫出了簡單的風格。另外有些作家，如福克納（Faulkner），則喜歡用複句和合複句，因而寫出了複雜的風格。寫學術論文的人，通常不必講究文筆的風格，而只需力求清晰明白。通常，多用簡單句和合句比較容易清晰明白，但卻也比較像口語，比較不凝煉。相對的，多用複句和合複句則比較莊重而有文氣，但卻容易因為繁複而不夠簡明。在此，我們建議：學術論文以寫簡單句、合句和複句為主，只需偶爾配一些合複句就好。

不管是什麼句子，句中都常常會有連接詞來連接字詞、片語、或子句，而句與句之間則有「起承轉折用語」（transition expressions）可以相互連接。英文的「起承轉折用語」通常分為下面三類：

a. **表示包括（Including）**：譯成中文為「還有、此外、另外、然後、同樣的」。

例如additionally/ in addition, also, besides, further, furthermore, likewise/ similarly, moreover, next, then等。另外，incidentally/ by the way, either, too, as well, for example, for instance以及表示時間順序的afterwards, later, finally, at first, at last等也是。

b. **表示對照（Contrasting）**：譯成中文為「不過、可是、但是、然而、相反的」。

例如but, however, instead, nevertheless, on the contrary, on the other hand, still, yet等。另外，all the same/ just the same, otherwise/ or eslse以及放在句尾的though也是。

c. **表示總結（Summarizing）**：譯成中文為「因此、於是、結果、那麼、接著、如此」。

例如accordingly, as a result/ consequence, consequently/ in consequence, hence, in concusion, so, then, therefore, thus, to sum up等。另外，像actually, after all, anyway, as a matter of fact, at any rate, at least, in a word, in brief/ short, in fact/ effect, in reality/ actuality, in other words, in that case等也是。

「起承轉折用語」通常都可放在句首而後面加逗點。例如：

a. You should not have told Bob the secret. *Furthermore*, Bob should not have repeated it.

b. Bob was asked to come at five. *However*, he appeared at six.

c. I have done a good job. *Therefore*, I am praised and well rewarded.

不過，"and"和"but"不加逗點，除非另插入修飾語。例如：

a. Derek stumbled over a fallen tree and broke his leg. *And* he cried for help./ *And, pitiably,* he cried for help.

b. A friend of his came at once. *But* he did not know how to help him./ *But, unfortunately,* he did not know how to help him.

有許多「起承轉折用語」也可放在句中（通常在主詞或動詞之後），而用逗點隔開。例如：

a. Water goggles and masks are often used for underwater swimming. Masks are forbidden, *by the way*, at some beaches.

b. I study very hard, indeed. My grades, *nevertheless*, are poor.

c. No formal complaint was made. The police, accordingly, took no action.

當「起承轉折用語」的too, either, though通常放在句尾，而前面加逗點。例如：

a. Martha has placed an order on the internet. She has paid the money, *too*.

b. She has not received the goods. She has not received any news, *either*.

c. She will complain to the company. She will not take any legal action for the time being, *though*.

注意："as well"等於"too"，但前面不加逗點，如"She has paid the money *as well*."

其實，許多「起承轉折用語」也都可放在句尾，而前面有時也要加逗點。例如：

a. He wants to bring an umbrella along with his briefcase. He wants to carry a laptop *besides*.

b. On second thought, he knows he can dispense with the laptop. He will use his iPhone 5 *instead/ , instead*.

c. It is more fashionable to do so. And it is more convenient, *after all*.

「起承轉折用語」是用以連接句子與句子。但有時候兩句子之間，如果含義相當密切，便有可能合成一句，只是用「半支點／分號」（semicolon）隔開而已。這種用分號隔開的句子中，其第二句也照樣會用到「起承轉折用語」。例如：

a. History is a record of mankind; different historians interpret it differently, *however*.

b. Icelanders complain about New York in the summer; *likewise*, Ecuadorians complain about the city during the winter.

c. The movie star has become very popular; news about him, *therefore*, spreads very fast.

到底某「起承轉折用語」可放在什麼位置，而其前或其後要不要加逗點，那是習慣的問題，學英文的人要隨時留意。其實，英文有許多成語（如to begin with, as it were, so to speak, that is, for sure, to be sure, among other things, into the bargain等）都隨時會跑到句首、句中、或句尾來修飾句意。這是想學好英文的人必須特別注意的。例如：*To begin with*, he gave me, *among other things*, a purse full of money and said he would support me *for sure.*

另外，句子中也常有「用逗點分開」或「放在括弧中」的「同位語」（appositive）。例如：在"We use morpholinos to reduce the expression of CoxVa, a structural subunit, and of Surf1, an assembly factor, both of which impair ..."這句子中，"a structural subunit"是說明"CoxVa"的同位語，而"an assembly factor"則是說明"Surf1"的同位語，在這裡用逗點隔開（其實放在括弧中也可以）。

複雜的英文句子，除了可能有「起承轉折用語」和「同位語」之外，往往裡頭還會有「補充說明或修飾的用語」。例如：在"To begin with, Betty Smith, the girl your cousin loves so much, is loved by many others as well, and, needless to say, she is very proud."這句子中，"To begin with"（「首先」）是起承轉折用語，"the girl your cousin loves so much"是"Betty Smith"的同位語，而"needless to say"（「不需說」）則是補充說明或修飾"she is very proud"的用語。

句子並非越長越複雜越好，有時反而越精簡越好。通常，寫文章時，會盡量用字詞或片語而不用子句。像"Have you heard of my son's success?"等於"Have you heard that my son has succeeded?"，但前者為簡單句，後者為複句。許多子句確實都可以變成字詞、片語，例如："Mitochondria have the potential of emitting oxidants. The potential is increased in skeletal muscle when the muscle recovers from exercise. It is possible that the muscle reovers because it has relied on lipid metabolism for a long time and/ or because its mitochondrial biochemistry has（been）altered."這麼多句子可以變成一句"The oxidant-emitting potential of mitochondria is increased in skeletal muscle during recovery from exercise, possibly as a consequence of prolonged reliance on lipid metabolism and/ or altered mitochondrial biochemistry."

最常把句子變成片語的方法就是把動詞變成名詞或動名詞，例如："Economic sanctions are imposed on the country"變成"the imposition of economic sanctions on the country"。"They respond violently"變成"their violent response"。由這種變化便可產生"The imposition of economic sanctions on the country leads to their violent response"這種句子。

又如："The soldiers faced defeat in such a situation"變成"the soldiers' facing defeat in such a situation"。"We knew"變成"our knowing"。而由這兩句又可產生"They deny our knowing the soldiers' facing defeat in such a situation"。

另一種常把句子變成片語的方法就是把形容詞變成名詞，例如："The general was ignorant of the defeat"變成"the general's ignorance of the defeat"。"We were angry at it"變成"our anger at it"。由這兩句又可產生"You cannot imagine our anger at the general's ignorance of the defeat"。

又如："She is jealous of her husband"變成"her jealousy of her husband"。"It was dangerous not to know it"變成"the danger of not knowing it"。而由這兩句又可產生"We did not foresee the danger of not knowing her jealousy of her busband"。

不管如何，論文裡的句子要力求簡要明瞭，句子與句子之間要連貫通順。因此，「起承轉折用語」的挑選、「同位語」以及「補充說明或修飾用語」的插入、整個句子的繁簡、乃至標點的使用等，都要留意。有關標點符號的使用，請特別注意下面幾點：

a. 英式英語先用單引號（'...'），後用雙引號（"..."）。美式英文剛好相反：先用雙引號，後用單引號。

b. 英式英語句尾的句點（.），有時放在引號前，有時放在引號後（依含義視情形而定）。美式英語則一律放在引號前。

c. 句子中如果有太多逗點（,），容易混淆。為清楚起見，必要時要用括號、長畫符號（—）、或分號。例如：

a. 用括號：She went in, tried on everything (bonnets, blouses, bras, and girdles, not to say furcoats), pretended to have no interest, and then left without buying anything.

b. 由長畫符號：All his belongings—his house, his car, and even his clothes—were seized by his creditors.

c. 用分號：Following this procedure: first, get your application forms; next, fill them out; last, pay the charges.

段落由句子組成。通常一個段落會有兩個以上的句子，而整個段落中會有一句所謂的「主題句」（topic sentence），那句話是該段落中最重要的話，其他的句子只是幫忙說明、引申、強化、修飾、舉證的功能罷了。例如：下面一段英文中，第一句是主題句，其他各句都只是進一步說出「鳥之美沒例外」的主題而已。

The beuty of birds is without exception. I have seen ugly beasts, ugly men and women, in films or in real life. But I have never seen an ugly bird. Even an owl, with its catlike face, has a majestic sort of beauty. As for the kiwi, the poor, weak-eyed bird in New Zealand, just look at its long bill, its tailless body covered with hair-like feathers, and you will be struck with its grotesque beauty.

就像上面的例子，大部分的主題句都是放在段落的第一句。不過，有時主題句也會出現在段落的中間或最後面。例如下面這兩段：

I grant that flowers are at times as beautiful as birds in shape and in color. Yet, flowers normally do not move themselves. They only sit or stand there waiting to wither and die. *The beauty of birds is not static; it is dynamic.* Every bird is constantly on the move unless it is sick or stopping to feed, to mate, or to rest. It moves mostly by flying. It glides, soars, flaps, or hovers in the air. And how gracefully a seagull glides! How handsomely an eagle soars! How artistically a kite flaps! How superbly a humming-bird hovers!

But, alas, we are unthinkingly destroying the birds' habitat—from the arctic tundras, through the woodlands, grasslands, wetlands, swamps, marshes, rivers, lakes, estuaries, mountain peaks, cliffs, and deserts. We are unreasonably preventing birds from nesting and feeding in every way imaginable. And we are unpardonably killing them in large numbers as game for sport or food, or as an unconsidered consequence of industrial development. *Under such circumstances, we are not just "as proud as a peacock"; we are"birdbrained"without any sense of beauty.*

但**請注意**：並非每一個段落都會有一個主題句。有時候整個段落只是一連串的描寫（description）或陳述（account），根本沒有一句話可以概括其他每句話的含義。其實，整段話要說的主題或重點，也是可以隱含不說的。例如下面一段，暗中要說的是：那隻名為"the Awesome One"的老虎won the election by dirty means。

The day for election came. All the beasts were qualified voters. But, in addition to those, there suddenly appeared a great multitude of hares at the glade where all electors were supposed to gather for the election. The hares had seldom been seen in the district. They said the tigers had kindly invited them from the neighborhood to the polls to watch the show of democracry. And they all raised their front feet when the Awesome One was announced to the voters. As a result, the tiger won the election by an absolute majority.

整篇論文是由各章節組成，分章或分節要有邏輯，也要有比例原則。有的章節太長或太短，就是不好，就應該重新切分或加以合併。同理，一個段落也要避免太長或太短，最好以幾句話共同說出一個重點為原則。當諸多段落一點一點說出章節的要點，而諸多章節又說出整篇論文的論點時，那便是組織嚴密的論文了。

作業

1. 請找出一期屬於你們學門的（紙本的或電子的）英文學術期刊來，選看其中一篇論文的一段話，據此做下面幾件事：

   a. 把該段話中的對等連接詞and, or, but, so全部畫底線，瞭解它們要用什麼字詞來譯成中文。

   b. 瞭解這些and, or, but, so連接的是什麼（字、詞、語、句）而有沒有對等。

   c. 把該段話中的從屬連接詞也全部畫底線，瞭解它們是關係代名詞、關係形容詞、或關係副詞。

   d. 如果有關係副詞，瞭解那是表示時間、地點、目的、原因、理由、結果、方法、方式、程度、條件、讓步或什麼。

2. 請再找出一期屬於你們學門的（紙本的或電子的）英文學術期刊來，選看其中一篇論文裡的較長的一段話，據此做下面幾件事：

   a. 數一數那段話裡有多少英文句子。

   b. 看一看那段話裡的句子是簡單句、合句、複句、或合複句。

c. 看一看那些句子有沒有用到「起承轉折用語」。

d. 如果有transition expressions，瞭解那是表示Including, Contrasting,或Summarizing的用語，而那些用語是放在句前、句中、或句尾，又那用語有沒有逗點跟它連用。

e. 另外瞭解有沒有句子的附帶修飾語或同位語。

f. 如果有同位語，瞭解那是補充說明什麼的同位語。

3. 下面一段英文有關space travel（太空旅行），請仔細閱讀後，再回答接著的問題。

There are immense problems to be overcome before space travel becomes possible. First of all, the spacecraft has to be aimed exactly at where the target planet is going to be when it arrives, perhaps several months later. But the target planet, say Mars, does not stay waiting there, you know. Like our Earth, it is revolving all the time on its axis and it is swinging through space round the Sun in an elliptical orbit of its own. How can we then aim exactly at a mobile object like that from afar, where the object we stand on, our Earth, is also spinning like a top and moving round the Sun in its own orbit? Fortunately, today we can do complex and accurate calculations beforehand with the help of computers, and with other high tech equipment we can send radioed instructiouns to the spacecraft and ask it to slightly alter its direction in time as it hurtles on toward the destination.

a. 第一句（There are immense problems to be overcome before space travel becomes possible.）有幾個子句？"before"所引導的子句是對等的或從屬的子句？因此，整個句子是簡單句、合句、或複句？

b. 第二句（First of all, the spacecraft has to be aimed exactly at where the target planet is going to be when it arrives, perhaps several months later.）裡有幾個子句？三個，對嗎？"where"引導的子句修飾"aimed ...at"的地點，而"when"引導的子句又修飾"going to be"的時間，看來整句是合句、複句、或合複句？

另外，"First of all"是起承轉折用語嗎？"perhaps several months later"是補充說明的用語嗎？其前的逗點可以省略嗎？

c. 第三句（But the target planet, say Mars, does not stay waiting there, you know.）是簡單句、合句、或複句？如果把"say Mars"（＝let us say Mars「就說火星好了」）以及"you know"（「你曉得的」）這兩個插入的補充用語不算為子句，那麼這句話便是簡單句，不是嗎？

d. 第四句（Like our Earth, it is revolving all the time on its axis and it is swinging through space round the Sun in an elliptical orbit of its own.）是由“and”連接兩個對等子句組成的合句嗎？起頭“Like our Earth”很像是起承轉折用語，但也是補充說明或修飾用語，不是嗎？

e. 第五句（How can we then aim exactly at a mobile object like that from afar, where the object we stand on, our Earth, is also spinning like a top and moving round the Sun in its own orbit?）有幾個子句？其基本結構是“How can we aim ... where something is also ...”，但“something”又等於“the object (which) we stand on”。因此，這個句子有三個子句（一個主要子句加上兩個從屬子句），不是嗎？

這句中的“then”（「那麼」）也可用逗點分開成為（“How can we, then, aim ...”），而它是起承轉折用語，不是嗎？另外，“our Earth”是“the object we stand on”的同位語，不是嗎？而“and”連結“spinning like a top”和“moving round the Sun in its own orbit”有對等嗎？

f. 第六句（Fortunately, today we can do complex and accurate calculations beforehand with the help of computers, and with other high tech equipment we can send radioed instructiouns to the spacecraft and ask it to slightly alter its direction in time as it hurtles on toward the destination.）這句有幾個子句？其基本結構為"we can do ... and we can send ... and ask ... as it hurtles ..."，因此，這句是由兩個用"and"連接的兩個對等子句加上一個由"as"引導的從屬子句，不是嗎？

至於"and ask"的"and"是連接"send ..."和"ask ..."，不是連接兩子句，不是嗎？而句首的"Fortunately"是起承轉折用語，不是嗎？

g. 在這一段話中，哪一句最像主題句（topic sentence）？應該是第二句，不是嗎？

4. 下面是一段有關the variability of grape berries（葡萄果粒之變異）的英文報告，請仔細閱讀後，再回答接著的問題。

　　We all know that the variability of grape berries is caused by both environmental factors (such as vineyard location, light, temperature, and soil moisture) and viticultural practices (such as weeding, irrigation, fertilization, pruning, and cluster thinning) and it is seen in the individual berries of a bunch, between one bunch and another on a vine, and among vines within an entire vineyard. We seldom realize, however, that such variability can be both advantageous and disadvantageous. On the one hand, variability in grape genes may mean plasticity and plasticity may help the existing cultivars adapt to a specific region. Furthermore, berry variability may help produce different sorts of wine from the same cultivar. On the other hand, the variability of grape berries can also be a disadvantage because it may cause uneven maturity among bunches, vines, or vineyards and it thus may bring about seasonal fluctuations in the produce for sale.

a. 第一句["We all know that the variability of grape berries is caused by both environmental factors (such as vineyard location, light, temperature, and soil moisture) and viticultural practices (such as weeding, irrigation, fertilization, pruning, and cluster thinning) and it is seen in the individual berries of a bunch, between one bunch and another on a vine, and among vines within an entire vineyard."]是合句、複句、或合複句？

在這句中，如果把兩組括號變成兩組逗點，好嗎？把它變成"environmental factors, such as vineyard location, light, temperature, and soil moisture, and viticultural practices, such as weeding, irrigation, fertilization, pruning, and cluster thinning ..." 會不會逗點太多而容易混亂？如果括號變成長畫符號使之成為"environmental factors—such as vineyard location, light, temperature, and soil moisture—and viticultural practices—such as weeding, irrigation, fertilization, pruning, and cluster thinning—and..."也會比較清楚嗎？

在"such as vineyard location, light, temperature, and soil moisture"以及"such as weeding, irrigation, fertilization, pruning,

and cluster thinning"的詞語中，把"and"去掉，可以嗎？中文
會說「諸如甲、乙、丙」，但英文習慣說"such as a, b, *and* c"
或"such as a, b, c, d, *and* e"，不是嗎？

在"in the individual berries of a bunch, between one bunch and
another on a vine, and among vines within an entire vineyard.這
話語中，第一個"and"連接"one bunch"和"another (bunch)"，
第二個"and"連接的是三個介系詞片語。請問哪三個？

b. 第二句（We seldom realize, however, that such variability can
   be both advantageous and disadvantageous.）是簡單句、合
   句、或複句？"however"是放在句中的起承轉折用語嗎？
   "both ... and"是連接兩個子句嗎？

c. 第三句（On the one hand, variability in grape genes may mean
   plasticity and plasticity may help the existing cultivars adapt to
   a specific region.）有幾個子句？用"and"連接的子句與子句
   間有對等嗎？因此，它是複句或合句？這句中的"on the one
   hand"是起承轉折用語嗎？

d. 第四句（Furthermore, berry variability may help produce
   different sorts of wine from the same cultivar.）是簡單句嗎？
   在這句中，"Furthermore"也是起承轉折用語嗎？

e. 第五句（On the other hand, the variability of grape berries can also be a disadvantage because it may cause uneven maturity among bunches, vines, or vineyards and it thus may bring about seasonal fluctuations in the produce for sale.）是不是另一個合複句？它的基本結構是不是"the variability ... can also be ... because it may cause ...and (because) it thus may bring about ..."？

在這句中，"On the other hand"也是放在句首的起承轉折用語嗎？它可改成"Furthermore," "Besides," "Also," "Additionally," "In addition,"等任何一個嗎？可以改成"However," "Nevertheless," "Yet,"或"Still"嗎？是不是應保留下來跟前面的"On the one hand"連用？

f. 在這五句組成的一段話中，哪一句是「主題句」（topic sentence）？是第一句或第五句嗎？或是段中的第二句（We seldom realize, however, that such variability can be both advantageous and disadvantageous.）？

5. 下面一段英文有關 nuclear energy（核能），請仔細閱讀後，再回答接著的問題。

According to Einstein's theory of equivalence, we know $E = mc^2$, where E is the energy in ergs, m is the mass in grams, and c is the velocity of light in centimeters per second. This means that

1 kilogram of matter will produce 25,000,000,000 kilowatt-hours of energy if it is entirely converted into energy. It is estimated that this amount of energy is nearly equal to 300,000,000 times the total amount of energy produced by the combustion of 1 kilogram of pure coal. This estimate, in turn, means that it is highly practical to obtain nuclear energy for power purposes by setting up a chain reaction in ordinary uranium (a mixture of U-234, U-235 and U-238) through the use of slow neutrons to control the release of atomic energy in the process of fission. What remains, then, is only this question: Can a power station, with all its design, construction, and equipment, guarantee 100% safety control of the release of such atomaic energy?

a. 第一句（According to Einstein's theory of equivalence, we know $E = mc^2$, where E is the energy in ergs, m is the mass in grams, and c is the velocity of light in centimeters per second.）有幾個子句？主要子句是"we know ..."，而"where"引導三個由"and"連接的子句（"E is ..., m is ..., and c is ..."），因此，這句是複句或合複句？

句首"According to ..."是起承轉折用語嗎？是補充說明或修飾用語嗎？或兼具該兩種功能？

b. 第二句（This means that 1 kilogram of matter will produce 25,000,000,000 kilowatt-hours of energy if it is entirely converted into energy.）有幾個子句？主要子句是"This means ..."，另外有由"that"引導的名詞子句，以及由"if"引導的（表示條件的）副詞子句。因此，這句是合句、複句、或合複句？

c .第三句（It is estimated that this amount of energy is nearly equal to 300,000,000 times the total amount of energy produced by the combustion of 1 kilogram of pure coal.）有幾個子句？主要子句是"it is estimated ..."，另外有由"that"引導的（算從屬的）一個名詞子句（"this amount of energy is ..."），所以它是複句，不是嗎？如果把"the total amount of energy produced by the combustion ..."改成"the total amount of energy *which is* produced by the combustion ..."，這句仍然是複句，不是嗎？其實，寫作時，能省則省，所以加"which is"大可不必，不是嗎？

d. 第四句（This estimate, in turn, means that it is highly practical to obtain nuclear energy for power purposes by setting up a chain reaction in ordinary uranium (a mixture of U-234, U-235 and U-238) through the use of slow neutrons to control the release of atomic energy in the process of fission.）有幾個子句？主要子句是"This estimate means ..."，另外有由"that"引導的一個名詞子句（"it is highly practical to ..."），不是嗎？
這句話較長，但長在有許多介系詞片語："for power purposes," "by setting up a chain reaction," "in ordinary uranium," "through

the use of slow neutrons," "of atomic energy"和"in the process of fission"等。這些片語可以改成子句而不感到囉唆不宜嗎？例如：改成"... it is highly practical to obtain nuclear energy *which is* for power purposes by setting up a chain reaction in ordinary uranium (a mixture of U-234, U-235 and U-238) through the use of slow neutrons to control *the atomic energy that is released* in the process of fission."好嗎？

e. 第五句（What remains, then, is only this question: Can a power station, with all its design, construction, and equipment, guarantee 100% safety control of the release of such atomaic energy?）的主要子句是"What remains, then, is only this question"，這子句的主詞（"What remains"）本身也是一個子句（由疑問代名詞"What"所引導），所以這已經是一個複句。至於冒號（colon）":"以後的那一句"Can a power station ... guarantee ...?"算是前面那句話的對等子句。所以，這整個第五句是合複句，不是嗎？

另外，"then"（「那麼」）是放在句中的起承轉折用語嗎？"with all its design, construction, and equipment"是插在句中來補充說明或修飾的用語嗎？如果把"guarantee 100% safety control of the release of such atomaic energy"改成"gurantee that when such atomic energy is released, its safety can be 100% controlled"，這樣好嗎？

第十一章

常用的詞語與句式

講解

　　講英語或寫英文，最常用的詞語當然是那幾個人稱代名詞和be動詞、那幾個包括冠詞在內的「確定詞」（determiners）[1]、以及那幾個介系詞和連接詞。在這一章裡，所謂常用的詞語，並非指出現頻率最高的那些字，而是指在寫英文學術論文時可能常常會用到的詞語。那些詞語也不是指各學門常用的術語或各行業的行話，而是指在寫學術論文時，在許多章節段落中，各學門各行業都常常會使用來引導、報告、講述、申論、和總結的共同詞語。其實，這種詞語也常跟隨某種文句的模式來出現，其中有些在本書前面各章中已經講過，在這裡我們想再綜合整理一下而加以勾要提示。

　　首先，在寫英文論文時，不論在哪一部分，常常都會用到一些原本是拉丁文的字詞來更精確或更正式地表達含義。像在報告實驗過程時，可能會說到*in vitro*（在實驗室內或在試管內）或*in vivo*（在活體上或在野生狀態）。有關使用那種拉丁字詞，我們的建議是：行文時，為了簡省或精確，可以用那些拉丁字詞，否則全用英文未嘗不好。例如："Many species of animals (e.g. dogs) are found to ..."比"Many species of animals (for example,

---

[1] 「確定詞」（determiners）指放在名詞前，用以確定是否特定或屬什麼特定種類的字眼，包括a(n), the; this, that, these, those; no, any, some, a little, a few, many, much, most, enough, another, both, several, all, each, every, a certain; my, your, his, her, its, their等。

dogs) are found to ..."寫起來更簡省。而"The corpse was to be kept intact *in situ*."比"The corpse was to be kept intact in its original (or appointed) place."更簡省又精確。可是，像有些經濟學者會用"*ceteris paribus*"來表示「別的條件一樣時」，這與英文"other things being equal"一樣的意思，只是用拉丁文似乎更正式而更有學問罷了。

原則上，寫論文使用外來語時（包括拉丁文在內），那些外來的字詞都要用斜體來標示。不過，有些外來字（像拉丁文的 e.g., etc., i.e.等）因為太常用了，所以現今也就都不再用斜體了。**附帶請注意**：使用拉丁字詞時，有時要配合使用逗點或句點，如在"Mary's property (i.e., her estate in Korea) is worth a million dollars."這句子裡，"i.e."自己有兩句點，其後還加一個逗點。寫論文時，至今仍然常用的拉丁字詞及其含義，請參考附錄二（常用拉丁字詞）。

除了拉丁字詞之外，寫論文時也常用一些英文縮寫，如：p.5 = page 5; pp. 42-57 = pages 42-57; l. 15 = line 15; ll. 3-8 = lines 3-8; ff. = and the following; no. 6 = number 6。還有各種度量衡單位的縮寫，如：h = hour(s), m.= meter(s), kg. = kilogram(s), lit.= liter(s)等等。至於在特殊學門裡，另外還會有一些特別專用的單位名稱及縮寫，如電磁學裡講到電磁場的單位mG = milligauss（毫高斯）便是。像這種在特別學門裡常用的縮寫，當然各學門要自己熟悉。

寫論文時，常常會說到類似「上一章／前一節」「下一段／後面幾章」這種指涉上下文的話。這種話的英文詞語與句式，可參考下面：

a. In the last chapter, we have pointed out that...（在上一章，我們已經指出……。）

b. In the foregoing section, x has already been mentioned.（在前一節，x已被提到。）

c. For y please see the passage above.（要知y請見上頭之段落。）

d. Reference can be made to a diagram like the above.（可參考如上之圖。）

e. Regarding the above-mentioned idea of z,（有關上頭提到的z的觀念，）

f. The aforesaid person（前面所說的人）

g. In the next part, we will touch on ...（在下一部分，我們將觸及……）

h. In the following pages, the topic will be elaborated on.（在接著幾頁裡，這題目將加以詳述。）

i. In the chapter that follows, our focus will be on ...（在跟著來的這一章，我們的焦點將在……上。）

j. The results are as follows:（結果如下：）

k. For y please see below.（要知y請看下面。）

l. ...（*v*. Table 5 below）. [……（見下面表5）。]

寫論文時，隨時也都會提到某（些）人講到某事（理），或某事（理）被某（些）人說過。這時可能用到如下的英文詞語與句式：

a. In his paper M says/ claims/ holds/ asserts/ suggests that A is B/ A influenced B. （在其論文中，M說／宣稱／堅持說／斷言說／提示說……）

b. In his paper M says,/ remarks,/ observes,/ adds,/ writes,"A is B."/ "A influenced B." （在其論文中，M說／評說／評說／補充說／寫說：「……。」

c. In 1995 M said/ thought/ was convinced/ declared/ proclaimed that A is B/ A influenced B. （在1995年，M說／認為／相信／宣告／宣布說……）

d. In 1995 M said:/ remarked: / observed:/ added:/ wrote:"A is B."/ "A influenced B." （在1995年，M說／評說／評說／補充說／寫說：「……。」

e. It is said/ suggested/ pointed out/ observed/ declared in a paper of M's that ... （在M的一篇文章中，說到／提示到／指出／評論到／宣告說……）

f. It was said/ believed/ held/ asserted/ written in1995 that ... （在1995年，人們說到／相信／堅稱／主張／寫到說……）

g. We are reminded of the report/ statement/ suggestion/ remark/ proclamation that ... （我們被提醒到……的報導／陳述／提示／評論／宣布。）

h. It leads us to the belief/ idea/ claim/ observation/ assertion that ...

（那把我們帶到……的信念／觀念／宣稱／評論／主張。）

　　本書第三章已經講過，論文的第一部分是講述研究背景（background）的「引言」（Introduction）。引言裡可能講到研究的「緣起」（cause）、「動機」（motivation）、「目的」（purpose）、「問題」（problem）、和「假說」（hypothesis）。研究的緣起、動機、或目的有百百種。面對某問題（problem）、疑問（question）或議題（issue），碰到某需要（necessity）、需求（demand）或要求（requirement/ request），或對某事物或人物感到興趣（interest）、困難（difficulty）、或引誘（temptation），都會想要去做個研究（make a study/ do a research），去探索（explore）、調查（investigate）、考慮（consider）、檢視（examine）、分析（analyze）、評估（assess）、或運算（calculate），或加以評價（evaluate）、說明（explain/ explicate）、闡釋（elucidate/ expound）、細察（scrutinize）、深究（probe into）、或者普查／量測（survey）。講述這部分的英文也是百百種。在此，我們依據第三章談到的要點，將常用的詞語與句式，撰寫出如下兩段，供你參考甚或模仿。

　　X is/ has been a popular topic/ a much-concerned topic/ an often-seen phenomenon/ a much-discussed issue in the world/ in the field of physics/ in modern society/ in women's circle. Over the past few decades/ During the last ten years/ Since 1980/ All this century/ This year/ In recent years/ Recently/ Lately/ So far/ Up to now/ Up to the present, there have been reports about .../ many scholars have noticed .../ enough attention has been paid to .../ great efforts have been made to .../ plenty of time has been used to .../ countless national resources have been employed to ... Last year/ In 2011/ Just last month/ During World War II/ At the time of the Great Fire, Peter Brown carried out a research into .../ made a thorough study of .../ was invited to investigate .../ was interested in .../ was led to explore .../ practically assessed .../ tried to elucidate .../ conducted an experiment on .../ made a survey of ... He found that .../ discovered that.../ He concluded his research by saying that .../ He proved the fact that .../ He showed us the truth that .../ He confirmed our idea that ... However, his finding/ discovery/ experiment/ investigation is still short of our expectation/ is still inadequate to account for .../ still leaves us enough room to question .../ still fails to ... For instance, he has not yet touched on the problem of whether or not A is contingent on B/ it is still unknown where and when such a phenomenon is most likely to occur/ he did not explain why A can result in B/ his focus was only on the herediary aspect of C. With his study and all other previous studies before us, we still do not understand why .../ it is still not known how .../ we still have no good reason for the fact that .../ still no sufficient evidence is provided for the finding that ... It is therefore our aim to learn from our further study the mechanism by which D ... / our intention to find the crucial role which E plays in F .../ our purpose to realize how G .../ our hope to know ... by scrutinizing .../ our goal to ... with this investigation.

It is generally understood/ It is well known/ It is an undisputed fact/ It is a confirmed truth that Y is .../ that Y has the effect of ... on Z/ that Y plays a significant part in .../ that Y is instrumental in obtaining Z. It is further understood/ It is also known/ There is also no denying/ It is a proved truth as well that V is .../ that V is closely related to W/ that V depends very much on W for .../ that V has a great deal to do with W. According to a recent report,/ several previous studies,/ Paul Greene,/ a distinguished biologist, A is much more important, compared with B. At this point, then, we may queston/ one may want to know/ it may be asked/ the researcher may be led to the problem as to/ you may doubt why C has .../ how C can ... Since this question is still unanswered,/ Since the problem is still unsolved,/ Since the issue is yet to be disputed,/ Since the topic still needs our concern, we think it will behoove us to do some further research on .../ it is time to make a full-scale investingation into .../ it will be a great contribution to conduct an experiment on .../ it is worth while to calculate ... and assess ... We hope/ It is hoped that this research/ investigation/ experiment/ assessment of ours can bring a satisfactory answer to the question mentioned above/ can give reliable evidence to the point doubted/ can provide a good result for the problem raised/ can reach an acceptable conclusion for the topic in question/ can shed some light on the issue discussed/ can throw light on the matter at issue.

　　在論文的引言部分，在做「文獻回顧」（literature review）時，也常會用到一些詞語與句式。在此，我們分別依據兩種寫作格式，也寫如下兩段供大家參考或模仿。

Regarding/ Concerning/ In regard to/ Related to the problem/ topic/ issue/ question of X, many papers have been published/ several reports have been issued/ a number of studies have been made/ enough research has been done. In 2002, John White was the first to *say/ state/ suggest/ prove/ find/ call our attention to* the fact and to notice the phenomenon/ to observe the truth that Y is ... Next,/ Then,/ After him,/ Later,/ Afterwards,/ Subsequently, George Pinker (2005) mentioned/ reported/ explained that ... In contrast, Jane Greene (2006) found/ believed/ argued/ held/ maintained/ assetted that ... And some scholars/ researchers echoed her ideas/ agreed with her, including Long (2006) and Johnson & Johnson (2007). Thenceforth,/ From then on, there have been findings of similar nature/ ideas in the same line (e.g. Black, 2007; Brown, 2008; and Newman & Smith, 2009). Most recently, however, Paul Gray (2010) gave new evidence that .../ had the resurgent idea that .../ reacted by saying that .../ brought us to the realization that ...

The topic/ problem/ issue / question of X has been much discussed/ has been variously considered/ has been interpreted by a variety of critics/ has been touched on by many different scholars. In his ..., for instance, Peter Brown says/ states/ claims/ suggests/ asserts that"..."(143). Similarly, in their ..., Samuel Kater and Ralph Walter hold/ maintain/ aver/ affirm that ... (98). These ideas, nevertheless, are modified/ balanced/ countered by the suggestion / the idea/ the opinion that ... (see, e.g., Tate 125-130 and Roller 306-309). And such ideas are referred to as/ are labeled/ are called/ are considered as/ are regarded as"..."(Tate 127). It is now/ nowadays agreed/

supposed/ believed/ stipulated, however, that ... (*v.* Fisher 2010, 86 *ff.*). Accordingly,/ Therefore,/ Finally, we have to admit that ... (Choi 71)/ it is confirmed that"..."(Cooper 49).

在論文的引言部分，如果將研究的目的／目標以及假說／問題寫成一段，或許會有類似下面的詞語與句式：

With a view to understanding .../ In order to realize ... we have set out to find the reasons for .../ we think it necessary to know the factors underlying .../ we count it all important to ... In the process of doing this research/ conducting this experiment/ making this study, it has been our supposition/ hypothesis/ rationale that ... This supposition/ hypothesis/ rationale is based on/ built on/ grounded on the fact that ... After this research/ experiment/ study, we hope we can answer these three questions: first, ...; second, ...; third, ...

在本書第四章中，我們說到：論文中要報告研究經過時，如果有徵求某些人做為研究對象，就要報告那些人的人數，以及那些人（跟該研究有關）的各項重要資料，如年齡、性別、習慣、病歷、教育背景等。同時，這些對象如果有加以分組，也要提到。這一部分的報告，可能會用到類似下面這一段裡的詞語與句式：

For this research, we have recruited 40 students as our study subjects./ Luckily, we have 40 volunteers participating in our program./ Sixty-three people responded to our recruitment and, after screening, 40 of them were considered fit for this study. Our recruitment/ screening was based on age, sex, habit, and educational background. The age of the participants was limited to 30 and under. We wanted an equal number of males and females. We paid special attention to whether they had the habit of smoking or not. And we selected only those who had college education. The forty students/ volunteers/ participants were divided into two groups at random/ by gender.

同樣的，論文中要報告研究經過時，如果有用到某種動物（如rats, mice, rabbits, frogs, zebrafish, etc.）來當「模式」（models），當然也要報告詳情。若還加以分組（如分成the control group and the experimental group），也要提及。這部分的英文或許類似下面一段：

Altogether 30 BALB/ c mice were used for this immunological experiment. They were divided into two groups, each group having 15 of them. The first group (Group A) served as the experimental group while the second group (Group B) served as the control group. We chose this strain of mice because they are known to have comparatively low mammary tumor incidence and because they have a long reproductive life-span. They were all acclimated in our lab before we began our experimental work.

報告研究經過時，有的會陳述「材料與方法」，有的會陳述「資料與分析」。從材料的準備或資料的收集，說到使用的工具、儀器、設備、空間等，或談到使用的問卷以及牽涉到的人員、機構等，再報告研究的手法或實驗的技術等。這一連串的話很長，各學門每篇論文的講述內容也大不相同，所以在此無法提供英文的共通詞語與句式供參考。反正，學習者應隨時留意自己學門內的論文，看人家的英文是怎麼寫的。

在本書第五章裡，我們說：在論文的「討論」部分，可能要提當初研究的目標或問題，也要說這次研究的結果或發現，然後要講這個結果或發現是否合乎研究前的期望或假定、是否合乎一般的理論或想法、是否應驗了某種機制、是否跟前人的研究結果一致、是否受到了某種（材料、方法、或其他的限制）、是否有特色或缺點、是否有應用的價值、是否有特殊的意義、是否有進一步研究的必要等等。而在檢討、比較、論說之後，就要下結論。在此，我們也提供一些常用的英文詞語與句式供參考：

a. As stated above,/ As stated in the first introductory chapter, this study was to .../ this paper is to ...

b. Now, our result shows that .../ our finding is: .../ we have discovered that .../ it is obvious that .../ we are led to find that ...

c. This result is in complete accord with our expectation/ anticipation/ presupposition/ hypothesis.

d. This finding fits in nicely with the theory we have tentatively produced for the problem facing us.

e. These results/ findings testify that .../ testify to the importance of .../ just go to show that .../ can prove that .../ can serve as evidence of .../ undoubtedly demonstrate that ...

f. Unfortunately, this result/ finding fails to meet with general approval/ falls short of our expectation/ cannot dovetail with the theory propounded/ is in direct contradiction to the conclusion of many previous studies/ is unable to explain the underlying mechanism/ is incongruous with the presupposition.

g. Owing to the limitation of time/ space/ financial support/ equipment/ method/ raw material/ supplementary material/ our budget, we were unable to .../ we have been unable to .../ we had to .../ we could not but ...

h. Since our ... was limited,/ Since we were short of ...,/ As there was no guarantee that ...,/ Because of the insufficiency of samples,/ For the sake of safety, we could only ...

i. We are glad to say that this study has had a significant result/ this research has resulted in a valuable finding/ this experiment proves to be fruitful as far as its result is concerned/ this discussion has clarified the idea of .../ this paper has verified the truth that .../ this finding can bear testimony to the fact that ...

j. However, it is sad to say that this study still has some shortcomings/ drawbacks: first/ in the first place, ...; second/ in the second place, ...; third/ in the third place, ...; and finally, ...

k. The greatest value of this study lies in .../ This study is most significant in that .../ The use of this study cannot be overestimated since it has solved the problem of .../ What counts is the fact that this finding can be applied to many other cases.

l. We suggest/ It may be suggested that some further research (should) be done in respect to .../ in regard to ...

m. We may add / It may be added that it is feasible/ profitable/ worth while/ advantageous to make an advanced and complete study of ...

n. With these results/ findings, we may conclude that .../ At this point we have arrived at/ come to/ reached this conclusion: ...

o. To sum up,/ In conclusion, A is ...

在本書第六章裡談到各種「副文」，其中有關「注釋」（Notes）的部分，前面只談到格式，還沒提到英文的詞語與句式。其實，注釋的內容也是百百種，因而用到的英文詞語與句式也是百百種，無法全部加以簡化提要。不過，許多注釋都或許會寫出類似這樣的英文：

a. Hereinafter the idea/ term/ device/ assay refers to ...（此後在本文中，該觀念／詞語／伎倆／測試指（涉）……）

b. In M's terminology/ system of thinking, A is referred to as ...（在M的術語中／思想體系中，A被指（涉）為……）

c. For more detail/ background information/ data/ related discussion, see M's ...（想要更多細節／背景訊息／資料／相關討論，見M的……著作。）

d. Regarding this topic, further information/ reference/ discussion/ investigation is available in M's ...（關於這題目，進一步的訊息／談論／討論／調查可在M的……著作中找得到。）

e. Related to this idea of A is the idea of B proposed/ suggested/ pointed out by M in his ...（與A這觀念有關的是M在其……著作中所提出的／提示的／指出的B的觀念。）

f. With this a significant/ valuable/ fruitful/ good comparison can be made of A in regard to its effect.（跟這個，可能做一個有意義的／有價值的／有收穫的／很好的比較，比較A的效用方面。）

g. *Interpretation/ Discussion* like this is confined to the *context/ circumstances/ social condition/ natural environment* of ...（像這樣的詮釋／討論僅限於……的上下文／情況／社會條件／自然環境。）

h. No related proof [evidence] has been found/ No related idea [theory] has been produced as yet *concerning/ regarding* this.

（關於這個，至今尚無 發現相關的證據[證明]／產生相關的理念[理論]。）

　　本章講到的常用的詞語與句式，在英文學術論文中確實常常會看到，也確實值得學習使用。可是，寫論文千變萬化，在各行各業之中，當然還有許多其他常用的英文詞語與句式在這裡沒有提到，而限於篇幅也無法提到。那就留給英文學術論文寫作者自我研究學習了。

作業

1. 請找出一期屬於你們學門的（紙本的或電子的）英文學術期刊來，選出其中至少三篇論文，據此做下面幾件事：

   a. 比較那幾篇論文的Introduction部分，看看有哪些詞語與句式是比較常出現的。

   b. 比較那幾篇論文的中間部分（包括有關material, method, data, discussion等），看看有哪些詞語與句式是比較常出現的。

   c. 比較那幾篇論文的Conclusion部分，看看有哪些詞語與句式是比較常出現的。

   d. 比較那幾篇論文的副文部分（包括摘要、注釋、參考書目／資料、謝詞、資助訊息、利益衝突宣告、前言等），看看有哪些詞語與句式是比較常出現的。

2. 請找出至少三篇屬於你們學門的（紙本的或電子的）英文學位（碩士或博士）論文來看，據此做下面幾件事：

   a. 比較那幾篇論文的Introduction部分，看看有哪些詞語與句式是比較常出現的。

b. 比較那幾篇論文的中間部分（包括有關material, method, data, discussion等），看看有哪些詞語與句式是比較常出現的。

c. 比較那幾篇論文的Conclusion部分，看看有哪些詞語與句式是比較常出現的。

d. 比較那幾篇論文的副文部分（包括摘要、注釋、參考書目／資料、謝詞、資助訊息、利益衝突宣告、前言等），看看有哪些詞語與句式是比較常出現的。

3. 下面各句中，請選出正確的詞語或句式：

a. X (is defined as/ is confined as) ...（X定義為……）

b. In the (last/ latest) few years, (in particular/ in particularity), ...（特別是在最近幾年，……）

c. As (the x case demonstrating/ demonstrated by the x case), (but/ however), ...（可是，誠如x案例所示，……）

d. The article is to discuss two problems (born in/ bearing on) the issue of y, which involves/ revolves) many organizations.（本文要討論與y議題有關之兩問題，那牽涉到許多組織。）

e. The article (structures/ is structured) as (following/ follows). （本文結構如下。）

f. (To begin/ Firstly), it clarifies ... (The next/ Secondly), it discusses ... (The third/ Thirdly), it examines ... (At last/ Finally), it analyzes ...

g. An (express/ expressive) reference to x is not (rare/ seldom) in (such/ those) countries as ... （在諸如⋯⋯那些國家裡，明白指涉x並不少見。）

h. (Furthermore/ Over more), it is clear (from/ with) the report that A and B have agreed to have (recourse/ intercourse) to ... （進一步說，那報導明白表示A和B已經同意訴之於⋯⋯）

i. Although this does not (relate/ concern) x in a case (of such/ as such), (but/ yet) we must ... （雖然這無關在如此場合中的x，可是我們必須⋯⋯）

j. (After all/ All in all), it seems (possibly/ likely) that a bad result will (ensue/ entail) if ... （畢竟，如果⋯⋯，似乎有可能壞的結果會產生。）

4. 下面各句中，也請選出正確的詞語或句式：

a. The (rational/ rationale) for linking A with B is (which/ that) x is identical to y (as long as/ only if) ... （把A連結B的理論基礎是：只要……，x就等同y。）

b. (Typically/ Standardly), A produces the following outputs: a, b, c, and d, to (say/ speak) nothing of e. （典型地，A產生下列產物：a, b, c,和d,更不用說e。）

c. Figure 2 (presents/ represents) a pattern of ..., the numbers on the figure (representing / presenting) ..., the triangles (indicating/ indicate) ..., and the circles (showing/ shown) ... （圖2呈現……的樣式，圖上的數字代表……，三角形表示……，而圓圈顯示……）

d. Two additional curves (outline/ underline) the wide (divergence/ distinction) of opinion on this issue, with the red curve and the blue curve standing for a and b (respectively/ respectfully). （兩條附加的曲線概示此議題上意見很分歧，紅色的曲線和藍色的曲線分別代表a和b。）

e. As (can/ it can) be seen in Table 4, A depends on B (for/ by) x, C corresponds roughly, not closely, (on/ to) D, and E (various/

varies) with F.（如表4可見，就x而言A有賴B，C是大約對應 而非極為對應D，而E隨F而變化。）

f. According to our (observance/ observation), A fully (reflected on/ reflected) the real situation of ..., but B (reacted to/ reacted) C (considerably/ considerable) far from our expectation.（按照 我們的觀察，A完全反映⋯⋯的真實情況，可是B對C的反應 跟我們的期待有相當距離。）

g. It was found that x did not (react/ reflect) to y in a (time-and dose-dependent/ times-and doses-dependent) manner while its effect on z was (dependent/ independent) on both time and dosage.（發現到的是：x對y的反應並非取決於時間與劑量， 而它對z的效用是取決於時間與劑量。）

h. Two hundred (of our questionnaires/ copies of our questionnaire) were distributed and 175 of them [about 90%] were filled (out/ up) and came back to us. Based on the (accepted/ received) copies, our analysis showed that ...（我們發出兩百份問卷，其中有175份[約90%] 填完後回到我們。根據回收的問卷，我們的分析顯示⋯⋯）

i. It is (common sense/ a common sense) that A (responds to/ responds) B by stopping ... and C responds to D (by/ with) laughter. But the (response/ respond) of E to F was simply beyond our imagination. （依常識，A藉停止……來回應B，而C以笑聲來回應D。但E對F的回應簡直就是我們想像之外。）

j. This paper has (touched/ attached) upon... and (revealed/ disclose) that ... The conclusion (reached/ arrived) herein is: ...（這篇論文談到了……，而揭露了……的事實。在這裡達到的結論是：……）

5. 下面各句中，請把畫底線的（有錯誤的）詞語改正過來：

a.Aknowledgement

At first, we would like to thank ... Our thank is also due to ... for ... We greatly indebted to ... because ... We were grateful, too, to ..., who ... Finally, we want to express our sincere gratitude for M. Wang, without whom encouragement this study work could not have been finished.

b. Note

(1)Here in after, x refers to ...

(2)As regard y, see ...

(3)For new messages concerned this, see ...

c. This research <u>had funded</u> by ...

d. The authors <u>declared on</u> no potential conflicts <u>in interest</u> with respect to the research, <u>author,</u> and/ or publication of this article.

第十二章

常犯的英文錯誤

講解

　　以中文為母語而以英文為外語的人，如果沒有把英文學好，在說、寫英文時難免常常會犯錯。在一般場合說英文時，因為沒有多少思考的時間，說錯話更是難免。可是，在寫英文時，即使有充分時間可以準備與修改，卻仍然會因母語的影響而犯許多種錯誤。一般來說，大家常犯的英文錯誤不外乎「用字不當」（improper diction）和「文法不對」（incorrect grammar）兩種。在寫英文學術論文時，英文太差的人因為字彙（vocabulary）有限，當然談不上diction（用字）、phraseology（用詞）、或wording（用語）；也因為練習不夠，往往連最基本的文法都無法遵守。可是，就連英文還算不錯的人，有時一不小心，便也會有用字與文法的問題。底下是華人寫英文學術論文時常犯的一些錯誤，請注意參考。

　　在用字方面，我們發現許多人常分不清"doubt"和"suspect"。通常"doubt"是否定的「懷疑」（認為不是或沒有），"suspect"則是正面的「懷疑」（認為是或有）。例如："I doubt that he is an artist/ he has a mistress"（我懷疑[不認為]他是藝術家／他有情人）。如果說成"I suspect that he is an artist/ he has a mistress"，便是「我懷疑[認為]他是藝術家／他有情人」。

　　有些人分不清rational（理性的）和rationale（理論基礎），還以為既然rational是「理性的」，ration就是「理性」。其實，

ration是「口糧、配給」，rationality才是「理性」。也有些人分不清avenge（為某人報仇）和revenge（為自己報仇），如："Caesar, I will avenge you"（凱撒，我要為你報仇），"I will revenge myself on you"（我要為自己向你報仇）。或許你也不知beginner是「初學者、生手」，它不等於initiator（起頭的人、先驅），也不等於starter（起跑發令員、比賽先發者、前菜、暖身活動、起動器）。

也有許多人混淆"lie, lay, lain"（躺）、"lied, lied, lied"（說謊）、和"lay, laid, laid"（放置）的三態變化。**請注意**，要說"He lay asleep in bed"（他躺睡在床裡），而非"He lied/ laid asleep in bed"。要說"He was laid on a stretcher"（他被放在擔架上）而非"He was lay/ lied on a stetcher"。要說"He lied to everybody"（他對每個人說謊）而非"He lay/ laid to everybody"。

有時，一說到「贏」，有些人就只想到 win, won, won。其實，「贏他們」是"defeat them"或"beat them"，不是"win them"（贏得他們）。「贏得比賽」才是"win the game"，而不是"beat/ defeat the game"。也有很多人一講到「讓」就想到"let"，所以會寫出"She let me very happy"這種錯誤的句子（應改為"She made me very happy"）。中文「花費」譯成英文不一定是"spend"。"I spent two hours cooking it"沒錯，"I spent 200 dollars on it"也沒錯。但是，"It took two hours to finish"和"It cost me 200 dollars"才對。這裡不能用spent代替took或cost。

許多人分不清alter和change，也分不清mend和repair。中文「修改衣服」譯成英文是"alter a garment"，「換穿衣服」是

"change clothes"，「修補衣服」是"mend clothes/ a garment"，修補橋樑則是"repair a bridge"。這些英文動詞不可混用。另外，要知道這些不同的「綁」：「綁鞋子」是"tie the shoes"，「綁標籤」是"attach tags"，「綁兩手」是"bind one's hands"，「綁馬到樹幹」是"hitch the horse to a trunk"。也要知道這些不同的「收集」：「採花」是"gather flowers"，「採水果」是"pick fruit"，「收垃圾」是"collect garbage/ rubbish"。而收稅、集郵也用"collect"。

有許多人把集合名詞的集體含義誤成個別含義，而把"He needs to enlarge his English vocabulary"說成"He needs to increase his English vocabularies"；把"His speech attracted a large audience"說成"His speech attracted many audiences"；把"The English alphabet has 26 letters"說成"English has 26 alphabets"；把"The Big Dipper is a constellation of Ursa Major"（北斗七星是大熊座的一個星群）說成"The Big Dipper is seven constellations of Ursa Major"；把"John and his company"（約翰及其伙伴）說成"John and his companies"；把"raise cattle and poultry"說成"raise cattles and poultries"；把"buy furniture or merchandise"說成'buy furnitures or merchandises'；把"They are the infantry/ gentry/ nobility/ peasantry"說成"They are the infantries/ gentries/ nobilities/ peasantries"等。

也有很多人把本來就應有-s的字，去掉-s，像gallows（絞架）變gallow；victuals（食物）變victual；debris（瓦礫堆）變debri。更多人不知或忘了有許多名詞在特定含義之下通常用複數形。如：depths（深處）、heights（高處）、precincts（境域）、premises（房地）、outskirts（郊外）、suburbs（郊區）、whereabouts（下落、所在）；belongings（所有物）、chippings（木、石碎片）、earnings（賺來之所得）、proceedings（會議論文）、savings（儲蓄）；ashes（灰燼）、dregs（渣滓）、embers（餘燼）、leftovers（剩菜剩飯）、relics（遺骸、廢墟）、remains（遺物、遺體）；arrears（欠款）、damages（賠償金）、gains（利潤）、proceeds（所得）、sales（銷售量／額）；advices（通知）、arms（武器）、colors（軍旗）、contents（目錄）、effects（財物）、goods（貨物）、honors（禮儀）、manners（禮節）、pains（努力）、waters（水流、水域）等等。

其實，英文有很多字都有同義字（synonym）和反義字（antonym）。字與字之間在含義和用法上的差異，往往要看thesaurus（類語詞典）才會清楚。有時，好的字典也會提供這方面的訊息。像外交要有「彈性」用"flexibility"，絲襪或市場有（伸縮）「彈性」用"elasticity"，而肌膚或棉被有（受壓）「彈性」則用"resilience"。像"delay"指「延遲」（be late），"adjourn"則是「休停或延期」（postpone）。

知道嗎？血管是vessel，動脈是artery，靜脈是vein。硬的（金屬、塑膠）水管是pipe，軟的（橡膠）水管是hose，排氣的導管是duct，吸管是straw/ tube，試管或喂食用的管子是tube。當管子、水道或機器油路在裡頭「堵塞」時，不是jammed，也不只是blocked或stopped，而是clogged。知道嗎？水結凍是freeze，豆汁、牛奶凝結成糊是curdle，血凝乾成塊是clot，蛋煮熟而凝固是coagulate。

或許你不知道：事情分possible或impossible。當possible 之後，有的very probable，有的則是improbable（或然率不高）。或許你也不知道：事情不管好壞，有的likely to happern，有的unlikely to happen，但不好的事才用liable to happen（如The glass is liable to break）。知道嗎？好事或壞事都會ensue或follow，而result in ...或lead to ...的結果，也可以是好事或壞事。但entail something的something，通常只有壞事。同樣的，aftermath是不好的後果，result/ outcome則是可好可壞。

許多用詞錯誤都是直接翻譯引起的。像「故事講到……」譯成"The story talks about ..."。其實，人才會talk，故事不會talk，你可以說"The story is about ..."，但不宜說"The story talks about ..."。不過，怪得很，你卻可以說"The paper discusses/ analyzes ..."（本論文討論／分析……），雖然那也是人（而非論文）在討論／分析。我們常看到"learn knowledge"（學習知識）這種翻譯。其實，learn a lesson, a skill, or a secret比較正確，what has been learned（所學的東西）會變成knowledge，而人會gain/ obtain（獲得）或increase/ augment（增加）knowledge，不是learn knowledge。

有人用"protect children's safety"來翻「保護孩子的安全」。這是贅語，protect children就是protect them for their safety。你可以說"protect children from danger"或"protect the old people against insecurity"，但不要說"protect children's safety"或"protect the old people's security"。也有人用"play the sports facilities"來翻「玩那些運動設施」。其實，人是用運動設施來玩（遊戲），不是直接玩（弄）運動設施。所以要說"play with the sports facilities"。另外，也經常有人說"discuss/ mention about ..."（討論／提到有關……）。其實，discuss/ mention是及物動詞，說"discuss/ mention the matter"就好，不要說"discuss/ mention about the matter"。

講到這裡，已經牽涉到文法了。本書第七章說了：英文名詞分為C或U，但許多人就是分不清哪些名詞是可數，哪些名詞是不可數。因此，會把"You have got some mail/ a piece of mail/ a letter/ a parcel/ a package"說成錯誤的"You have got a mail"。會把"I eat rice and beans"說成"I eat rice and bean"或"I eat rices and beans"。另外，大家也常忘了單數普通名詞前面要加a/ an。因此，會把"She wore a black skirt"說成"She wore black skirt"。會把"He is in a yellow T-shirt"說成"He is in yellow T-shirt"。

說到衣物，你知道嗎？衣物統稱為"clothing"或"clothes"或"garment"或"apparel"，或"dress"。這些字中"clothing/ apparel"是U，要說a piece of clothing, women's apparel。而"clothes"是複數，怪的是：前面可加many，但不可加two, three, four ...。可以說"many clothes"，不能說"two/ three clothes"，只能說"two/ three suits of clothes"。至於"garment"，它是C，可以說"some waterproof outer garments"，也可以說"a winter garment"。最後，"dress"很特別，它指女人或小孩穿的「洋裝」時是C，指特殊的

「禮服」或尋常穿的「服裝」時，卻是U。衣服又分outerwear（外衣）和underwear（內衣），而兩字都是U。在outwear中，blouse, cape, cloak, coat, frock, gown或jacket都是C。在underwear中，sweater, vest, waistcoat也都是C。但各種褲子，包括breeches, drawers, knickers, panties, pants, shorts, slacks, trousers等，都是複數。中文說「一條」短褲、內褲、長褲時，英文說"a pair of"shorts/ knickers (panties)/ trousers (pants)。

不少人懶得重複冠詞，把"An alligator and an ant went to see the walrus and the whale"說成"An alligator and ant went to see the walrus and whale"。其實，只有兩者合成一體時才可省去第二個冠詞，如"a rod and line"（一組釣竿釣線）、"a cup and saucer"（一組杯碟）、"the bread and butter"（那奶油麵包）、"the editor and publisher"（那編者兼發行人）。

許多人不習慣用虛字it來代替不定詞片語，所以把"I find it safe to go out at night"講成"I find safe to go out at night"。其實，在許多類似的句型中，也要記得用it來代替動名詞片語、that- 子句、和wh-子句。例如：

a. We think *it* wrong *for you to lie to your parents.*

b. They considered *it* no good *trying to please her.*

c. She counted *it* an honor *that he proposed to her.*

d. I put *it* to you *whether or not the thief should be sent away.*

很多人常在文句中用it, they, this, that,等代名詞，但卻看不出那代名詞指什麼，那就是"unclear reference"（指涉不明）的錯誤。例如：在"The need to supply the city with enough clean water and air is a big problem the government is now facing. The increasing population here has *it* and will complain to *them* about *it*."這兩句中，"it"和"them"指什麼呢？說話者可能想說"The increasing population here has the problem of clean water and air supply and will complain to the government about the problem"，但突然跑出的"it"只能指涉前一句中的"the need to supply ..."，而"them"無法直接等同"the government"。

本書第八章說過，英文的動詞常造成句型。像consider一字，可以有"He considered"，"He considered it/ the issue"，"He considered buying a used car"，"He considered her (to be) lucky"，"He considered her (to be) a respectable woman"，"He considered her as a female, not as an old person"，"He considered that she might react differently"，"He considered whether to stay or not"，"He considered how she could manage to escape"，"He considered it impossible to seduce her"，"He considered it necessary that she should be moved away"等等的句型。其中，許多人常分不清"consider ... (to be) ..."和"consider ... as ..."的不同。要知道："consider him (to be) a spy"是「認為他是間諜」，而"consider him as a spy"則是「以間諜來看待他／考量他」。

並非每個動詞都像consider這個字一樣可以用在許多句型中。我們最常看到的句型錯誤是suggest (somebody) to do something，例如："I suggest to leave earlier"和"They suggested us to invest more money in the stocks"都是錯誤的句法。應該改為

"I suggest leaving earlier"和"They suggested that we (should) invest more money in the stocks"或"They suggested our investing more money in the stocks"才對。

另一個常看到的句型錯誤是：把對的"We provide them with instant information"或"We provide instant information for them"寫成錯的"We provide them instant information"。同樣的，把對的"The Mayor presented the medals to the winners"或"The Mayor presented the winners with the medals"寫成錯的"The Mayor presented the winners the medals"。

只有所謂「與格動詞」（dative verbs）才可以同時加間接受詞和直接受詞，如gave him a book, brought the children many gifts, bought me an i-phone, sent everyone a precious present 等都對。但 provide和present不是「與格動詞」，不適用這種句型。我們通常也說"I can suggest a good topic for you"，而不說"I can suggest you a good topic"。倒是很多人不知道可以說類似"He denied her nothing," "She envied him his wisdom," "I refused him only the right to cheat"這樣的句子。另外，有人把"He promised me five months"（他答應給我五個月）誤以為"It is five months since he promised me"（他答應我到現在已經五個月）。

講到這裡一定要提「無持續的動詞」（verbs with no duration），像promise（答應）是瞬間的事，不可能一個答應的動作持續幾天幾月，所以不能說"He has promised five months"，而要說"It is/ It has been five months since he promised"。同理，

畢業或死掉也是一下子的事，因此不能說"I have graduated ten years"或"The dog has died three hours"，而要說"It is/ It has been ten years/ three hours since I graduated/ the dog died"。這一類的動詞不少，像capture a thief, catch cold, contract a disease, discover a secret, fall in love, kill an animal, meet a friend, realize a problem, take medicine等都是「無持續的動作」，不能用完成式加for two hours, weeks, months, years等。倒是可以說"I have had a cold for three days"/ "We have held them captive for a week"/ "He has been in love with her for four years"/ "The animal has been dead for eight hours"。這樣的話，因為都是指持續的狀態，不是一時的動作，所以可以加"for多久"的詞語。

　　另一個常犯的句型錯誤是：把*v. i.*當*v. t.*而直接加受詞，忘了要有介系詞。例如：把"You must *respond/ react to* it quickly"寫成"You must respond/ react it quickly"。把"I will *reply to* your letter soon"寫成"I will reply your letter soon"。把"They *rebelled/ revolted against* the government"寫成"They rebelled/ revolted the government"。把"A *depends/ relies on* B"寫成"A depends/ relies B"。把"She *attends on* her master"寫成"She attends her master"。其他像"*intervene/ meddle in* something"或"*interfere/ meddle/ tamper with* something"也都不能沒有in或with。

　　附帶**請注意**：我們說"reach the destination"，但卻說"*arrive at/ get to* the destination"。我們說"*wait for* a person"，卻說"await a person"。也**請注意**："A reflects B"是「A反映B」，"A *reflects on/*

upon B"則是「A反省B」。"elaborate a plan"是「精心做計劃」，"*elaborate on/ upon* a plan"則是「詳細說明計劃」。"believe him"是「相信他（的話）」，"*believe in* him"則是「相信他（的人格、才能）」。像這種有無介系詞的對錯或差別，一定要隨時留意。

反過來，也有不少人把*v. t.*當*v. i.*而多加了介系詞。像把" to *access* something"或"to *have access to* something"說成" to access to something"，把"*approaching* the platform"說成"approaching to the platform"，把"*ascend* the throne"說成"ascend on the throne"，把"*attained* his goal"說成"attained to his goal"，把"*resume* his work"說成"resume to his work"，把"*recall* his past"說成"recall to his past"，把"*pervade* the air"說成"pervade in the air"，把"*transgress* the bounds"說成"transgress over the bounds"等。附帶說：attend = participate in, comprise = consist of, intimate = hint at, oppose = object to, ridicule = laugh at。

有些動詞該用主動或被動，在某些場合不好斷定，因此容易產生錯誤。像人賣書（He sells books），書被賣（The book is sold），主動被動很清楚。但「這本書賣得好」的英文是"The book sells well"，不是"The book is sold well"。感覺起來，那本書因為本身的特色所以好像自己會主動的賣。像下面的例子也是一樣，用主動都是因為本身性質的關係。

    a. The lesion meansures 2cm x 3cm in size. （傷處量起來2 x 3公分大小）

    b. The bull's eye counts five. （靶心算起來5）

    c. The spectators number more than 500. （觀眾數起來超過500）

d. The food tastes delicious.（那食物嚐起來味道好）

e. The door does not open easily.（那門開起來不容易）

f. The ball throws straight.（這球丟起來很直）

從這些例子，加上" She looks beautiful"（她看起來美），"It sounds good/ smells bad/ feels soft"（那聽起來好／聞起來差／摸起來軟）這種句子，可見講到「……起來如何如何」時，就是用主動的時機了。

英文有一類動詞叫「反身動詞」（reflexive verbs）。這一類動詞常用 -self/ -selves的字來當受詞。許多人不知道這緣故，便犯錯了。例如，你不能說"I have decided to devote to education"而要說"I have decided to devote myself to education"（我已決定奉獻於教育）。其他例子如：

a. She prides herself on her good looks.（她傲於美貌）

b. He absented himself from all meetings.（他缺席於所有會議）

c. I will avail myself of this opportunity.（我會利用這機會）

d. They always conduct themselves nobly.（他們總是行為高尚）

e. We are really enjoying ourselves here.（我們在此確實享樂）

f. Please exert yourself to educate the young.（請你致力教育年輕人）

注意："devote oneself to something"也可改成"be devoted to something"，但上面六個例子中的其他反身動詞不能改成被動。倒是seat oneself = be seated, engage oneself = be engaged, expose oneself = be exposed。

有不少人常常在該用完成式時只用簡單式，尤其在不定詞或動名詞的狀況下。例如：要講「她被說曾是美女」，英文應該是"She is said to have been a beauty"，不是"She is said to be a beauty"。"She is said to be a beauty"是「她被說（目前）是個美女」。同理，請瞭解下面例子中為何用完成式：

a. He is found *to have been* dead for two weeks.

b. They were supposed *to have arrived* before you came.

c. You are expected *to have submitted* your papers by Friday.

d. She seems *to have known* the secret already.

e. The boys appeared *to have been punished* in school.

f. I am sorry *to have kept* you waiting for so long.

g. We regret *having told* them the secret.

h. I cannot remember *having stolen* anything from you.

i. We apologize for *having insulted* you on that occasion.

反正如果是過去「曾經」或「已經」做的事或存在的事實，在不定詞或動名詞中也要記得用完成式。

英文句子中，如果把放在句首的從屬子句的主詞省去，或把它改成沒有主詞的分詞構造句、介系詞片詞、或不定詞片語，那麼其主詞就被視為等同後面主要子句的主詞。例如：在"Finding a rat, she screamed"這句中，"finding a rat"（看到老鼠）的也就是"screamed"（尖叫）的"she"（她）。現在問題來了：許多人因為中文的習慣會說出這種錯誤的英文："Walking on the bridge, my hat was blown off"（走在橋上時，我的帽子被吹掉）。它錯在：

文法上，"my hat"被視為既是"was blown off"也是"walking on the bridge"的主詞，但帽子只會被吹，不會走在橋上。華人常會犯這種錯誤。其他例子如下：

a. Having finished my work, my boss let me go home.（錯）

After I had finished my work, my boss let me go home.（對）

Having finished my work, I was allowed to go home.（對）

b. Obsessed with fame, his health was neglected.（錯）

As he was obsessed with fame, his health was neglected.（對）

Obsessed with fame, he neglected his health.（對）

c. When tired, rest is needed.（錯）

When（you are）tired, you need rest.（對）

d. In shopping with Jane, my cell phone was lost.（錯）

In shopping with Jane, I lost my cell phone.（對）

e. In returning home, a car knocked him down.（錯）

In returning home, he was knocked down by a car.（對）

f. Upon arrival, they were already waiting for me at the airport.（錯）

Upon arrival, I found them already waiting for me at the airport.（對）

g. To do my duty, the task was finished in time.（錯）

To do my duty, I finished the task in time.（對）

The task was finished in time to do my duty.（對）

有非常多人，因為直接翻譯中文的關係，常錯誤的用and來代替with或from。例如：把「結合A和B」翻成"combine A and B"，而把「區別A和B」翻成"distinguish A and B"。其實，應該是"combine A with B"和"distinguish A from B"才對。其他像"blend/ mingle/ balance/ compare/ connect A with B"和"tell/ know/ separate/ differentiate/ discriminate A from B"也會有用and取代with/ from 的相同錯誤。其實，"connect/ link/ glue A to B"的to也會被誤換成and。但注意：是可以說"A and B are combined"和"distinguish between A and B"。

也有非常多人忘了要重複不同的介系詞。例如：把"We were informed of, and interested in, the news"寫成"We were informed and interested in the news"。其他類似的錯誤如下：

a. They hope *for* and rely on his integrity.（忘了for）

b. I will neither agree *to* nor vote against the proposal.（忘了to）

c. You are to save him *from*, not get him into, the danger.（忘了from）

d. We should believe *in*, and abide by, the law.（忘了in）

e. They took pity *on*, and gave alms to, the poor.（忘了on）

f. He gazed *at*, and yelled to, the girl.（忘了at）

g. He was at first deprived *of*, and then provided with, their daily necessities.（忘了of）

某些動詞固定的接某些介系詞，當動詞在句中變成名詞時，通常會跟隨同樣的介系詞。可是，有許多人常錯誤的用of來取代原來該用的其他介系詞。例如："I am interested in music. He knows my interest *in* music." 不能改成"I am interested in music. He knows my interest *of* music." 其他類似的錯誤如下：

    a. We need their protection of intrusion.（錯）

       We need their protection from/ against intrusion（對）

    b. We must consider your intrusion of others' privacy.（錯）

       We must consider your intrusion on/ upon others' privacy.（對）

    c. I have just received their congratulations of my success.（錯）

       I have just received their congratulations on my success.（對）

    d. I know my boss's dissatisfaction of my work.（錯）

       I know my boss's dissatisfaction with my work.（對）

    e. We are informed of their safe arrival of the destination.（錯）

       We are informed of their safe arrival at the destination.（對）

    f. You need to make reference of the book.（錯）

       You need to make reference to the book.（對）

    g. They opposed your inquiry of the cause of his death.（錯）

       They opposed your inquiry into the cause of his death.（對）

    h. Such preparation of reaction needs some time.（錯）

       Such preparation for reaction needs some time.（對）

    i. I do not care about his annoyance of my conduct.（錯）

       I do not care about his annoyance at my conduct.（對）

但**請注意**也有例外：雖然我們說"He was charged with murder"，卻說"He was arrested on a charge of murder"，不說"He was arrested on a charge with murder"。

另一個許多人常犯的錯誤是：按中文習慣在否定句中用any/ all/ both ... not 的句法。例如：把「任何人不得知道這祕密」說成"Anybody must not know the secret"。其實，這句話應該改成"Nobody must know the secret"才對。同樣的，「我們都沒被邀請」也要說成"None of us are/ is invited"，不能說成"All of us are not invited"。而「他們兩人都沒死」是"Neither of them died"，不是"Both of them did not die"。其他例子如下：

a. Anything should not be done for that purpose.（錯）

　　Nothing should be done for that purpose.（對）

b. Any dog is not allowed to enter the gate.（錯）

　　No dog is allowed to enter the gate.（對）

c. Any man did not reach the top before.（錯）

　　No man reached the top before.（對）

d. Any ideas have not been thought out yet.（錯）

　　No ideas have been thought out yet.（對）

e. All projects are not accepted.（錯）

　　No projects/ None of the projects are accepted.（對）

f. All of his time is not spent on the work.（錯）

　　None of his time is spent on the work.（對）

g. Both thieves were not caught.（錯）

　　Neither thief was caught.（對）

h. Both you and I are not successful.（錯）

　　Neither you nor I am successful.（對）

按中文習慣也有許多人說類似"No matter you love her or not, you should not blame her"這樣的話。其實，那句話應該改成"No matter whether you love her or not, you should not blame her"或至少改成"Whether you love her or not, you should not blame her"才對。其他類似的例句如下：

a. No matter you are right or wrong, you must obey the rules. （錯）

(No matter) whether you are right or wrong, you must obey the rules. （對）

b. No matter you are who, you must apologize. （錯）

No matter who you are, you must apologize. （對）

c. No matter you may have what reason, you must not beat her. （錯）

No matter what reason you may have, you must not beat her. （對）

d. No matter you have tried how hard, they will not appreciate it. （錯）

No matter how hard you have tried, they will not appreciate it. （對）

e. No matte you did it for what reason, I would support you. （錯）

No matter *why/ for what reason* you did it, I would support you. （對）

英文學術論文寫作：講解與作業

按中文習慣，更多人會說："The weather is different in Taipei and Kaohsiung"。其實，那是錯誤的英文，除非你前面先說了東京的天氣如何如何，而接著說台北和高雄的天氣（跟東京）不一樣。如果你只是說台北的天氣和高雄的天氣不一樣，那就應該改成"The weather in Taipei is different from that in Kaohsiung"才對。其他類似這種對錯的例句如下：

a. American food and British food are similar.（可能錯）

American food is similar to British food.（對）

American food and British food are similar to each other.（對）

American food and British food are similar to French food.（對）

b. Oranges and apples are the same in shape.（可能錯）

Oranges are the same as apples in shape.（對）

Oranges and apples are the same as tangerines in shape.（對）

c. Taiwan and China are related.（可能錯）

Taiwan is related to China.（對）

Taiwan and China are related to each other.（對）

Taiwan and China are related to Japan.（對）

d. Red and yellow are blended.（可能錯）

Red is blended into yellow.（對）

Red and yellow are blended into each other.（對）

Red and yellow are blended into blue.（對）

在做比較時，很多人也按中文習慣說出類似"The weater of Tokyo is colder than Taipei"的話，忘了要說"The weather of Tokyo is colder than that of Taipei"。同樣的，有人也說"Chinese food is more delicious than America"，忘了要說"Chinese food is more delicious than American food"。這種因比較不對等而發生的錯誤，有其他例子如下：

a. The tail of my dog is longer than yours. （錯）

The tail of my dog is longer than that (= the tail) of yours. （對）

b. The ears of a cat are much shorter than a rabbit. （錯）

The ears of a cat are much shorter than those (= the ears) of a rabbit. （對）

c. Your income is equal to me. （錯）

Your income is equal to mine (= my income). （對）

d. The hostess' manners are much more reported than the guests. （錯）

The hostess' manners are much more reported than the guests' (= the guests' manners). （對）

e. His share is the same as her. （錯）

His share is the same as hers (= her share). （對）

中文的說話習慣甚至於常常讓人講出這樣的英文："I take pity on the man that his son was run over by a car"。其實，這句話應該改成"I take pity on the man whose son was run over by a car"才對。其他類似的例句如下：

a. Do not use words that you do not know their meanings. （錯）

Do not use words *whose meanings/ the meanings of which* you do not know. （對）

b. He bought the car which they had cut down the price 25%. （錯）

He bought the car *the price of which* they had cut down 25%. （對）

c. She mentioned an awful event that they could not bear to retell its result. （錯）

She mentioned an awful event *the result of which* they could not bear to retell. （對）

d. He has submitted a paper which we know nothing about its points. （錯）

He has submitted a paper *whose points/ the points of which* we know nothing about. （對）

e. I have written a book that you will find its value inestimable. （錯）

I have written a book *whose value/ the value of which* you will find inestimable. （對）

也有一些人忘了"between"是指兩者之間，而按中文的習慣說出"There are always some secrets between each person"這種句子。其實，應改成 "There are always some secrets between two persons"才對。其他類似的錯誤如下：

a. There is misunderstanding between each character. （錯）

There is misunderstanding between one character and another. （對）

b. We are now between the tunnel. （錯）

We are now between the (two) tunnels. （對）

c. Food was distributed *between* the 100 odd refugees. （錯）

Food was distributed *among* the 100 odd refugees.（對）

d. Hamlet had to choose between"to be"*or*"not to be."（錯）

Hamlet had to choose between"to be"*and*"not to be."（對）

e. It is a choice between the devil *or* the deep sea.（錯）

It is a choice between the devil *and* the deep sea.（對）

　　要講完所有常犯的英文錯誤是不可能的。經驗告訴我們：華人最常犯的英文錯誤是冠詞、時態、介系詞和名詞的U或C以及*sg.*或*pl.*的使用。那方面的錯誤只能在不斷的改正與磨練中，才能漸漸改善。在此，講到的只是英文有程度的人也常常會犯錯的一些樣板例子而已。寫英文學術論文的人，一定要經常留意人家怎麼精確的用英文表達某種含義，自己才會不犯錯，也才會寫出精確的英文。

作業

1. 把過去你曾寫過的英文學術論文拿出來看。不管裡頭的英文有
   沒有被老師改正過,請瞭解:
   a. 你也犯過本章所講到的英文錯誤嗎?

   b. 你還犯過哪些英文錯誤本章沒有提到?

2. 請拿一篇你寫的英文學術論文給一位英文好的人看,藉以瞭解:
   a. 你也犯過本章所講到的英文錯誤嗎?

   b. 你還犯過哪些英文錯誤本章沒有提到?

3. 找出一期屬於你們學門的(紙本的或電子的)英文學術期刊
   來,選看其中一篇論文的一段話,據此做下面幾件事:
   a. 把那段英文譯成中文。

   b. 不看原來的英文,而把譯成的中文再譯回英文。

   c. 比比看你譯回的英文和原來的英文有何文字或文法的差異。

   d. 瞭解你在用字和文法方面有何弱點。

4. 如果有空，再看另一篇別人刊出的好的英文學術論文，重複做上一題要你做的那幾件事。

5. 下面各段英文中，畫底線的部分都有錯誤，請將之改正過來。

a. Hepatocellular carcinoma is one of the most frequently-found human <u>cancer</u>. During our experiment we <u>find</u> that dietary administration of SNWE could <u>marked</u> suppress the AAF-induced cancers in wistar rats. We observed the serum levels of some important enzymes <u>in liver</u>. Remarkably, SNWE <u>increases</u> the detoxifying enzyme in the AAF-induced liver and reduced the <u>damages</u> of the liver.

b. Three basins are tributary to the river <u>flows</u> into that province. The river provides <u>them surface water</u> for domestic use. One of the basins <u>is covered</u> an area of about 1,000 km^2, <u>which</u> 60% is located in the province. Good management of this basin is becoming <u>uttermost importance</u>.

c. <u>At time</u> of recession, a sub-national government can either <u>resort capital</u> markets or use inter-governmental grants to implement <u>their</u> counter-cyclical fiscal policy. Inter-goveenmental grants, however, often cannot be <u>relied,</u> since the grantor governments may have <u>its</u> own fiscal difficulties. Incurring public debt in economic downturns <u>are</u> theorectically sound. Still, drastic fiscal measures <u>taking</u> by state or local governments to balance their <u>budget</u> ofen affect their credit ratings adversely, thus <u>erode</u> their borrowing capabilities <u>at</u> the capital market.

d. <u>Despite of</u> the influence which social forces exhibit, as <u>evidence</u> by the previous discussion, partisanship is different from many of the <u>belief</u> that are <u>subjected</u> to social influence. It is often formed early in life <u>though</u> a process of socialization, and it is <u>relative</u> stable through an individual's life. <u>Such as</u>, it is a product of social forces only for <u>a period of short time</u>. This <u>suggested</u> that partisanship may be one of the few <u>attachment</u>, if not the only one, formed early and held <u>by individual</u> for a long time; it is insulated <u>off</u> and unaffected by social <u>surrounding</u> in the individual's adulthood.

e. Table 3 <u>showed</u> descriptive statistics and correlations of all study <u>variable</u>. According to this table, <u>no matter an organization</u> is based in Taipei or not, there are significant correlations <u>among</u> location and all other variables. This fact justifies its inclusion <u>of</u> the control variables. Moreover, <u>because the</u> strong correlations, we can consider the possibility <u>which</u> location may act as a moderator of relationships.

f. Bone remodeling depends upon the balance of bone formation and bone resorption, wherein bone forming osteoblasts and bone-resorbing osteoclasts play crucial role. Chronic inflammatory disease, including rheumatoid arthritis, periodontitis, and osteoporosis, will induce bone loss, that in turn increases the number of bone-resorbing osteoclast. Recent studies have indicated n-3 polyunsaturated fatty acids can reduce the production of inflammatory cytokines in a number of condition, whereas n-6 polyunsaturated fatty acids have opposite effect.

g. Falstaff lives on words and escape ill fortune through word. We all love to hear him to war with words. He may be a coward by sword, but never a coward by words. This knight's eloquence has talked into a braggart soldier, into a man big with bluffs and wag. Nevertheless, he is a sophist who is able to talk us into awareness of all the"false stuff."His frank reflection of living and lying have earned himself the name of"a fundamentally honest man."

附錄一　書面英式英語與美式英語的對照

一、拼字方面
英式英語／美式英語

> -ise/ -ize 如civilise/ civilize, modernise/ modernize
>
> -gue/ -g或-gue 如catalogue/ catalog or catalogue, dialogue/ dialog
>
> 　　　　　　or dialogue
>
> -our/ -or 如endeavour/ endeavor, valour/ valor
>
> -re/ -er 如centre/ center, theatre/ theater
>
> -wards/ -ward 如afterwards/ afterward, towards/ toward
>
> -xion/ -ction 如inflexion/ inflection, reflexion/ reflection
>
> -yse/ -ize 如analyse/ analyze, catalyse/ catalyze

其他像check/ cheque（支票）, disc/ disk（圓片、磁碟片）, defence/ defense（保衛）, programme/ program（計劃）, scepticism/ skepticism（懷疑論）, storey/ story（樓層）, tyre/ tire（輪胎）。

二、用詞方面

英式英語／美式英語

不同之處甚多，詳見Norman Schur, *British English A to Z*一書，下面僅是一些例子：

airways/ airlines（航空公司）, biscuit/ cookie（餅乾）, chips/ French fried potatoes（炸薯條）, cooker/ stove（爐子、炊具）, fender/ bumper（保險桿）, flats/ apartments（公寓）, lift/ elevator（電梯）, luggage/ baggage（行李）, motorway/ freeway（高速公路）,notice board/ bulletin board（佈告欄）, petrol/ gasoline（汽油）,public convenience/ public rest room（公廁）, railway/ railroad（鐵路）a reading glass/ a magnifying glass（放大鏡）, referee/ reference（幫寫介紹信者）, a small ad/ a classified ad（報上小廣告）, rubbish/ garbage（垃圾）,rubbish bin or dustbin/ garbage can（垃圾箱、垃圾桶）, subway/ underpass（地下道、陸橋下車道）, traffic block/ traffic jam（交通阻塞）, underground/ subway（地下鐵）, vest/ waistcoat（背心）, wing/ fender（汽車之翼子板、擋泥板）, zip/ zipper（拉鍊）。

三、文法方面

1. [英式] Have you any sister? I have not a house of my own.

   [美式] Do you have any sister? I do not have a house of my own.

2. [英式] I can help you to do everything. He helped to carry the box.

[美式] I can help you do everything. He helped carry the the box.

3. [英式] You used to live in London, use(d)n't you? Used he to play tennis at school?

[美式] You used to live in London, didn't you? Did he use to play tennis at school?

四、標點方面

1. [英式] 先用單引號，如：The expression 'restrictive measures' is used in that article.

[美式] 先用雙引號，如：The expression "restrictive meansures" is used in that article.

2. [英式] 先單而後雙，如：He said, 'By "a public convenience" I mean what you call "a public rest room" or a toilet for public use.'

[美式] 先雙而後單，如：He said, "By 'a public convenience' I mean what you call 'a public rest room' or a toilet for public use."

3. [英式] 引全句時，句點在（第二個）單引號前，如：She said, 'I prefer not to use any public toilet.'

[美式] 引全句時，句點在（第二個）雙引號前，如：She said, "I prefer not to use any public toilet."

4. [英式] 引詞語時，句點在（第二個）單引號後，如：The expression 'restrictive measures' is used in an article entitled 'Restrictive Measures and EU Law'.

[美式] 引詞語時，句點在（第二個）雙引號前，如：The

expression "restrictive measures" is used in an article entitled "Restrictive Measures and EU Law."

附錄二　常用拉丁字詞

字詞、詞類

中文含義、英文含義

例子

（註：請同時注意大小寫、斜體、與標點符號之使用）

A.D. (AD)　adv.

　　公元後Anno Domini, after the birth of Christ

　　"it occurred in A.D. 300"

ad hoc　adj. & adv.

　　專門的、臨時的、特別的for a specific occasion, improvised

　　"a very *ad hoc* approach, on an *ad hoc* basis, do something *ad hoc*"

ad infinitum　adv.

　　至無限地、無止地 to infinity, forever without end

　　"to multiply something *ad infinitum*"

A.M. (a.m.)　adv.

　　上午ante meridiem, before noon

　　"to arrive at 7 A.M., to come at 9 a.m."

a posteriori   adj. & adv.

     後天的、依經驗的、按事實的based on experience

     "using *a posteriori* evidence, to acquire the knowledge *a posteriori*"

a priori   adj. & adv.

     先驗的、推理的 deductive reasoning, reasoning deductively

     "adopting an *a priori* method, to learn it *a priori*"

B.C. (BC)   adv.

     公元前Before (the birth of) Christ

     "he died at 476 B.C."

bona fide   adj.

     真實的in good faith, real, genuine

     "a *bona fide* business transaction"

***c.* or *ca.* (*circa*)**   prep.

     大約about

     "it happened *c.* 500 B.C."

cf.   v.

     比較compare

     "The result of Group A is good (cf. that of Group B)."

CV   n.

     履歷、簡歷curriculum vitae, resume

     "Bring with you your CV."

de facto   adj.

     實際的existing by fact (not by right)

"a *de facto* government"

de jure adj.

法理上的existing by right, from the law

"a *de jure* inheritor"

e.g. adv.

比方說、例如for example

"A bird, e.g. a dove, is ..."

et al. n.

及其他人（作者）and others, and other authors

"Trager Smith, et al., say ..."

etc. n.

等（等）et cetera, and others

"This is suitable for prints, maps, blueprints, etc."

i.e. adv.

那就是（說）that is (to say)

"the nitwit, i.e. the fool ..."

infra adv.

在下面below

"See *infra*, p. 30."

in situ adv.

在原（指定）處in its original (appointed) place

"an experiment conducted *in situ*"

in vitro adj. & adv.

在實驗室裡、在試管中in the lab/ tube

"an *in vitro* experiment, the result found *in vitro*"

in vivo adj. & adv.

在活體上、在野生狀態in life, on living organisms

"to observe the *in vivo* effect, cells cultured *in vivo*"

loc.cit. adv.

在前引述處loco citato, in the place cited

"See the explanation *loc.cit.*"

op.cit. adv.

在所引著作中opera citato, in the work cited

"See examples *op.cit.*"

passim adv.

（此點見）各處the point is made here and there

"He says,"A is B"(*passim*, Becker)."

per capita adj.

每人平均的 per head

"a rise in *per capita* income"

P.M. (p.m.) adv.

在下午post meridiem, after noon

"at two o'clock P.M./ p.m."

P.S. adv.

附記post scriptum

"P.S.: Please remember me to the Mayor."

sic   adv.

如原文thus, the error is in the original quote

"Then 'I like the clientel [*sic*],'he wrote."

sine quo non   n. & adj.

必要條件without which not, essentially necessary

"It is a *sine quo non* (item for consideration)."

v.   verb

參見see

"it is believed that ... (*v.* Keller 34)."

vice versa   adv.

反之亦然the reverse (of what is said) is true

"The man blames his wife and *vice versa.*"

viz.   adv.

即namely

"He had three sisters, *viz.*, Alice, Ella, and Jane."

附錄三　各章作業參考答案

第一章
第一章第5題

下面各題畫線部分可視為technical terms。

a. For health one should drink pure water, not alcohol.

b. Water is composed of <u>oxygen</u> and <u>hydrogen</u>.

c. The conclusion Einstein arrived at was the equation: $\underline{E} = \underline{MC^2}$.

d. The word"<u>morphemes</u>"contains three <u>morphemes</u>: two <u>bound morphemes</u> ("morph-" and"-eme") and one <u>free morpheme</u> ("-s").

e. Marx and Engels formulated the principles of <u>dialectical materialism</u>. They maintained that economic structure is the basis of history, and determines all the social, political, and intellectual aspects of life.

f. We found <u>calcium levels</u> to be decreased by <u>RA</u> and <u>D3</u> but increased when <u>AG1296</u>, in addition to <u>RA</u> or <u>D3</u>, was given.

g. <u>Quantum phenomena</u> are particularly relevant in systems whose dimensions are close to the <u>atomic scale</u>, such as <u>molecules</u>, atoms, electrons, protons, and other subatomic particles.

h. The aerostructures are for horizontal stabilizers, engine nacelles, fan cowls, etc.

第二章
第二章第2題

應改成如下：

a. "Stress and Depression among Latina Women in Rural Southeastern North Carolina"

b. "Lagged Associations between Overall TV News Viewing, Local TV News Viewing, and Fatalistic Beliefs about Cancer Prevention"

第二章第3題

應改成如下：

a. "Circulating insulin-like growth factor binding Protein-1 and the risk of pancreatic cancer"

b. "Pattern of migration: how Paleo-Indians crossed Beringia and settled in the Americas"

第二章第4題

斜體字應刪除，畫底線部分或許可刪除。

a. "*An* Exposure Assessment of Mercury and Its Compounds by

Dispersing Modeling: A Case Study <u>in the Sea of Japan Coastal Area</u>"

b. "Hybrid Materials: Monodisperse Hollow Supraparticles via Selective Oxidation <u>Using an in situ Assembly Method</u>"

c. "*The* liver function in humans <u>with borderline liver dysfunction</u> is improved by a mixture of schisandra fruit extract and sesamin: <u>a randomized, placebo-controlled study</u>"（同時第一個liver改成 Liver）

d. "*A Study of* a photon-fueled gate-like delivery system using i-motif DNA functionalized mesoporous silica nanoparticles"（同時a photon-fueled改成A photon-fueled）

第三章
第三章第4題

Over the past two decades, the crucial role A plays in B *has become* a topic of practical interest. Available evidence suggests that if A increases in amount, then the welfare of B is increased as well. However, it is noted that the amount of A cannot grow unlimitedly. It may bring danger if it grows to a certain extent. Now, the question is: what is the extent? We have probed into this question, gathered enough data, made a good analysis, and provided an answer, which may be convincing to those interested in this topic.

a. 文中用"has become"而不用"became"，因為要表示「已經變成……」。

b. 文中說"it is noted that ..."而不說"I/ we note that ..."，因為不只I/ we note此事，是大家都注意到此事。

c. 文中的前兩句是在泛論A與B的關係。

d. 文中的第3、4、5句（"However"~"extent?"）是帶出特定問題。

e. 文中最後一句（"We"~"topic."）不只直接說出「研究目的」，還說出研究過程。

f. 文中最後一句是簡述了整個研究的作為。

g. 文中最後一句的"We"不是指眾人，而是指整個研究團隊／發表論文的群體。

h. 文中最後一句若改成"This question has been probed into, enough data have been gathered, a good analysis has been made, and an answer has been provided, which may be convincing to those interested in this topic."，就不知誰是做那研究行為的人了。

第三章第5題

　　A is an infectious viral disease associated with chickens. It is caused by B, a virus belonging to the family of C. In 2010, a spread of the disease *was found* in the area of D. In that same year, some biosecurity measures（生物安全措施）were taken to control the spread. However, the control was not very effective. Some time later, some scientists found that the outbreak of the disease is mostly due to certain vaccine-related strains（與疫苗有關的類型）of B. We, therefore, made an attempt to confirm the fact.

a. 文中前兩句是泛泛地在介紹A這種傳染病，第3、4、5句（"In 2010"~"effective"）是具體說出一個想控制那傳染病的案例，第6句（"Some"~"of B"）指出前人有關那傳染病的發現。這些話是研究的「背景」。

b. 這段話的最後一句（"We, therefore, made an attempt to confirm the fact."）是「動機」與「目的」。要"confirm"的"fact"是the outbreak of the disease *is* mostly due to certain vaccine-related strains。研究者只是想 confirm前人的發現。

c. 文中的"was found"不可改成"has been found"，那會不合於文法。

d. 文中的"some biosecurity measures were taken"若改成"we took some biosecurity measures"，就會改變含義，指生物安全措施是研究者做的。

e. 在"some scientists found that the outbreak of the disease *is* mostly due to certain vaccine-related strains" 這句子中，"is"若改成"was"， 就不是恆常事實。

f. 文中"We, therefore, *made* an attempt to confirm the fact."這句的"made"不可以改成"make"，因為只是過去某時在做那企圖。全句不可改成"Therefore, an attempt was made to confirm the fact"，因為要說出誰在made an attempt。

第三章第6題

第一段有兩句話，一句談到：限制措施一直是歐聯的一種最重要的外交政策。另一句講到"限制措施have been imposed on a large number of occasions, including ..."

第二段話講到："採用限制措施has raised several difficult legal questions, including ..."

第三段話講到："本文章discusses ..., including ... , and examines ..."

第四段話講到："本文章is structured as follows. First, ... Finally, the article analyses ..."

a. 在這四段話裡，第一段是泛談情勢，第二段是指出問題，第三段講到目的或目標。

b. 在這四段話裡，第四段是在講文章的結構。那不是小論文的Introduction常有的內容。

c. 第一段裡要說限制措施"have been imposed"而不說"were imposed"，也不說"we have imposed restrictive measures"，因為限制措施已經被imposed了，而imposed措施的人不知是誰，反正不是we。

d. 從第四段裡的"analyses"一字（而非analyzes），可以推論出那期刊是用英式英語在編排。

第四章

第四章第6題

　　The boilers fed with *B. subtilis* supplementary diets gained much more body weights than the control group (Table 3). ... No significant difference in body weight was found, however, among those groups which received different *B. subtilis* diets, when they were compared with the control group.

a. *B. subtilis*即*Bacillus subtilis*，因為是拉丁字學名所以要斜體。

b. *Bacillus subtilis*（枯草桿菌）是研究的material。

c. 該研究有divide the boiler chickens into groups。

d. 句中the control group是指受控制而沒吃枯草桿菌的肉雞。

e. 該研究中的experimental group不只有一組。

f. 句中"those groups which received different *B. subtilis* diets"就是指實驗組，而且表示不只是一組。

g. 第一句中"much"可用"significantly"取代。而第二句中"significant"也可用"great"取代。

h. 用"gained"和"was found"，表示過去研究當時的發現。

i. 第一句後面印上"(Table 3)"，為了補充說「如表3所示」。

j. 出現"than ..."時有比較級，出現"compared with ..."時，不一定有比較級的字眼。

第四章第7題

a. 利用Markov model來設立自己的theoretical models，就像利用某theory/ approach來開發自己的theory/ approach。在論文中報告研究過程時，應該包含像這樣的細節。

b. 被使用的the Opportunistic Network Environment (ONE) simulator，就像別的學門所使用的科學儀器或設備。在論文中報告研究過程時，也應該包含像這樣的細節。

c. 模擬所根據的the Random Waypoint (RWP) mobility model，就像別的學門所使用的assay（測試法）。在論文中報告研究過程時，也應該包含像這樣的細節。

d. 在論文中，把某一部分再細分成若干部分，並分別給標題，當然可以。給heading的字體（大、小寫或粗、細體與正、斜體之分），沒有硬性規定。像這裡的SIMULATION AND NUMERICAL RESULTS分成*Simulation Result*與*Performance Analysis with Numerical Results*，是可以接受。

e. 這裡全用現在式的動詞（run, is, shows, kill, becomes等）來講述研究的過程與結果，這是電子學門的普遍作法。

f. 既然有Figure 5，該論文應至少有五個graphs。

g. Figure 5的heading如果寫成Simulation result with RWP mobility model，是可以。要把這heading放在圖後（下方）。

h. Figure 5是應該顯示"if the worms kill nodes ..., they may bring ... Furthermore, if the anti-virus software becomes ..., the worms will bring ..."這兩個事實。

第五章
第五章第3題

    The availability of insects for food *depends* very much on the temperature of the season (Taylor 1963); therefore, choosing the right season for releasing the bats *may be* crucial to their survival (Fleming & Eby 2003; Wang *et al* 2010). ...

    Like hawks in the air, those bats usually *foraged* in certain restricted areas during the first 4 or 5 hours of the night (Barak & Yom-Tov 1989)... *It is not unlikely* that our bats *directed* the suitable sites for their foraging by eavesdropping on their conspecies (Balcombe & Fenton 1988; Fenton 2003).

a. 動詞用現在式（depends）表示恆常事實，用過去式（*foraged, directed*）表示僅過去某時之作為。

b. may be若改為might be，語氣（mood）變成高度假設。

c. It is not unlikely若改為It was not unlikely，就是說那件事只在過去那時候有可能，現在不一定可能。

d. 括弧中專有名詞是作者的姓。不連名帶姓，是因為在參考書目中以姓排列，而且一定跟著有名。數字是著作年分。*et al*就是and others（等人）。Fleming & Eby就是Fleming and Eby兩人。Yom-Tov是一個姓。

第五章第4題

Two *primary contributions* have emerged from this significant research. ... Aside from the contributions, these results have several *implications* for further practical as well as theoretical consideration regarding organizational diversity.

After examining all the factors involved, we found that the ethnic diversity among the employees seemed to get in the way of their civility towards the service recipients and it seemed to have negatively affected the organizational performance. These findings should be *interpreted* in contrast with those previous findings which suggest the positive effects of ethnic diversity on organizational performance [e.g., Richard et al., 2004, 2007] ... Our findings certainly suggest that demographic diversity among employees might create or deplete resources for civility and ultimately influence the performance of organizations.

a. 第一段談到研究的primary contributions（主要貢獻），不算離題（digression）。

b. 第一段另談到研究結果的implications（意涵），也不算離題。

c. 第二段第二句講到的These findings是指前一句中所說的這兩件事：

(1)雇員的種族歧異，似乎妨礙到給予服務對象的禮節。

(2)雇員的種族歧異，似乎妨礙到組織的作為。

d. 第二段談到「應該如何interpreted（詮釋）發現的事實」，這不算離題。

e. 第二段提到前人的認定：他們認為種族歧異對組織作為有正面效用。像這樣在討論中提前人的結論，很正當。

f. 這裡最後一句"Our findings certainly suggest that"這幾個字後面的那句話說：「雇員中人口分布的歧異會創造或用盡 助長禮節的資源而最終影響到組織的作為。」這句話是這篇論文的結論。這結論是牴觸前人的結論。

g. 在這兩段話中：

Have emerged不可改成had emerged 。

seemed to get in the way不可改成seem to get in the way 。

把might create or deplete改為may create or deplete，語氣會更肯定，但無所謂更好或更壞。

h. 這裡用中括弧[ ]取代小括弧( )，沒有關係。像這種格式的細節，是跟刊物的體例一致就好，不必太計較。

第五章第5題

For Eugenio Barba, ... the body is a network of energy and the"whole body thinks/ acts, with another quality of energy"(*Paper Canoe* 52).

a. 把Eugenio Barba的名與姓一起寫出（而不僅僅寫其姓Barba），是因為文中第一次提到他。

b. 引言後的（*Paper Canoe* 52）是表示*Paper Canoe*那著作的第52頁。

c. 這裡不可以把（*Paper Canoe* 52）改為（Barba 52），就是因為這裡有兩個事實：(1)同一句中前頭已經提到Eugenio Barba。(2)文中引用到的Barba的著作不只*Paper Canoe*那一本（從「引用書目」中，可知文中總共引用到Barba三個著作）。

In *A Thousand Plateaus*, Deleuze and Guattari *stretch* the image even further and *describe* the Body without Organs as a"worldwide intensity map"(165) and they *argue* that"... The BwO is opposed not to the organs but to that organization of the organs called the organism"(158).

a. Deleuze and Guattari是指Gilles Deleuze and Felix Guattari這兩人。但文中不用全名，因為這裡並非文中第一次提到他們兩人。（文中前面確實已經提過他們）

b. 這裡的（165）和（158）是指著作第165頁和第158頁。作者就是句中提到的Deleuze and Guattari。著作就是句前提到的*A Thousand Plateaus*。如果句前沒有提到*A Thousand Plateaus*這著作，（165）和（158）就必須改寫成（*A Thousand Plateaus* 165）和（*A Thousand Plateaus* 158）。（「引用書目」告知：在文中，那兩人被引用的著作有兩本，其一為*A Thousand Plateaus: Capitalism and Schizophrenia*，其二為*Anti-Oedipus: Capitalism and Schizophrenia*）。

c. 在這段話中，用stretch, describe和argue而不用stretched, described和argued，是因為兩作者在那著作中確實永遠（過去、現在、及未來）都會stretch, describe和argue。

The performance of the dilated body is indeed the mystery of theatre. ... In this sense, to make a dilated body is both the foundation and the possibility of performance. It is an act to create a "secular sacrum" (Grotowski 49) in the theater ...

a. 文中（Grotowski 49）不放在句後，而放在"secular sacrum"之後，是因為應該放在直接引用的話語後（不管一句或一詞）。

b. 「引用書目」告知：在文中，Grotowski就是Jerzy Grotowski這個人。這裡不寫（Jerzy Grotowski 49）是因為括弧中只需引作者姓氏來告知出處。

c. 「引用書目」也告知：Grotowski在文中被引用的著作只有 *Towards a Poor Theatre*這一本。就是因為只有這一本，所以寫（Grotowski 49）就好，不必寫（Grotowski, *Towards a Poor Theatre*, 49）。

d. 如果文中沒提到Grotowski，光在引言後寫（*Towards a Poor Theatre*, 49）就無法知道書的作者。

第五章第6題

第一句話說：「我們已顯示（"We have demonstrated"）*Cysticapnos* 是可以實驗栽培而對基因研究不會有困難的。」這種話像是「研究的結果／發現」，但也像「研究的結論」。

第二句話推測取得某種資料會便利（will facilitate）對*Cysticapnos*基因的研究，像這種推測（surmise）是可以放在結論中。

第三句話說*Cysticapnos*是第一個有基因功能研究資料的花種（species），這等於說出該研究的意義／重要性。這種定位的話也是可以放在結論中。

第四句話說：「我們當初發展（we developed）這套研究系統是為了進行有關*Cysticapnos*的比較研究。」第五句話說：「可是，這套系統也可以用來（can be used to）研究別的東西。」這兩句話合起來也可當結論的一部分。在這裡"developed"不可以改成"develop"，"can be used"也不可以改成"could be used"。

最後一句話說：「比較各種罌粟花（poppies）的基因結構有了見地之後，未來的研究可以延伸到（may extend to）更基礎的延胡索的種類（basal fumitory species）。」這顯然是一個建議（suggestion）。建議是可以當結論的一部分。"may extend to"若改為"might extend to"，語氣會太假設、太沒自信了。

第六章
第六章第3題

a. 不可以把Acknowledgements改成Acknowledgment。

b. 文中的I（我）不改成We（我們），那是因為研究者／論文撰寫人都僅自己一人。

c. 如果把I（我）改成The author/ researcher（作者／研究者），感覺起來會欠親切。期刊論文中常用the authors來取代we指感謝人，那是因為"we"太籠統，指涉的人可能不只有論文的作者。

d. 感謝許多人，每次都用不同的感謝用詞，有這種變化，是比較好。如果從頭到尾都用"I thank So and So for ..."的模式，就太單調了。

e. 這些感謝用詞中，有一個用得不妥當，那是"appreciate"。

f. 這段謝詞的第三句是應該改為：I appreciate the valuable comments and suggestions which Professor A and Professor B gave me when they served as my oral examiners.

g. 感謝時，用複數的thanks（are due to ...）而不用單數的thank（is due to ...），那是英文的習慣。用gratitude而不用gratitudes，那是因為該字是不可數的抽象名詞。

第七章
第七章第3題

a. 從這段英文，可知"cancer"和"mortality"是U，"cause"是C。

b. "The high mortality of lung cancer"不可以改成"High mortality of the lung cancer"，而"lack of effective methods for therapy"也不可以改成"the lack of the effective methods for the therapy"。前者應限定在前面提到的「屬於肺癌的那個高致死率」，後者不必限定在哪一種「有效治療法的缺乏」。

c. "Berberine"（黃連素）是物質名詞，是U。而"alkaloid"（生物鹼）也是，但前加an表示某一種類。"... berberine (an isoquinoline alkaloid) is known to have ..."不可以改成"A berberine (isoquinoline alkaloid) is known to have ..."。

d. 第三句中"...a number of biochemical and pharmacological effects"這些字裡的"effects"用*pl.*是因為前面有"a number of (= many)"，它不可改成"effect"。

e. 第四句中"NSCLC"是"non-small cell lung cancer"的「略語」。"A549, H460, H1299 and H1355"是某些"cell lines"（細胞株）的代號。"MRC-5 and HUVEC"是兩種 normal cells。

f. 英文"cell"（細胞）一字是C，所以會加-s，如"normal cells"。但在"human non-small cell lung cancer"一詞裡，用"cell"而不用"cells"，那是因為該"cell"已經當形容詞（如her boy friends裡的"boy"）。

第七章第4題

a. 把USA寫成U.S.A.也可以。但the President和the Senate不可以改成the president和the senate，因為特指美國總統與參議院。

b. Congress不說成the Congress，而the Senate也不說成Senate，這都是習慣用法。

c. "Normally, it is he who, either in his own utterances or through his Secretary of State, points the path to be followed."這句中的"who"是可以改成"that"，而It is ... that ...是「強調語氣」的句法。美國總統不一定是男的，因此這句中的he, his是可以改成he/ she, his/ her，但即使在女權高漲的今天，英文裡還是習慣用he, him, his來泛指每一個人。

d. "This is part of the leader's power that American presidents enjoy most." 這句中的"This"是指前一句"It is he who ..." (「是他指出路徑讓人跟隨」) 這個事實。這個"that"可以改成"which"或省略。但"part of"不可以改成"a part of"，那是習慣用語。

e. "It is his constitutional prerogative to appoint the ambassadors, ministers and consular representatives of the United States." 這句中的"It"是「虛字」（expletive），它代替後面的"to appoint ... States"這些字。

第七章第5題

a. 專有名詞像Mississippi, Atlantic, Rocky, Pacific, Continental Divide, Connecticut River等，前面都有the，那是因為英文習慣在河流、湖泊、山脈、海洋、群島等名稱前加the。

b. 文中waters一字是由U的物質名詞water（水）變成C的普通名詞而指「水流」，The Rockies是指the Rocky Mountains。

c. 動詞divide可當名詞指「分水嶺」，落磯山做為the Continental Divide也叫the Great Divide。那大分水嶺分開的Continent叫the Continent of North America。

d. 在"... a visitor may throw two snowballs in opposite directions and know that each will feed a different ocean." 一句中，"in opposite directions"不可改成"in the opposite directions"或"in opposite direction"，因為不指特定的某些「相反的方向」，

而且這裡所說的「相反的方向」一定是兩個。另外，each 指each snowball 。

e. 第二段開頭"Life in England"（英格蘭的生活）不可改成"A life in England"（英格蘭的一條命）或"The life in England"（英格蘭的那種生活）。動名詞"planning"是U，與C的"plan"含意上不同，它是比較強調計劃的動作而非完成的某計劃。

f. 英文specialty一字是C，Land當「土地」是U，當「地方」才是C。而cigar是C，但tobacco是U。

g. 在"The tobacco is grown with great care, under acres (hectares) of thin cloth which shades the delicate leaves."這句中，"The tobacco"是泛指「菸草」。而care和cloth均為U是因為前者是抽象名詞而後者是物質名詞。至於"the delicate leaves"，它是指the delicate leaves of the tobacco (plants)。

h. 英文cattle一字是*pl.*，也通常當複數使用。在"The stony farms are devoted to dairy cattle."一句中，"cattle"是*pl.*。

i. "The farmers also tap the sweet juices from maple trees to make maple sugar."這句不可以改成"Farmers also tap sweet juice from the maple tree to make maple sugars"，因為：要特指「那些農夫」，要特指（從楓樹來的）「那些甜汁」，但不特指從「哪些楓樹」取甜汁，而"sugar"是U的物質名詞。

第八章第3題

a. 這段話的第一句裡，"were invited"是因為"in recent years"（最近幾年）而用過去式。它是可以改成"have been invited"，表示一些學者在最近幾年「已經被邀請」去調查。

b. 第一句的後半"given that ... test"這個子句，是「分詞構造」（participial construction）。但它的「含義主詞」並非主要子句裡的"some scholars"，也就是這子句不等於"as some scholars were given (the fact) that each time the used sample had already passed the ... test"這意思。

c. 這個"given that"是個成語。它等於"on condition that"或"if"。它是表示條件的假設法，在這裡是一種「有可能」的假設。句中"had passed"是表示之前「已經通過」必要的、先期的、適合度的檢定。用"had passed"表示"passed"的時間是在調查之前。

d. 第二句（"The data ... populations."）裡，"collected"一字是"collect"的過去分詞，它的意思是「被收集的」。"The data collected for their investigation"這句話等於"The data which were collected for their investigation"（「為他們之調查所收集的資料」），它是整句話的主語。而這句話的述語是"were, as we know, sampled carefully from certain normal, uniform, and exponential populations"（「是（如我們所知）仔細地由

某些正常的、一致的、指明的口數來形成樣本」）這句話。

句中"were ... sampled"不可改成"was ... sampled"，因為主詞"data"是複數。它也不可以改成"are ... sampled"，因為講的是過去某時的行為動作。

e. 第三句（"After analyzing ... GOF test."）裡，"analyzing"一字是動名詞，它是"After"的受詞。它後面的"the collected data"又是它自己的受詞。

f. 第三句中"they ... agreed"不可改成"they ... agree"，因為要表示他們當時同意而非現在同意。「他們同意A導致B」，英文說成"they ... agreed that A *results* in B"，是可以的。不改成"they ... agreed that A *resulted* in B"，是因為要表示那是恆常的事實。

g. 第三句中，在"A results in B"的句型裡，A是"screening of samples by a pretest for normality"（為常態而藉前測來篩選樣本）。這裡的"screening"是名詞。把"screening of samples"改成"screening samples"也可以，這時的screening便是動名詞。

h. 第三句中，在"A results in B"的句型裡，B是"a more conservative, conditional, Type-I error rate ..."（一個更保守而有條件的第一型錯誤率……）。這句話的核心是"rate"這個字。"error rate"是名詞修飾名詞，"Type-I error rate"是複合名詞，"Type-I"修飾複合名詞"error rate"。

i. 第三句中，在"A results in B"的句型裡，B其實是"a more conservative, conditional, Type-I error rate than application of the one-sample *t*-test without doing any preliminary GOF test"（比起應用無任何先期合適檢測的單樣本t測試，有一個更保守而有條件的第一型錯誤率）。在這裡，"application of the one-sample *t*-test"是可以改為"applying the one-sample *t*-test"。

第八章第4題

a. 確實：當「反射、反映」之意時，reflect是*v.t.*，而當「省思」之意時是*v.i.*。

b. 在"the plants and animals which have been cultivated, and which have varied during all ages"這句話中，不說成"... which have cultivated, and which have been varied ..."，是因為plants and animals是「被（人）栽培／培養」，而自己「變種／變異」。也是因為"cultivate"是*v.t.*而"vary"是*v.i.*。如果把這句話譯成中文，應該是「那些已被培養（了）而在各年齡中已產生（了）變化的動植物」或「那些曾被培養（過）而在各年齡中曾產生（過）變化的動植物」都可以，但前者更通。

c. 在"I think we are driven to conclude that ..."這句中，"think"之後是可加"that"。但加了以後變成"I think that we are driven to conclude that ..."，一下子來了兩個"that"並不好。另外，句中只說「我們被驅使去下結論」，沒說「我們被什麼驅使去下結論」，那確實是因為「其實很難說出被什麼驅使」。

d. 在"this greater variability is simply due to our domestic productions having been raised under conditions of life"這句

中，"having been raised"是完成又被動的動名詞，它是due to 的受詞。其實，our domestic productions就是它的「含義主詞」。它沒用「所有格」，不寫成our domestic productions' 是因為「我們家裡的產物」不是人，本來就不能加(')。如果改成代名詞，是應該用"their"(due to their having been raised)。

e. 在"those to which the parent-species have been exposed under nature"這句中，用的是"A is exposed to B"（A暴露於B）的句法，只是不僅被動，還是完成的時態。用被動語態而不說 "The parent-species have exposed to those conditions of life"是 因為"expose"這字是v.t.。

f. 在"No case is on record of a variable being ceasing to be variable under cultivation"這句中，"a variable"是"being ceasing"的含義主詞。

附帶說：把達爾文的"a variable being ceasing to be variable" 改成"a variable being ceasing being variable"當然不好。

g. 在"It has been disputed at what period of life the causes of variability, whatever they may be, generally act"這句中，"act"是v.i.。

在"whatever they may be"這句中，不說"whatever they are"，是講「或許是」，不講「就是」。用may來跟whatever, however, whoever, wherever, whenever, whichever這種字，是一種「有可能的假設」。如果把may改成might，文法也對。可是，那就變成一種比較「不可能的假設」。

h. 可以把"during the early or late period of development of the embryo"這片語改成"during the early or late period of/ in developing the embryo",可見"develop"可當*v.t.*。

i. 在"Sterility has been said to be the bane of horticulture"這句中,"has been said to be"應譯成「曾經被說是」。如果把本句改為"Sterility is said to have been the bane of horticulture",意思就變成「不結果實被說成一直是園藝的致命傷」。

j. 在"I may add that ..."這句中,"add that ..."是「補充說」的意思。在此,"I may add"等於"I may say additionally"。

k. 在"as some organisms will breed ...; so will some animals and plants withstand ..."這句中,"showing that ..."是個分詞構造,它的「含義主詞」是前面整句話所說的「這件事」。這句法就像"He comes to see her every day, indicating that he is in love with her"一樣。

l. 在"so will some animals and plants withstand domestication or cultivation, and vary very slightly"這句中,"withstand"(抗拒)後面有受詞"domestication or cultivation"(馴養或培養),"vary"(變異)後面只有修飾語"very slightly"。可見"withstand"是*v.t.*而"vary"是*v.i.*。如果把"withstand"後的"domestication or cultivation"改成"domesticating or cultivating",並不好。同理,要把「所有生物體都抗拒死亡」譯成"All organisms withstand death"。

第九章

第九章第4題

a. 在第一句（Very few of us, even including clever speculators, are skilled at and fond of using crystal balls for investment.）中，"even" 是修飾"including ..."的副詞，"skilled"是分詞轉成的形容詞，"crystal"是名詞轉成的形容詞。"at"和"of"的受詞都是動名詞 "using ..."。"at"是跟"skilled"連用而"of"是跟"fond"連用。

b. 在第二句（We know it is hardly possible to tell with any certainty whether prices will go up or go down between the time when we make an investment and the time when we want to use the money.）中，"It is hardly possible ..."不可以改成"We are hardly possible ..."。"tell ... whether ..."不可以改成"tell ... about/ of whether ..."。"with any certainty"不可以改成"in/ by any certainly"。"the time *when* we make an investment and the time *when* we want to use the money"中的"when"是可以省略。

c. 在第三句（Experience tells us that the key to true wisdom in personal investment is in the word *diversification*.）中，"the key to ..."不可以改成"the key of/ for ..."。"in personal investment"不可以改成"of personal investment"。"in the word *diversification*"的"in"不可以省略。

d. 在第四句（That means: money, like eggs, should not be put in just one basket; it should be placed in a variety of channels with different attributes.）中，"like"是介系詞，"a variety of"是等於"various"的成語，"with different attributes"是等於"having different attributes"而用以修飾"channels"的介系詞片語。

e. 在第五句（For instance, against the funds placed in insurance, banks, and bonds, there should be some invested in corporate stocks or in real estate as a hedge against inflation.）中，"against the funds ..."的"against"是表示「對比」。"some ..."是等於"some funds ..."。"corporate"是"corporation"的形容詞，它跟"corporal"有區別。"a hedge against inflation"的"against"是表示「對抗」的含義。

f. 在第六句[You know, when prices rise, the value of your corporate securities or of your real estate would rise as well (in some cases by larger amounts, on the average)]中，"the value of your corporate securities or *of* your real estate"這句若省去第二個"of"並不好。用兩個"of"會更清楚地表示"the value of your corporate securities"or"the value of your real estate"。"rise by larger amounts"的"by"是表示「差距」。"on the average"是成語，它是「平均而言」的意思。

g. 在第七句（When prices fall down, your money in insurance, banks, and bonds would then increase in value.）中，"down"是由介系詞轉成的副詞。

第九章第5題

a. 在第一句（In anthropology the word"culture"is defined far more comprehensively than it is ordinarily understood.）中，"far"修飾"more"，可換成"much"或"a great deal"。"comprehensively"不改為"comprehensive"，因為要修飾動詞"defined"。"ordinarily"是修飾動詞"understood"。

b. 在第二句（For many ordinary people culture is synonymous with development or improvement acquired by training or education.）中，"For many ordinary people"的"For"是「就／對……而言」。"is synonymous with"可以改成"is synonymous to"，也可以改成"has the same meaning as"。"acquired by"之"by"等於"by means/ way of"。

c. 在第三句（For them, accordingly, a"cultured,"or more properly,"cultivated,"individual is one who has acquired a certain command of knowledge or skill in certain specialized fields, usually such as literature, art, and music.）中，"cultured," "cultivated"和"specialized"都是分詞轉成的形容詞。"more properly"不可以改成"properlier"。看得出"certain"可接單數或複數名詞。"usually"不可以改成"usual"。

d. 在第四句（Such cultivated individuals are expected and often found to have good manners as well.）中，"manners"不可以改成"manner"。

e. 在第五句（Consequently, those who are not so well educated in these fields, or those whose manners are considered"bad"as they were learned in the streets rather than in polite society, are often called uncultured people.）中，"those who ..."和"those whose ..."的"those"都等於"those people"。"as they were learned in the streets"的"they"，是指"their manners"。"rather than"是成語，等於"instead of"的意思。"uncultured"像"uneducated"一樣，是否定而且是分詞形式的形容詞。

第九章第6題

a. 在第一句（According to statistics, by far the most common organisms used in the psychology laboratories are firstly the white rat and secondly the college sophomore.）中，"by far"是成語，表示「差距很大」。"by far the most common"就是「（比起來）遠最為平常」的意思。"the most common"可以改成"the commonest"。"the psychology laboratories"(= the laboratories for psychology) 不可以改成"the psychological laboratories"。（同理，history teacher不等於historical teacher）。"the white rat and the college sophomore"不可以改成"white rat and college sophomore"。用單數加the是代表全體。"firstly"和"secondly"在此不宜變成"first"和"second"。"first"會有「起先」之意。

b. 在第二句（The underlying reasons are: first, both are readily available; second, both are inexpensive to use.）中，

"underlying"是分詞的形容詞。"first"和"second"可以改成
"firstly"和"secondly"。"readily available"不可以改成"ready
available"，也不等於"ready and available"。"inexpensive to
use"的"to"是不定詞的"to"。

c. 在第三句（Other animals are sometimes used, of course.）中，
"Other animals"不可以改成"The other animals"，但可以改成
"Some/ Certain other animals"。

d. 在第四句（The rhesus monkey and the chimpanzee also get
their share of attention in many fields of study.）中，"The
rhesus monkey and the chimpanzee"也是用單數加the來代表全
體的物種。"their share of attention"不可以改成"their attention
of share"。"in many fields of study"不可以改成"in many field
of studies"。

e. 在第五句（Sometimes even the sow bug, cockroach, and the
amoeba are used instead of the frog or the rabbit in learning
experiments.）中，"cockroach"不說成"the cockroach"是因
為它是同位語，等於the sow bug。"the amoeba"是「阿米巴
（變形）蟲」。"the frog"和"the rabbit"是指青蛙／兔子這
一類動物。"in learning experiments"等於"in learning to make
experiments"。

第十章

第十章第3題

a. 第一句（There are immense problems to be overcome before space travel becomes possible.）有2個子句。"before"所引導的子句是從屬的子句。因此，整個句子是複句。

b. 第二句（First of all, the spacecraft has to be aimed exactly at where the target planet is going to be when it arrives, perhaps several months later.）裡是有3個子句。"where"引導的子句修飾"aimed ...at"的地點，而"when"引導的子句又修飾"going to be"的時間，看來整句是複句。

另外，"First of all"是起承轉折用語。"perhaps several months later"是補充說明的用語，其前的逗點不可以省略。

c. 第三句（But the target planet, say Mars, does not stay waiting there, you know.）是簡單句，如果把"say Mars"（= let us say Mars「就說火星好了」）以及"you know"（「你曉得的」）這兩個插入的補充用語不算為子句。

d. 第四句（Like our Earth, it is revolving all the time on its axis and it is swinging through space round the Sun in an elliptical orbit of its own.）是由"and"連接兩個對等子句組成的合句。起頭"Like our Earth"很像是起承轉折用語，但也是補充說明或修飾用語。

e. 第五句（How can we then aim exactly at a mobile object like that from afar, where the object we stand on, our Earth, is also spinning like a top and moving round the Sun in its own orbit?）

有3個子句：一個主要子句加上兩個從屬子句。

這句中的"then"（「那麼」）也可用逗點分開成為（"How can we, then, aim ..."），而它是起承轉折用語。另外，"our Earth"是"the object we stand on"的同位語。而"and"連結"spinning like a top"和"moving round the Sun in its own orbit"，是有對等。

f. 第六句（Fortunately, today we can do complex and accurate calculations beforehand with the help of computers, and with other high tech equipment we can send radioed instructiouns to the spacecraft and ask it to slightly alter its direction in time as it hurtles on toward the destination.）這句有3個子句，由兩個用"and"連接的對等子句加上一個由"as"引導的從屬子句。

至於"and ask"的"and"是連接"send ..."和"ask ..."，不是連接兩子句。而句首的"Fortunately"是起承轉折用語。

g. 這一段話中的主題句（topic sentence）是第二句。

第十章第4題

a. 第一句["We all know that the variability of grape berries is caused by both environmental factors (such as vineyard location, light, temperature, and soil moisture) and viticultural practices (such as weeding, irrigation, fertilization, pruning, and cluster thinning) and it is seen in the individual berries of a bunch, between one bunch and another on a vine, and among vines within an entire vineyard."]是合複句。

在這句中，如果把兩組括號變成兩組逗點，會逗點太多而容易混亂。如果括號變成長畫符號也會比較清楚。

在"such as vineyard location, light, temperature, and soil moisture"以及"such as weeding, irrigation, fertilization, pruning, and cluster thinning"的詞語中，把"and"去掉，不可以。中文會說「諸如甲、乙、丙」，但英文習慣說"such as a, b, *and* c"或"such as a, b, c, d, *and* e"。

在"in the individual berries of a bunch, between one bunch and another on a vine, and among vines within an entire vineyard.這話語中，第一個"and"連接"one bunch"和"another (bunch)"，第二個"and"連接的是三個介系詞片語：in the..., between ..., and among ...。

b. 第二句（We seldom realize, however, that such variability can be both advantageous and disadvantageous.）是複句。"however"是放在句中的起承轉折用語。"both ... and"是連接兩個形容詞。

c. 第三句（On the one hand, variability in grape genes may mean plasticity and plasticity may help the existing cultivars adapt to a specific region.）有2個子句。用"and"連接的子句與子句間有對等。因此，它是合句。這句中的"on the one hand"是起承轉折用語。

d. 第四句（Furthermore, berry variability may help produce different sorts of wine from the same cultivar.）是簡單句。在這句中，"Furthermore"也是起承轉折用語。

e. 第五句（On the other hand, the variability of grape berries can also be a disadvantage because it may cause uneven maturity among bunches, vines, or vineyards and it thus may bring about seasonal fluctuations in the produce for sale.）是另一個合複句。它的基本結構是"the variability … can also be ... because it may cause ...and (because) it thus may bring about ..."。

在這句中，"On the other hand"也是放在句首的起承轉折用語。它不可以改成"Furthermore," "Besides," "Also," "Additionally," "In addition,"等任何一個，也不可以改成"However," "Nevertheless," "Yet,"或"Still"，因為應保留下來跟前面的"On the one hand"連用。

f. 在這五句組成的一段話中，「主題句」（topic sentence）是段中的第二句（We seldom realize, however, that such variability can be both advantageous and disadvantageous.）。

第十章第5題

a. 第一句（According to Einstein's theory of equivalence, we know $E = mc^2$, where E is the energy in ergs, m is the mass in grams, and c is the velocity of light in centimeters per second.）有4個子句。這句是合複句。

句首"According to ..."是起承轉折用語，也是補充說明或修飾用語。

b. 第二句（This means that 1 kilogram of matter will produce 25,000,000,000 kilowatt-hours of energy if it is entirely converted into energy.）有3個子句。這句是複句。

c. 第三句（It is estimated that this amount of energy is nearly equal to 300,000,000 times the total amount of energy produced by the combustion of 1 kilogram of pure coal.）有2個子句，它是複句。如果把"the total amount of energy produced by the combustion ..."改成"the total amount of energy *which is* produced by the combustion ..."，這句仍然是複句。其實，寫作時，能省則省，所以加"which is"大可不必。

d. 第四句（This estimate, in turn, means that it is highly practical to obtain nuclear energy for power purposes by setting up a chain reaction in ordinary uranium (a mixture of U-234, U-235 and U-238) through the use of slow neutrons to control the release of atomic energy in the process of fission.）有2個子句，主要子句是"This estimate means ..."，另外有由"that"引導一個名詞子句（"it is highly practical to ..."）。

這句話較長，但長在有許多介系詞片語，這些片語如果改成子句就會感到囉唆不宜。例如：改成"... it is highly practical to obtain nuclear energy *which is* for power purposes by setting up a chain reaction in ordinary uranium (a mixture of U-234, U-235 and U-238) through the use of slow neutrons to control *the atomic energy that is released* in the process of fission."並不好。

e. 第五句（What remains, then, is only this question: Can a power station, with all its design, construction, and equipment, guarantee 100% safety control of the release of such atomaic energy?）的主要子句是"What remains, then, is only this question"，這子句的主詞（"What remains"）本身也是一個子句（由疑問代名詞"What"所引導），所以這已經是一個複句。至於冒號（colon）":" 以後的那一句"Can a power station ... guarantee ...?"算是前面那句話的對等子句。所以，這整個第五句是合複句。

另外，"then"（「那麼」）是放在句中的起承轉折用語。"with all its design, construction, and equipment"是插在句中來補充說明或修飾的用語。如果把"guarantee 100% safety control of the release of such atomaic energy"改成"gurantee that when such atomic energy is released, its safety can be 100% controlled"，是可以，但太長。

第十一章
第十一章第3題

畫底線者為正確的詞語或句式：

a. X (<u>is defined as</u>/ is confined as) ...（X定義為……）

b. In the (<u>last</u>/ latest) few years, (<u>in particular</u>/ in particularity), ...（特別是在最近幾年，……）

c. As (the x case demonstrating/ demonstrated by the x case, (but/ however), ... （可是，誠如x案例所示，……）

d. The article is to discuss two problems (born in/ bearing on) the issue of y, which involves/ revolves) many organizations.（本文要討論與y議題有關之兩問題，那牽涉到許多組織。）

e. The article (structures/ is structured) as (following/ follows).（本文結構如下。）

f. (To begin/ Firstly), it clarifies ... (The next/ Secondly), it discusses ... (The third/ Thirdly), it examines ... (At last/ Finally), it analyzes ...

g. An (express/ expressive) reference to x is not (rare/ seldom) in (such/ those) countries as ...（在諸如……那些國家裡，明白指涉x並不少見。）

h. (Furthermore/ Over more), it is clear (from/ with) the report that A and B have agreed to have (recourse/ intercourse) to ...（進一步說，那報導明白表示A和B已經同意訴之於……）

i. Although this does not (relate/ concern) x in a case (of such/ as such), (but/ yet) we must ...（雖然這無關在如此場合中的x，可是我們必須……）

j. (After all/ All in all), it seems (possibly/ likely) that a bad result will (ensue/ entail) if ...（畢竟，如果……，似乎有可能壞的結果會產生。）

第十一章第4題

畫底線者為正確的詞語或句式：

a. The (rational/ <u>rationale</u>) for linking A with B is (which/ <u>that</u>) x is identical to y (<u>as long as</u>/ only if) ... （把A連結B的理論基礎是：只要……，x就等同y。）

b. (<u>Typically</u>/ Standardly), A produces the following outputs: a, b, c, and d, to (<u>say</u>/ speak) nothing of e. （典型地，A產生下列產物：a, b, c,和d,更不用說e。）

c. Figure 2 (<u>presents</u>/ represents) a pattern of ..., the numbers on the figure (<u>representing</u> / presenting) ..., the triangles (<u>indicating</u>/ indicate) ..., and the circles (<u>showing</u>/ shown) ... （圖2呈現……的樣式，圖上的數字代表……，三角形表示……，而圓圈顯示……）

d. Two additional curves (<u>outline</u>/ underline) the wide (<u>divergence</u>/ distinction) of opinion on this issue, with the red curve and the blue curve standing for a and b (<u>respectively</u>/ respectfully). （兩條附加的曲線概示此議題上意見很分歧，紅色的曲線和藍色的曲線分別代表a和b。）

e. As (<u>can</u>/ it can) be seen in Table 4, A depends on B (<u>for</u>/ by) x, C corresponds roughly, not closely, (on/ <u>to</u>) D, and E (various/ <u>varies</u>) with F. （如表4可見，就x言A有賴B，C是大約對應而非極為對應D，而E隨F而變化。）

f. According to our (observance/ <u>observation</u>), A fully (reflected on/ <u>reflected</u>) the real situation of ..., but B (<u>reacted to</u>/ reacted) C (<u>considerably</u>/ considerable) far from our expectation. （按照我們的觀察，A完全反映⋯⋯的真實情況，可是B對C的反應跟我們的期待有相當距離。）

g. It was found that x did not (<u>react</u>/ reflect) to y in a (<u>time-and dose-dependent</u>/ times-and doses-dependent) manner while its effect on z was (<u>dependent</u>/ independent) on both time and dosage. （發現到的是：x對y的反應並非取決於時間與劑量，而它對z的效用是取決於時間與劑量。）

h. Two hundred (of our questionnaires/ <u>copies of our questionnaire</u>) were distributed and 175 of them [about 90%] were filled (<u>out</u>/ up) and came back to us. Based on the (accepted/ <u>received</u>) copies, our analysis showed that ... （我們發出兩百份問卷，其中有175份[約90%]填完後回到我們。根據回收的問卷，我們的分析顯示⋯⋯）

i. It is (<u>common sense</u>/ a common sense) that A (<u>responds to</u>/ responds) B by stopping ... and C responds to D (by/ <u>with</u>) laughter. But the (<u>response</u>/ respond) of E to F was simply beyond our imagination. （依常識，A藉停止⋯⋯來回應B，而C以笑聲來回應D。但E對F的回應簡直就是我們想像之外。）

j. This paper has (<u>touched</u>/ attached) upon... and (<u>revealed</u>/ disclose) that ... The conclusion (<u>reached</u>/ arrived) herein is: ... （這篇論

文談到了……，而揭露了……的事實。在這裡達到的結論是：……）

第十一章第5題

畫底線部分更正後如下：

a. <u>Aknowledgements</u>

<u>First</u>, we would like to thank ... Our <u>thanks are</u> also due to ... for ... We <u>are</u> <u>greatly indebted</u> to ... because ... We <u>are</u> grateful, too, to ..., who ... Finally, we want to express our sincere gratitude <u>to</u> M. Wang, without <u>whose</u> encouragement this study work could not have been finished.

b. <u>Notes</u>

(1)<u>Hereinafter</u>, x refers to ...

(2)<u>As regards</u> y, see ...

(3)For new messages <u>concerning</u> this, see ...

c. This research <u>was funded</u> by ...

d. The authors <u>declared</u> no potential conflicts <u>of interest</u> with respect to the research, <u>authorship</u>, and/ or publication of this article.

第十二章
第十二章第5題

畫底線部分更正後如下：

a. Hepatocellular carcinoma is one of the most frequently-found human <u>cancers</u>. During our experiment we <u>found</u> that dietary administration of SNWE could <u>markedly</u> suppress the AAF-induced cancers in wistar rats. We observed the serum levels of some important enzymes <u>in the liver</u>. Remarkably, SNWE <u>increased</u> the detoxifying enzyme in the AAF-induced liver and reduced the <u>damage</u> of the liver.

b. Three basins are tributary to the river <u>flowing</u> into that province. The river provides <u>them with surface water</u> for domestic use. One of the basins <u>coveres</u> an area of about 1,000 km², <u>of which</u> 60% is located in the province. Good management of this basin is becoming <u>of uttermost importance</u>.

c. <u>At a time</u> of recession, a sub-national government can either <u>resort to capital</u> markets or use inter-governmental grants to implement <u>its</u> counter-cyclical fiscal policy. Inter-goveenmental grants, however, often cannot be <u>relied on,</u> since the grantor governments may have <u>their</u> own fiscal difficulties. Incurring public debt in economic downturns <u>is</u> theorectically sound. Still, drastic fiscal measures <u>taken</u> by state or local governments to balance their <u>budgets</u> ofen affect their credit ratings adversely, thus <u>eroding</u> their borrowing capabilities <u>on</u> the capital market.

d. <u>Despite</u> the influence which social forces exhibit, as <u>evidenced</u> by the previous discussion, partisanship is different from many of the <u>beliefs</u> that are <u>subject</u> to social influence. It is often formed early in life <u>through</u> a process of socialization, and it is <u>relatively</u>

stable through an individual's life. <u>As such</u>, it is a product of social forces only for <u>a short period of time</u>. This <u>suggests</u> that partisanship may be one of the few <u>attachments</u>, if not the only one, formed early and held <u>by an individual</u> for a long time; it is insulated <u>from</u> and unaffected by social <u>surroundings</u> in the individual's adulthood.

e. Table 3 <u>shows</u> descriptive statistics and correlations of all study <u>variables</u>. According to this table, <u>no matter whether an organization</u> is based in Taipei or not, there are significant correlations <u>between</u> location and all other variables. This fact justifies its inclusion <u>in</u> the control variables. Moreover, <u>because of the</u> strong correlations, we can consider the possibility <u>that</u> location may act as a moderator of relationships.

f. Bone remodeling depends upon the balance of bone formation <u>with</u> bone resorption, wherein bone forming osteoblasts and bone-resorbing osteoclasts play crucial <u>roles</u>. Chronic inflammatory <u>diseases</u>, including rheumatoid arthritis, periodontitis, and osteoporosis, will induce bone loss, <u>which</u> in turn increases the number of bone-resorbing <u>osteoclasts</u>. Recent studies have <u>indicated that n-3</u> polyunsaturated fatty acids can reduce the production of inflammatory cytokines in a number of <u>conditions</u>, whereas n-6 polyunsaturated fatty acids <u>have the opposite</u> effect.

g. Falstaff lives on words and <u>escapes</u> ill fortune through <u>words</u>. We all love to hear him <u>war</u> (或<u>warring</u>) with words. He may be a coward by sword, but never a coward by <u>word</u>. This knight's eloquence has <u>talked himself into</u> a braggart soldier, into a man big with bluffs and <u>wags</u>. Nevertheless, he is a sophist who is able to talk us <u>into an awareness</u> of all the"false stuff."His frank reflection <u>on</u> living and lying <u>has</u> earned himself the name of"a fundamentally honest man."

秀威經典　　　　　　　　學習新知類　PD0030　學語言09

英文學術論文寫作：
講解與作業

作　　　者／董崇選
責任編輯／陳佳怡、杜國維
圖文排版／楊家齊
封面設計／蔡瑋筠

出版策劃／秀威經典
發 行 人／宋政坤
法律顧問／毛國樑　律師
印製發行／秀威資訊科技股份有限公司
　　　　　114台北市內湖區瑞光路76巷65號1樓
　　　　　電話：+886-2-2796-3638　傳真：+886-2-2796-1377
　　　　　http://www.showwe.com.tw
劃撥帳號／19563868　戶名：秀威資訊科技股份有限公司
　　　　　讀者服務信箱：service@showwe.com.tw
展售門市／國家書店（松江門市）
　　　　　104台北市中山區松江路209號1樓
　　　　　電話：+886-2-2518-0207　傳真：+886-2-2518-0778
網路訂購／秀威網路書店：http://www.bodbooks.com.tw
　　　　　國家網路書店：http://www.govbooks.com.tw

2016年7月　BOD一版
定價：450元
版權所有　翻印必究
本書如有缺頁、破損或裝訂錯誤，請寄回更換

國家圖書館出版品預行編目

英文學術論文寫作:講解與作業 / 董崇選著. --
一版. -- 臺北市:秀威經典, 2016.07
　　面;　公分
BOD版
ISBN 978-986-92498-7-4(平裝)

1. 英語　2. 論文寫作法

805.175　　　　　　　　　　105003827

讀者回函卡

感謝您購買本書，為提升服務品質，請填妥以下資料，將讀者回函卡直接寄回或傳真本公司，收到您的寶貴意見後，我們會收藏記錄及檢討，謝謝！
如您需要了解本公司最新出版書目、購書優惠或企劃活動，歡迎您上網查詢或下載相關資料：http:// www.showwe.com.tw

您購買的書名：＿＿＿＿＿＿＿＿＿＿＿＿＿＿＿＿＿＿＿＿＿

出生日期：＿＿＿＿＿年＿＿＿＿＿月＿＿＿＿＿日

學歷：□高中 (含) 以下　　□大專　　□研究所 (含) 以上

職業：□製造業　□金融業　□資訊業　□軍警　□傳播業　□自由業
　　　□服務業　□公務員　□教職　　□學生　□家管　□其它＿＿＿＿

購書地點：□網路書店　□實體書店　□書展　□郵購　□贈閱　□其他

您從何得知本書的消息？

　□網路書店　□實體書店　□網路搜尋　□電子報　□書訊　□雜誌
　□傳播媒體　□親友推薦　□網站推薦　□部落格　□其他＿＿＿＿＿＿

您對本書的評價：(請填代號　1.非常滿意　2.滿意　3.尚可　4.再改進)

　封面設計＿＿＿　版面編排＿＿＿　內容＿＿＿　文／譯筆＿＿＿　價格＿＿＿

讀完書後您覺得：

　□很有收穫　□有收穫　□收穫不多　□沒收穫

對我們的建議：＿＿＿＿＿＿＿＿＿＿＿＿＿＿＿＿＿＿＿＿＿

＿＿＿＿＿＿＿＿＿＿＿＿＿＿＿＿＿＿＿＿＿＿＿＿＿＿＿＿＿

＿＿＿＿＿＿＿＿＿＿＿＿＿＿＿＿＿＿＿＿＿＿＿＿＿＿＿＿＿

＿＿＿＿＿＿＿＿＿＿＿＿＿＿＿＿＿＿＿＿＿＿＿＿＿＿＿＿＿

11466
台北市內湖區瑞光路 76 巷 65 號 1 樓

秀威資訊科技股份有限公司　　　收

BOD 數位出版事業部

....

（請沿線對折寄回，謝謝！）

姓　　名：＿＿＿＿＿＿＿＿＿　年齡：＿＿＿＿　性別：□女　□男

郵遞區號：□□□□□

地　　址：＿＿＿＿＿＿＿＿＿＿＿＿＿＿＿＿＿＿＿＿＿

聯絡電話：(日) ＿＿＿＿＿＿＿＿＿　(夜) ＿＿＿＿＿＿＿＿＿

E-mail：＿＿＿＿＿＿＿＿＿＿＿＿＿＿＿＿＿＿＿＿＿